What People Are S[illegible] Bringing [illegible]

By Elizabeth Wiens

"*Bringing Them Home* is **packed with both encouragement and practical information for homeschool families, or those considering homeschooling.** The author is a homeschool mom, as well as a passionate advocate, educating others about the problems with government-run education.

"Although it is a fictional account, the dialogue and the characters mirror a real life family that begins as so many do, with doubts about the schools where their children attend. Meet the Knight family, and follow them on their journey from thinking homeschooling is 'weird' to fully embracing the lifestyle. Along the way, they are supported by other, more experienced homeschool families, deal with some who don't understand their decision, and share their struggles and successes as they figure out what works for their family.

"The best thing about this novel is how the author lets you inside the head and heart of these parents who are striving to do what is best for their children. Parents, especially moms, will find themselves relating to the inner struggle that we face when we navigate the days, months, and years of our homeschooling journey. I found myself encouraged and my ideals reinforced, which we all need when we are swimming upstream in this culture!"

—HOMESCHOOLING FROM THE HEART

http://www.homeschoolingfromtheheart.com/blog/

"**An excellent read!** Wiens provides a thoroughly enjoyable read as she takes her readers through one family's journey from public school to home education."

—PAUL D. FARIS

Executive Director and Senior Legal Counsel, HSLDA Canada

As for Me and My House

A Novel

Elizabeth Wiens

OakTara
Waterford, Virginia

As for Me and My House

Published in the U.S. by:
OakTara Publishers
P.O. Box 8
Waterford, VA 20197
www.oaktara.com

Cover design by Yvonne Parks at www.pearcreative.ca
Cover image, Happy Bride © www.shutterstock.com/Dmitriy Shironosov
Cover image, Seeking Truth © www.iStockphoto.com/kk5hy
Author photo © Jylisa Wiens

ISBN: 978-1-60290-284-8

Printed in the U.S.A.

⌘⌘⌘

To my husband, Gary,
and our four daughters—
Jessica, Jylisa, Justina, and Tamara.

Without our own homeschool journey,
I would not have had this story to tell.

Family Tree

Cassy's Family
Mike & Joyce Harris
(Pastor in B.C.)

- Don & Kathy Harris
  - Connor (20)
  - Christy (16)
- Debbie & Rob Spencer
  - DJ (17)
- Cory & Trish Harris
  - Kiera (17)
  - Daniel (14)
  - Justin (12)
- **Cassy & David Knight**
  - **Nicole (14)**
  - **Jeremy (13)**
  - **Kimberleigh (11)**
  - **Anika (9)**

David's Family
Paul & Jean Knight
(Farmer in Alberta)

- Andrew & Laura Knight
  - Mandy (16)
  - Mark (13)
- **David & Cassy Knight**
  - **Nicole (14)** Birthday September
  - **Jeremy (13)** Birthday July
  - **Kimberleigh (11)** Birthday June
  - **Anika (9)** Birthday April
- Anthony & Sarah Knight
  - Timmy (10)
  - Lissy (8)
  - Samantha (5)

Lauren & Richard Andrews
(Homeschool friends)

- Melissa (16)
- Brianne (14)
- Christian (12)
- James (9)
- Kegan (8)

Prologue

Cassy crossed the cozy fireside room of their church to retrieve the beautiful, pearl-studded headpiece from the tissue-lined box where she had left it just an hour before. The gauzy veil flowed over the edge of the box and onto the table. She fingered the sheer material for a moment, struggling to get her emotions under control before returning to her radiant daughter with the final piece of adornment. Kimberleigh and Anika clamored excitedly around their sister. Each was dressed in their own sleek bridesmaid gown of teal satin.

"I can't wait until it's my turn." Kimberleigh sighed as she admired Nicole's dress. "I hope I can find someone as awesome as you did!"

"I'm sure you will," Nicole bent forward slightly to hug her sister. "Just make sure that you don't settle for less than God's best."

Cassy wiped a stray tear from her eyes at the familiar phrase she had repeated so often to her girls throughout their teen years. She paused to savor the moment as her daughters huddled together. Nicole stood between them, her face beaming. Tiny, beaded pearls adorned her fitted bodice, and they shimmered as she moved. The dress's satin skirt just graced the floor in front and cascaded out behind her in a gorgeous, traditional train. A modest neckline revealed the delicate strand of pearls around her neck, a present from her father for this special day. Capped sleeves covered Nicole's shoulders, completing the enchanting effect. The cut of the gown suited Nicole's graceful form. Her dark curls were loosely gathered up on the sides and hung nearly to her waist, standing out in sharp contrast to the shimmering white gown. A soft fringe of curls framed Nicole's face.

"I'm going to miss you!" Anika whispered.

"I'm not going to be living very far away. You can come see me whenever you want." Nicole's voice trembled ever so slightly.

"I know, but it won't be the same."

"No, I suppose it won't," Nicole answered gently.

"But think how much fun it will be when we become aunties, Anika, and we get to go babysit our new little niece or nephew," Kimberleigh teased, brightening the mood once again. "Before you know it, we'll all be married and getting together for an afternoon of shopping with a string of little ones tagging along."

Nicole giggled. "Or better yet, maybe we'll drop the little ones off with Grandma and all go out for lunch!" Nicole glanced up at her mother, and her smile faded.

Cassy was sure that, even from a distance, Nicole had noticed the unshed tears in her eyes as she watched them from across the room. Nicole would understand. Just last night Cassy had gotten out of bed and wandered to the kitchen for a cup of tea. She hadn't been able to sleep. Though she was thrilled with Nicole's choice in a husband, Cassy still struggled with a sense of loss as her eldest daughter prepared to leave home. Cassy had been surprised to find Nicole sitting alone in the dark kitchen, and the two had sat together for some time reminiscing.

In the wee hours of the morning, Nicole had voiced her own conflicting emotions. Feelings of joy mixed with sorrow over having to say good-bye to the family who had become so dear to her. After sharing a few tears, they had finally returned to bed, in hopes of a few hours of sleep before the big day.

Now Nicole spread her arms in a tender invitation. Cassy crossed the room, holding up the veil she was carrying so it wouldn't drag. Encircling her daughter with her free arm, she kissed Nicole's cheek. She knew her daughter could read her struggle, but Cassy didn't want Nicole to think for a minute that she wasn't happy for her on this special day.

"Let's get this veil on you," Cassy stated as she glanced at the clock on the wall. I can already hear the music starting."

After carefully pinning Nicole's veil in place, Cassy stepped back to examine the final effect. Gently Kimberleigh lifted the front layer over her sister's head and deftly arranged the soft folds covering Nicole's face. Anika hurried to gather Nicole's bouquet of baby roses nestled in a bed of trailing ivy and handed it to her sister.

"Oh," Cassy breathed with a radiant smile, "you look breathtaking!"

"Thanks, Mom," Nicole murmured.

Just then Melissa scurried into the room to join the other bridesmaids. She had been in another classroom helping to pin boutonnières on the groomsmen. "Everyone's ready." She collected her bouquet from the table as the door opened once again.

David entered and stopped a minute before crossing the room to hug his daughter. "When did my little girl grow into a princess?" he said huskily, his words causing Nicole's smile to widen further. David straightened to gaze into her face. "You ready to go sweetheart?"

"I think so, Daddy." Nicole shifted nervously, smoothing imaginary wrinkles from the front of her dress before taking her father's arm.

"You'd better go so you can be seated," he urged Cassy.

With one last look at her daughter, Cassy turned and exited the room. Once she had been ushered to her seat in the front row, Cassy tried to relax as the prelude music swirled around her. *How time has flown.* Her mind wandered over the past years and all that had gone into preparing Nicole for this moment. It seemed such a short time ago that she and David had pulled their children out of the public school system to bring them home. That had been a true turning point in their family, and Cassy would never regret that decision. She thought with fondness of their years of working and learning together; those years were quickly drawing to a close. Cassy blinked back her tears once again.

Those first few years of homeschooling had been so full that, as Cassy tried to think back, it almost felt as though she were trying to sort out the hazy details of a dream. Had she really been homeschooling for thirteen years? So much had happened in that time, and Cassy was amazed at how far they had come. God had been changing their family in so many ways, but it had been a gradual process.

As she and David had sought direction in the training of their children, they had felt a renewed desire to study God's Word and apply His principles more thoroughly in their everyday family life. Soon Cassy realized their decision to homeschool was only the first step in a journey that would entrench their family in an ongoing battle to walk counterculture to the world around them.

Early in their second year of homeschooling, she and David had decided to disconnect their television. Not that they had watched a lot of it prior to that decision, but as they analyzed the direction media was going and the negative influence it tended to be, David had decided to remove the temptation. And once they stepped away from all Hollywood had to offer, Cassy had slowly begun to realize just how desensitized to the language and worldly thinking she had become.

That was one of many decisions that had helped them to stay the course. The true test had come during the teen years, when she and David had been challenged to rethink so many things they had never questioned before. And it was those years that really shaped who their children had become....

1

The Concert

It was Friday night, and David hopped out of the van to go in search of Jeremy and Nicole. They were at a youth function at the church, and David could tell by the heavy beat of the drums and the whine of an electric guitar that the concert was still in progress.

"Who is this band anyway?" David mumbled under his breath as he entered the church. Nicole had called him less than half an hour ago to come pick her up early, and David had wasted no time in making the drive back into the city. She had sounded upset.

It didn't take David long to find his fourteen-year-old daughter sitting on the floor in the corner of the foyer. She sat all alone, her head down with her fingers in her ears. When she saw her father approaching, she jumped up with a look of relief.

"Hi, Dad." She hurried toward him.

"Where's Jeremy?" David had to raise his voice, even though Nicole stood right beside him.

"He's still inside." Nicole motioned toward the open doors leading into the sanctuary. "He's sitting in the fifth row from the front, on the left."

David headed into the sanctuary and stopped short at the scene before him. Well over two hundred youth filled the room, many of whom were crowded around the stage and in the aisles, jumping in time to the beat of the music. On the platform were four young men wearing torn jeans and T-shirts. The drummer had jet-black hair and wore a shirt with a large skull plastered across the front of it.

The exaggerated antics of the guys playing electric and bass guitars reminded David of images he'd seen of secular rock stars. Inside the sanctuary, the music was almost deafening. The lead singer leaned forward as he yelled into the microphone. David couldn't tell whether this was just so that he could be heard, or whether he considered yelling in rhythm to be equivalent to singing. His bleached blond hair stood up straight in all directions, stiff with gel. Vibrations from the pounding drums and heavy bass started to churn David's stomach.

He stood watching in shock for several minutes, straining to catch the words being sung, before remembering he was supposed to be looking for Jeremy. David headed to the side aisle to avoid the crush of teens in the center. It didn't take long for him to locate his son right where Nicole said he would be. Standing between two of his friends, Jeremy seemed mesmerized by the show. Finally, David caught his son's attention and motioned for him to come. With an expression of disappointment, Jeremy squeezed past the others in his row to where his father stood.

"What's up?" Jeremy mouthed.

Motioning for his son to follow, David led him out to the foyer to join Nicole.

"It's only eight o'clock." Jeremy stopped to look at his watch. "Why did you come back so early?"

"Because your sister called and wanted to come home. She said she had a headache, and I can see why!"

"Marcy said I was a party pooper for wanting to leave early." Nicole frowned at her dad.

"I'm glad you called; it's not the kind of concert I thought it was." David gave his daughter's shoulder a squeeze as he headed for the door.

"Why, what's the matter with it?" Jeremy reluctantly followed his Dad out of the church. "I mean, besides the fact that it was a little loud."

"A *little* loud?" David raised his eyebrows. "You mean a *lot* loud, and they looked, and sounded like a rock band!"

"They're a Christian punk band," Jeremy clarified.

"And what makes them different from any secular punk rock band?" By now they had reached the van and David climbed in behind the wheel.

Jeremy took a seat in the front beside his dad. "Well, the guys are all Christians and their words are Christian."

"What were they singing about that was so Christian?"

Jeremy was silent for a moment. "I don't remember exactly, and some of it was hard to understand, but I'm sure they were singing about God."

"The little bit I got out of it sounded like they were singing about themselves and all their struggles," Nicole said as her father started the van and pulled out of the church parking lot.

"Maybe that's part of it, but they didn't use any swear words or anything," Jeremy countered.

"So the absence of foul language is all it takes to classify something as 'Christian'?"

Frustration crossed Jeremy's face. "It's more than that," he mumbled.

"So it's okay for Christian singers to look, act, and sound like the world, as long as they don't use raunchy language? Just how does that glorify God?"

"But Dad, Pastor Jim checked them out and thinks they're okay. They weren't that bad."

David sighed. "I don't know, Jeremy. I don't know much about the group, but some people might think that's the kind of music teens like and it doesn't matter. They think it's okay to take what the world has to offer, clean it up a bit, and label it as 'Christian' without giving it much thought. But the Bible calls us to be different. We are not supposed to be conformed to the world, and we should be aiming for a much higher standard than what the world has to offer. I just want you to think about it."

"Yeah." Jeremy stared sullenly out his window.

"I couldn't believe how many kids were there tonight, and they seemed to really get into it," Nicole, commented.

"Oh, they were getting into it all right, but my guess is they were responding to the frenzy of the music—not to God. Music is a powerful thing; it affects your mind and emotions. There may have been a big turnout, but it doesn't matter how many people you get in the door of a church if they don't hear the gospel while they are there. Sitting in a church building isn't what changes your life. And if the kids think church is just a place to go for fun and entertainment, then we've done them a big disservice."

"I wouldn't call that fun or entertaining," Nicole muttered. "All it gave me was a headache! I don't care if the other girls teased me for leaving; I couldn't stand listening to that all night."

"You did the right thing to call. I should have checked into this band a little more before we let you come. That is not the type of music your mother or I want you becoming accustomed to or filling your mind with."

⌘⌘⌘

Cassy had Kimberleigh and Anika in bed by the time she heard David come in the back door. She had just curled up on the couch with her book, but she closed it and set the book aside. When the three of them entered the living room, she asked David, "So what was going on?"

"I guess the name 'Psychic Rush' should have been an indicator as to what kind of band this was going to be, but so many of the Christian bands have bizarre names anymore that I didn't think too much of it. I'm not really up-to-speed on what the kids are listening to nowadays, but I think it's time we get more informed. I don't know how anyone can call that music, let alone Christian music." David took a seat beside her on the couch.

"So, what did you guys think of it?" Cassy turned toward Jeremy and Nicole.

"It was different, but I didn't think it was so bad." Jeremy shrugged.

"I didn't like it," Nicole stated emphatically.

After discussing the concert a little longer, Cassy got an idea. "How would you like to make a school project out of researching a few of the popular Christian bands? The two of you can work on it together. You can analyze their dress, lifestyle, music, and lyrics and keep track of what you think brings glory to God and what draws attention to themselves or focuses on worldly things. I want you to learn to be discerning and not just accept something because everyone else accepts it."

"That could be fun! I'm sure once you read some of the lyrics, you'll see that they have a good message." Jeremy sounded enthusiastic.

"I already know what I think about it, but I'll do it anyway." Nicole stood up and stretched. "I'm ready for bed." She leaned down to kiss both of her parents good night. "Thanks for coming to get us, Dad."

"You're welcome."

"Do you think we need to talk to Pastor Jim about the concert?" Cassy asked once both of the kids had disappeared down the hallway.

"I don't know. I might ask him about it, but I definitely think we need to be more involved in what is going on in the youth group. The last thing I want is for the influences there to be counteracting what we are trying to do at home."

Could the youth group actually have a negative impact on her children? Cassy wondered. She knew there would be some issues—there had been a few already—but Cassy hadn't really considered that possibility. One thing she had noticed, though, was that the focus of many local youth groups seemed to be quite different than the small youth group she had grown up in. Cassy thought of her best friend, Lauren Andrews. Recently the Andrews' kids had quit attending youth, but Cassy had never asked her friend why. Maybe it was time to take a closer look at the whole youth culture phenomenon.

2

Learning Discernment

Now that her children were entering their teens, Cassy saw the benefit of giving them more independence in their studies. For some subjects and for read aloud time, they still worked together. However, she had discovered that she could assign her older children a project, or let them choose different topics they were interested in, and give them the freedom to study it out on their own with a little guidance along the way. It was neat to see them learn and grow and get excited about what they were studying. Jeremy and Nicole were also marking much of their own work, using the answer keys and then correcting their mistakes. The Knights had entered a different phase in their homeschooling, and Cassy was enjoying it immensely. She watched as Jeremy cornered Nicole the following week, eager to get started on their newest assignment.

⌘⌘⌘

Hauling his sister over to the computer, Jeremy suggested they choose five bands he knew some of the youth in church often listened to. He couldn't wait to prove to his father there was nothing wrong with Christian rock music. One by one he pulled up different websites, searching for information about each of the band members and studying their pictures.

"That guy looks plain weird!" Nicole pointed to the lead singer of a punk band called Crash Dummies. His hair was shaved on both sides of his head with scraggly black tufts sticking out all over on top and a long tail hanging down the back. His face was scruffy looking, and he wore a black muscle shirt and black leather pants. Both arms sported tattoos, and he had a large earring in one ear and a black leather band with silver spikes around one wrist. "He looks more like a guy I would expect to see in prison than a Christian who wants to tell people about Jesus."

"You can't judge someone by the way they dress." Jeremy scowled at his sister. He scrolled down the page, scanning it for some testimony about the fellow's walk with God...but found nothing. With a frown, he returned to the top and read through it more slowly, before clicking to another page. After looking over the whole site, Jeremy leaned back in his chair with a look of surprise. "I don't get it. God isn't even mentioned on this site. They talk a lot about their concerts, their fans, and all the places they are touring, but nothing about God at all!"

Nicole had been jotting down notes, and she pointed to the screen with her pen. "Let's check out this video link and hear what their music sounds like."

Jeremy clicked on the play button to start the music video. It was a clip from a live concert, and he watched as the man danced crazily around the stage to the wild roar of the packed stadium. The singer repeatedly urged his fans to raise their arms, then proceeded to throw himself into their uplifted hands to be bounced along above the heads of his frenzied audience. All the while, he shouted indiscernible words into the microphone to the raucous rhythm of the band. Jeremy's eyes widened as he watched in amazement.

"Are you sure this is a Christian group?" Nicole eyed her brother skeptically.

"Yes! Their CDs are at the Christian bookstore, and lots of the guys at church listen to them. They were even at the MusicFest weekend some of the youth went to last year." Jeremy smirked. "At least now I know how they got the name Crash Dummies. I wonder if the audience ever drops him?"

"I can't understand a thing he is saying, but he sure doesn't look like he is singing about God!"

"Let's see if we can find some of the lyrics to their songs; I'm sure the words are better than he sounds." Jeremy searched for the name of one of the band's albums and soon came up with a site posting the lyrics to all their songs. He clicked on the first one and started reading aloud, his voice fading as he progressed. When he had finished, he stared at his sister in shock. "That has nothing to do with God."

Nicole shook her head. "It's all about suicide and death! Most of it doesn't even make sense."

Jeremy clicked on the next song. It wasn't any better, and after reading the lyrics of twelve songs, Jeremy sat dumbfounded. Not one mention of God or anything clearly having to do with God in a single song. The lyrics were, however, full of references to violence, drugs, revenge, depression, and living to please oneself. It was not at all what he'd expected. "I can't believe that's what they're singing about."

"I can see why Mom and Dad don't want us listening to that stuff. There's nothing pleasing to God about it, and nothing about living for Him. I don't get why anyone who claims to be a Christian would sing about those things or act like that."

⌘⌘⌘

When the week was done, Cassy asked the kids what they'd discovered. With dismay Jeremy collected their notes, and after supper he and Nicole shared their findings. Only two of the five groups they had checked out made much reference to God on their website or in their songs, but even those references were vague. Most of their songs focused on popular issues and feelings rather than God.

The other three groups failed the test on all counts. Their lyrics were worldly and nonsensical, and their music was every bit as loud and rocky as the world had to offer. The band members gave no Christian testimony on their sites or in their blogs, and their dress was sloppy or made them look more like members of a gang than disciples of Christ.

Cassy glanced at David in shock when she read through some of the lyrics the kids had found. "I knew I didn't like the rock music, but I assumed that rock bands who called themselves Christian would have Christian lyrics, or at least positive lyrics. Those are horrible!" Cassy read from the words still on the computer screen: "'Darkness sucks me in, I'm afraid to sleep. I dream of blood, voices in my head, tell me what to do. I must silence the laughter, I will watch them die, then I will be free, yes I will be free.' Do parents know what their kids are listening to?"

"My guess is no. If it comes from a Christian bookstore, they assume it is safe." David reached down and exited the page on the computer screen. He looked at Jeremy and Nicole. "So, do you understand why we want you to be discerning about what you are putting into your minds?"

Jeremy gave a subdued nod. "Yeah, Dad, I didn't realize it was like that."

David patted his son on the shoulder. "Now you know."

⌘⌘⌘

A couple of days later, Cassy decided to give Lauren a call. She wanted to invite her for a visit, and Lauren agreed to come over that afternoon. Soon the two were enjoying coffee at the kitchen table while their kids took advantage of the mild spring weather outside. It reminded Cassy of a similar visit five years ago, when they had sat around the same table for the first time discussing homeschooling. Cassy was so thankful for Lauren's friendship and for all the encouragement she had given over the years.

"I told you on the phone that I wanted to talk to you about the youth group. First, I want to know what you think about it and why your kids don't go anymore." Cassy took a sip of coffee and gazed intently at her friend.

Lauren shrugged. "We decided we didn't want the kids getting caught up in the whole youth culture mentality. The philosophy of creating a separate youth program and segregating our teens from the rest of the church is really a recent idea. It's not a biblical practice, and I think the youth need to interact with and be mentored by the adults. Pastor Jim is a great guy and has a real heart for the teens, but he can't mentor all the youth, and he shouldn't have to. That's a parent's job."

"I hadn't thought about it like that before," Cassy admitted. "I mean I've had some concerns about peer influences, but it's hard to know where to draw the line. I agree that the kids need to be mentored by parents and the church as a whole, but don't you think they also need some interaction as a peer group?"

"Sure, they need to interact with kids of all ages; they do that within our homeschool group. I guess you have to determine whether you want that interaction to be within a family context, or a predominantly peer context. The focus of the group and level of influence over your kids will vary greatly depending on the setting. Our kids weren't in youth group very long before we started to see some of the attitudes rubbing off on them. Melissa started wearing more makeup and wanting to dress to impress the guys. That whole guy/girl dating thing is so big among teens, she couldn't escape it."

Cassy nodded. "I know what you mean. Nicole is facing that too. The girls are always talking about guys and who likes who, and when we want her to wait and pursue courtship, it gets pretty tough."

"Then Christian started begging to go play video games and hang out with his friends all the time. We noticed that both of them seemed to be gradually shifting to be more materialistic and entertainment oriented, and we didn't like that. We also found that often when a bunch of kids were getting together to watch a video, we would have to say no because we didn't approve of the movie. The other kids would give them a hard time over it. I guess we just found it more of a battle to instill the values we wanted to see in our kids, when we felt our standards were always being challenged by the kids in youth."

"Did you get a lot of negative feedback when you pulled them out?"

"Oh, sure. Pastor Jim wanted to know why they weren't coming. Of course it was difficult to explain without giving the impression that we were being critical of him personally. Then there were those who told us we were being too controlling and overprotective. They felt we were harming our kids spiritually by pulling them out, but frankly, most of their time in youth was spent in social activities. If we were depending solely on the youth group to give our kids the bulk of their spiritual training, they would not have the level of spiritual maturity they have now. But people just assume they aren't getting any training at home. Our kids are miles ahead of where I was at their age."

"Did you and Richard have a problem with any of the activities that were planned?"

"Some of them, but most were okay. The activities were just becoming too much of the focus, and we wanted our kids to see their walk with God as something more than that. We wanted them to have a vision for serving others rather than seeing entertainment as their chief goal. When entertainment becomes the norm, kids come to expect it. It's sad when you hear about youth groups who no longer hold a weekly Bible study because few kids will come if they don't think it's going to be any fun. Instead, they sandwich a short devotional between a bunch of games to make it appealing. Whatever happened to helping kids develop a heart for God and a love for His Word?"

"I think you're right." Cassy set down her coffee mug as she sorted out her thoughts. "I've recognized some of these issues over the last year; I've just never stopped to analyze it and put it all together before. Somehow it almost seems *un-Christian* to not send your kids to youth group, but I don't want to train my children to pursue pleasure more than God! So how did your kids take it when you pulled them out?"

"They were disappointed at first, but it didn't take them long to settle back into their old routine. In some ways, I think they are more relaxed now because they don't have to battle the pressure to conform on a weekly basis." Lauren stared into her coffee. "Richard and I have been thinking about starting a family Bible study at our place, just something informal. Would you be interested?"

"You mean getting together with all our kids?" Cassy was intrigued.

"Yeah. We could work through a book of the Bible and pray together, give the kids a chance to interact and ask questions. Whatever."

"What, no punk rock bands?"

Lauren laughed. "No! Is that what started all this?"

"That was part of it," Cassy admitted. "I'll have to talk to David about the Bible study, but I think I would be interested in something like that."

Just then nine-year-old Anika came bounding in the back door. "Mom, Jeremy wants me to ask if we can have some ice cream bars."

"I guess so, but how come Jeremy didn't come ask himself?"

"'Cause he's all wet and muddy."

"And how did that happen?" Cassy wasn't at all surprised.

Anika gave her mother a crooked grin. "Oh, he was trying to prove to Christian that he can jump across the creek, but he can't."

Cassy just shook her head as Anika left to get the box of ice cream bars from the deep freeze. "I think that boy makes as many dirty clothes as the three girls combined. I've finally come to realize that boys and dirt go hand-in-hand and have given up on trying to keep him clean."

Lauren laughed. "Yeah, but you can't expect boys to behave like girls. They need adventures and an outlet for all their energy."

"I know. I think that's why I often got frustrated with him when he was younger. I didn't get that. Boys aren't wired the same as girls, and Jeremy certainly wasn't wired to sit in a school desk all day. He's much happier being home, and I'm coming to understand him a little better." Cassy thought about the transition in her son since they had begun homeschooling five years earlier. Over the years, David had worked to channel Jeremy's energy and to get him involved in helping with projects around the house or working on the vehicles. It had made a huge difference in her son's life. "Boys really need to be mentored by their fathers."

Lauren nodded. "I'm afraid there are a lot of boys out there who don't have any strong role models in their lives."

The two enjoyed visiting for a while longer, until Lauren decided she'd better head home and went in search of her children. Before she left, Cassy promised once again to talk to David about the family Bible study.

3

Evaluating Youth

That night, Cassy discussed with David the possibility of pulling their kids out of youth and joining a study at the Andrews. Though the concept of the Bible study appealed to both of them and their philosophy of mentorship for their children, they had mixed feelings. After all, they both had fond memories of their youth group days, and they didn't want to feel like they were depriving their children of that experience. They also wanted to avoid hurting others in the church and feared that such a decision would be misunderstood by family and friends. They decided to present the matter to the kids and get their input. Following supper the next evening, David broached the subject.

"How would you guys like to be part of a Bible study with the Andrews' family one night a week?"

"Sure!" Kimberleigh was the first to respond. "I love getting together with the Andrews."

David turned to his two eldest children. "What if we were to go to this Bible study instead of youth group?"

"What!" David had Jeremy's full attention now. "You mean we'd miss all the youth activities? How come?"

"Well, your mother and I want to make sure that you are getting the biblical teaching that we feel is important, and we believe that God has given that responsibility to us as your parents. We also want you to develop strong character and convictions, which is sometimes more difficult in a peer setting that doesn't necessarily share those convictions."

"Does the Bible say kids aren't allowed to have any fun?"

"Of course not, Jeremy." David let out a heavy sigh. "We aren't trying to take away all your fun. We merely want you to keep it in perspective, and we don't want you to start placing the values of your peers over the values we are trying to teach you."

Cassy turned to Nicole. "What about you, honey?"

"I don't know, Mom." Nicole's eyes filled with tears. "It took me so long to feel a part of the group and like I was accepted. Everyone already thinks we are kinda weird for homeschooling, but if we drop out of youth group, we're really going to be alienated. I would enjoy getting together with the Andrews, but I don't want to feel like an outsider among all the youth."

"Why can't we do both?" Kimberleigh piped up. "I want to go to the Andrews, but I still want a chance to go to youth next fall."

"Well, your mother and I are trying to sort out the biblical role of church and family, and we feel the Bible presents a more family integrated approach to meeting together and discipleship. I don't see anything in Scripture that promotes segregating families into separate peer groups apart from their parents, but that's where our culture is at right now. Rightly or wrongly, it has become a part of how we do church. I'm trying to figure out how God would have me lead my family His way."

Cassy reached to place her hand on David's knee as she surveyed each of her children around the table. "We don't want you guys to feel alienated, and we don't want to cause problems in the church. But we want to do what is best for the family."

"I'll tell you what," David said. "I'll talk to Pastor Jim and see if we can help out with the youth for the rest of the spring. That way we can be more involved and see how it goes. Then we can decide what God wants us to do come fall and make a change then if necessary."

The kids seemed to perk up at that suggestion and all agreed to give it a try. Cassy phoned to tell Lauren their decision, and learned that the Hendersons were maybe interested in a family study as well. Lauren admitted that starting something right before summer was probably not the best timing anyway, so they would keep in touch regarding plans for fall.

⌘⌘⌘

After the service the following Sunday, Cassy followed David as he sought out Pastor Jim. They found him in the corner of the foyer chatting with the Copelands, a young married couple who helped with the youth. When the conversation ended, the Knights made their way over to the pastor.

"Hi David, what can I do for you?" He shook David's hand.

"Cassy and I want to get more involved with the youth group and were wondering if you could use some help."

"Well, a youth pastor is always looking for help." Jim laughed. "We have our big carnival night coming up in two weeks and are still looking for volunteers to monitor the inflatables, organize games, or help with food. I would have no trouble finding something for you to do."

"That's great. Anika and Kimberleigh can help too, but we are interested in helping out on a weekly basis."

"Oh, well, Troy leads the worship, and Alana leads the girls' discussion time while I lead the boys, but you could probably fill in on occasion if the Copelands are away. We usually need more helpers on our monthly activity nights. I could keep you posted, but you wouldn't need to come every week."

"Would it be a problem if we wanted to come every Friday anyway? That way we can be a part of what is going on and interact with the kids more as a family."

"You mean you plan on bringing the whole family every week?" Jim's eyebrows went up at that. "Kimberleigh and Anika aren't really old enough to take part in youth yet, and that might cause problems for other kids their age who aren't allowed to come. It might not hurt to bring them to a few of the larger events if they are helping, but some of the older teens probably won't like younger kids tagging along to all their events. Besides, the studies and discussions aren't really geared for them, and they would probably get restless."

"I think it would be good for teens to interact with whole families," David said thoughtfully, "but I understand. Could Cassy and I still come weekly and bring Kimberleigh and Anika to the carnival night and see how it goes? We would really like to be involved."

"I'll check with the Copelands and see if they are okay with that and let you know. I guess we could try letting the girls help with the carnival," he added rather reluctantly. "There's lots to do, but they're a bit young."

"Thank you." David nodded and gripped Cassy's elbow as he turned to go.

Though Cassy was disappointed that Kimberleigh and Anika were not really welcome to attend youth with them on a regular basis, she had to admit she wasn't surprised. There was little attention given in the church these days toward encouraging families to come together for any type of ministry program or event. In fact, it was more and more the trend to plan different weekly programs even for couples. The church seems to feel called to provide a separate program for each member of the family—seniors' events, men's night, ladies' day out, programs for moms of pre-schoolers, nursery care, kids' programs for all ages and separate programs for Jr. and Sr. high teens. *How more disjointed can our families and society get?* she wondered.

With resignation, Cassy called Lauren and made arrangements for Kimberleigh and Anika to spend the next few Friday evenings at their house. The regular youth schedule would break for summer in five weeks. Cassy hoped that would be long enough for them to make their decision regarding the fall.

⌘⌘⌘

Friday evening David and Cassy followed Nicole and Jeremy into the youth room at the church. An odd assortment of couches and overstuffed chairs, donated by church families, filled half of the long room. Against one wall sprawled an entertainment system complete with large screen TV and a stereo. The other end of the room sported a fooseball table, air hockey table, pop machine, and a cluster of small tables and chairs. Colorful graffiti art covered the far wall.

The room reverberated with noise. Nicole went to join some girls lounging on the couches, talking over the music emanating from the CD player, while Jeremy made his way over to a group of boys around the game tables. Spotting Alana Copeland organizing some snacks on a table in the corner, Cassy went to help.

"Hi, what can I do?"

The young woman glanced up as she stretched some plastic wrap over the trays she was preparing. "Jim said you might be coming tonight. I have the cookies ready to go, but if you want to get some Styrofoam cups from the kitchen, that would be great. We'll leave the juice in the fridge until the break."

By the time Cassy returned with the cups, Pastor Jim was calling the kids together in order to start. Troy turned off the CD player, then picked up his guitar and perched himself on a tall stool. Following Jim's opening prayer, Troy led the youth in some lively choruses. After about fifteen minutes of singing, he turned the time over to Jim.

Looking around the circle, Cassy noticed that few of the kids had Bibles with them. It seemed a little odd, but she turned her attention to the youth pastor.

"I don't want you to answer me out loud; just think about my next questions. First, how many of you have disagreements with your parents?" Jim glanced around the room, and Cassy followed his gaze. Several teens were smiling or nodding in response. "Now, when you disagree, think how you respond to your parents' authority.... As you may have guessed, our topic for tonight is honoring your parents."

Jim opened his Bible and read Deuteronomy 5:16. "'Honor your father and your mother, as the LORD your God has commanded you, that your days may be long, and that it may be well with you in the land which the LORD your God is giving you.' There are many passages in Scripture that command us to honor our parents. In Deuteronomy chapter 21, the Bible tells us how seriously God views this command. According to Jewish law, if a son was rebellious and disobeyed his parents, they were to take him to the elders and have him stoned to death. I guess that's one reason God says in the Ten Commandments that if you honor your parents, your days may be long. I wonder how many teens today would make it into adulthood if we still practiced that?"

"Not many," someone called out, and a few others snickered.

"So why do you think God commanded the Israelites to stone their rebellious sons?" Jim gazed intently at the young people around him.

"Because boys cause all the trouble," Marcy stated saucily, causing the girls next to her to giggle.

"That's what you think," one of the older boys countered. "Adam didn't get into trouble until Eve messed things up!"

Pastor Jim held up his hand and waited for the group to calm down before continuing. "This isn't a girls-are-better-than-boys issue. God doesn't look any more favorably on a girl's disrespect toward her parents. I think the issue was that rebellious young men would grow up and lead the people into disobedience. God was trying to cleanse the Israelite nation from evil and rebellion toward Himself. If you can't honor and obey your earthly fathers, you're not likely to obey your Heavenly Father. We may not stone rebellious teenagers anymore, but that doesn't mean God doesn't take the attitude we have toward our parents seriously."

Jim spoke a little longer about the meaning of honor. Cassy noticed a number of kids whispering back and forth while he talked, and some shifted restlessly in their seats. After the short devotional, they broke up into their discussion groups. The girls stayed in the youth room with Alana, while the boys headed to the fireside room with Jim.

Once the boys had vacated, Cassy moved from where she had been standing to take an empty seat on one of the couches. Some of the girls glanced at her curiously, as though wondering why she was there, but Cassy just smiled back at them.

Alana pulled out her paper with the discussion notes and asked the girls the first question. "Do you sometimes find it hard to honor your parents, and if so, why?"

The girls were quiet for a minute; then Marcy spoke up. "Sure, everyone does. I think it's because parents don't understand us, and it gets frustrating."

"You don't think your parents were ever your age?" Alana questioned gently.

"Well, yeah!" Marcy rolled her eyes. "But that was like ages ago, and it was different then. They don't understand our music or what it's like to be a teen nowadays. It's hard to communicate with them."

"Yeah," agreed a girl who sat directly across from Cassy. "My dad doesn't like the clothes I wear or the guys I date, but he needs to let me be the person God created me to be. It's not right that he tries to force me into his own mold. I don't think God ever expected us to give up our personal desires and opinions just because our parents don't agree."

Cassy couldn't help but stare at the girl in surprise. She glanced toward the front to see how Alana would respond, but the young leader just smiled.

"Uh, I don't think…," Cassy began.

"I know; just let the girls respond for now," Alana quietly interrupted.

"I think God gave us parents to give us guidance, and they understand more than you think. We are to obey them and show respect even if we don't agree, and that is how we honor them." Nicole spoke softly, but with conviction.

Cassy smiled, proud of her daughter. She heard a couple girls snicker and whisper loudly, "She had to say that; her mom is in the room!"

Cassy turned to the girls in annoyance but held her tongue.

Alana asked a couple more questions, and then the short discussion time was over. Cassy could hear the boys already racing toward the youth room as Alana got up and headed toward the snacks at the back of the room. She stood up to follow, her mind still on some of the comments made by the girls. When she reached the table, Alana asked if Cassy would mind going to the kitchen to retrieve the juice while she uncovered the plates of cookies.

Not until snack time was over and all the youth headed to the gym for some games did Cassy find a chance to talk to Alana. They had stayed behind to clean up. Cassy started collecting Styrofoam cups, which had been discarded all over the room. She searched for the right words to say.

"Alana."

"Yes?" Alana barely glanced up as she swept up cookie crumbs around the tables.

"This is my first week here, but I was wondering why you didn't confront some of the things the girls said during the discussion."

"Well, the purpose of discussion time is to give the kids a chance to voice some of their struggles and thoughts in a non-threatening atmosphere. Some weeks it is hard enough to even get them to comment on what Pastor Jim presents. If I start jumping on everything they say, they won't want to comment at all."

Cassy threw a stack of cups in the garbage can and studied the young woman. She knew that Alana and Troy had only been married about a year, and as of yet had no children of their own. Still, Cassy was struggling to conceal her frustration. "I understand that, but don't you want them to be able to apply what Jim taught biblically? I mean, what if the girls' comments don't line up with Scripture and they all go away thinking that what they said is right?"

"It's a process, Mrs. Knight. Some of these girls are new Christians, and some I don't think have made a decision at all. They are trying to work out what it means to be a Christian in their own minds, and we don't want to discourage them."

Although not satisfied, Cassy let the matter drop. *How are the kids supposed to understand what it means to be a Christian if you don't tell them the truth?* Cassy bit her tongue. Rather than creating tension on her first visit, she would wait and talk to David and see how the boys' session had gone.

When they were done cleaning up, the ladies flicked off the lights and headed to the gym to watch the games. It was another hour before the last of the kids had been picked up, and the Knights headed out into the peaceful night to find their van in the nearly empty parking lot. Pastor Jim was just locking the church doors.

On the way home, Cassy commended Nicole for speaking up earlier that night. As they discussed the evening, Cassy got the impression that the boys' session had gotten a little more direction than she felt the girls' session had. However, David agreed that the bulk of the discussion time was simply opinion sharing. Jeremy admitted that some nights the boys tend to goof around a fair bit and that many didn't take the discussion time too seriously.

"We'll see how the next few weeks go," David said.

4

The Carnival

Over the last couple of years, Cassy had set aside Wednesday afternoons to teach the girls homemaking skills. Some weeks were too busy and this schedule was interrupted, but she had tried to be as consistent as possible. The girls were all learning to cook and to sew, and Cassy encouraged them to develop a variety of skills. They had each found a special niche they enjoyed—Nicole loved her piano, reading, and sewing her own clothes, Kimberleigh especially loved singing, art and drama, and Anika loved to bake and help in the kitchen.

Jeremy usually joined his dad at work for the day, and Cassy knew her son lived for Wednesdays—no books or assignments, just following his dad around and learning about construction. It made Cassy nervous having him on construction sites, but she knew David was teaching him proper safety precautions. She remembered how excited her son had been the first day he had been allowed to use the power tools, and Cassy still found herself checking to see if he had all his fingers when he came in the door each Wednesday night.

Today Cassy had given Kimberleigh, who has just turned twelve, the task of fixing supper while she helped Anika sew a simple skirt. Once Anika had finished cutting out the pattern pieces, she headed downstairs to the sewing room. Cassy paused long enough to make sure Kimberleigh had everything she needed. This was the first time she would be preparing supper entirely on her own, and she had chosen to make her favorite—sweet-and-sour chicken with rice. As Cassy made her way downstairs, she could hear Nicole practicing the piano in the living room. The occasional noise drifting down from the kitchen told her Kimberleigh was at work.

⌘⌘⌘

Kimberleigh had the counter scattered with recipes, trying to decide what to make for dessert. She settled on brownies and began mixing up her ingredients. Once the pan was in the oven, she got the chicken breasts out of the fridge and set to work cutting them up. It was difficult cutting the slippery chicken, and Kimberleigh grimaced at the feel of raw meat beneath her fingers.

Just then the phone rang. Kimberleigh let it go, but then remembered she was the only one in the kitchen. Quickly washing her hands, she grabbed the phone. It was Grandma Knight. Kimberleigh chatted away, proudly telling her grandma what she was doing and listing off her menu. Finally, she took the phone down to her mother. When she returned to the kitchen, she smelled the distinct odor of something burning.

"Oh no, my brownies!" Kimberleigh raced to the oven to rescue her dessert. She poked the top of the brownies cautiously with her finger. "A little crispy, but edible," she declared, before returning to her chicken. With the meat cubed, she checked her recipes again. "The chicken needs an hour, the rice needs twenty minutes, and the biscuits need twenty minutes," she mumbled to herself. "Sorry Mrs. Chicken, but your time is up. You are the first to go into the pot." She peered down at the pile of meat in pity. "I know, it is a terrible way to go, but someone has to sacrifice themselves for my supper, and tonight it is you." With a heavy sigh she scraped the chicken off the cutting board into a frying pan and placed it on the stove.

⌘⌘⌘

Cassy, who had come to the kitchen to return the phone, stood smirking in the doorway. "Everything okay in here?"

Kimberleigh glanced up with a smile. "Oh yes, I was just mourning for Mrs. Chicken, but I'll be over it by suppertime."

With a laugh, Cassy shook her head and returned to the sewing room. Anika's skirt was coming along nicely, and it was almost finished when she heard David and Jeremy come in the back door.

"Whoa!" Jeremy stopped in the doorway. "It looks like a tornado went through the kitchen!"

Cassy left Anika to finish her seam and came to check on how supper was coming along. Kimberleigh was busy at the stove wiping up water that had just boiled over from the peas. The counters were scattered with dirty dishes, measuring cups, and baking supplies. Flour and bits of sticky biscuit dough still coated the surface of the island.

"Nicole, come set the table," Cassy called before turning to help Kimberleigh. "How's it going?"

"Okay." She sounded a little uncertain. "There's a lot more things to watch when you are doing this alone! I didn't realize making supper was so much work."

Cassy smiled sympathetically. "Yeah, the first time is the hardest, but it gets easier to organize things with a little experience."

Together they finished getting supper on. The biscuits weren't done yet, so Cassy left them in the oven as they dished up the rest of the food. Besides the messy kitchen, it looked like Kimberleigh had done not too bad. The peas were a little overcooked, but that would come with practice.

"You did great, honey," she encouraged, before calling the family to the table. By the time everyone was seated and David had prayed for the meal, the biscuits were ready.

⌘⌘⌘

"Hey, if you cut these in circles, I can use them for hockey pucks," Jeremy teased when they got to the brownies.

"Very funny. Why don't you try fixing all this stuff *and* talking to Grandma on the phone at the same time and see how *you* do!"

"Jeremy," David said sternly to his son, "someday you will need to show appreciation to your wife for all the meals she makes for you, and you can start by practicing on your sisters."

"Yes, sir." Jeremy appeared remorseful. "I was just teasing Kimberleigh; they aren't so bad." To prove it, he took a large bite, which broke off with a crunch.

Kimberleigh cracked up laughing. "Yes they are," she admitted as she poked her brownie with a fork.

"It's my turn for dishes," Anika moaned as she surveyed the kitchen. "Do I have to clean up all that mess?"

"I'll help, since I made it," Kimberleigh offered her younger sister, "but you still have to do the dishes."

⌘⌘⌘

That Friday the whole family climbed into the van and headed to the church for the youth carnival night. Pastor Jim had assigned them each a job the previous Sunday. He had given Kimberleigh and Anika the task of helping Cassy manage the refreshment booth, and they were excited. Cassy would be in charge of operating the cotton candy machine, and the girls would collect tickets in exchange for candy bars and pop. David had been asked to supervise the large inflatable.

The Knights arrived at the church half an hour early and went to work helping set up before the youth arrived. Alana showed Cassy how the cotton candy machine worked and quickly explained the ticket system to the girls. Kimberleigh and Anika nodded and started arranging the boxes of candy along the kitchen counter at one end of the gym. In no time the room started filling up with teens eager to run through the inflatable obstacle course or try their hand at an assortment of carnival games in order to earn tickets.

Halfway through the evening, the games and refreshment stand were shut down and everyone gathered to one end of the gym to watch a Christian illusionist perform. Cassy was glad for the break, and she ushered the girls over to take a seat toward the back just behind Nicole.

Marcy glanced over her shoulder and whispered to Nicole, "Too bad your little sisters have to tag along."

Nicole turned to her friend in surprise. "Why? I love having my sisters around."

"Yeah, whatever."

Cassy glanced down at the girls and could tell that they had heard the exchange. It was sad to see the attitude so many teens had toward their siblings—*another product of our age-segregated society.* Thankfully, her children were developing strong friendships with each other.

David soon joined them and they watched the show together. By the end of the night, Cassy felt exhausted. Some of the youth pitched in to fold the inflatable and put away the games, so David came over to help her clean up the kitchen.

"Dad." Nicole walked over to the counter. "Randy just asked me to go to a movie with him tomorrow night."

David looked up at his daughter. "What did you tell him?"

"I told him what you said to tell guys, that he has to talk to my father. I just thought you might want to know."

As Nicole left, Cassy spotted Randy across the gym making furtive glances toward the kitchen. Matt gave him a shove, but Randy shook his head. She glanced at David. A tiny grin tugged at the corner of his mouth, indicating he had been watching as well. "What are you going to tell him?"

David laughed. "Wait and see if he gets up the courage to come talk to me first."

After a few moments, Cassy glimpsed Randy slowly approaching the kitchen. She noticed her husband watching from the corner of his eye, as the boy repeatedly paused to look back at his friend, who shooed him on. Finally, Randy entered the kitchen and awkwardly cleared his throat.

"Uh, Mr. Knight?"

"What can I do for you, sir?" David stopped what he was doing and gave the young man his full attention.

"Uh, I was just wondering..." Randy's voice cracked. "I was wondering if I could take Nicole to a movie tomorrow night."

"Just the two of you, like on a date?" David looked the boy in the eye, causing him to flush a deep scarlet.

"Yeah." Randy shifted uncomfortably beneath David's gaze.

Cassy observed from the corner of the kitchen. She felt sorry for the lad, but her husband didn't let up. Randy was tall and rather good-looking, and she figured most girls would be flattered to have him ask them out. She also knew that David wanted to protect his daughters.

"How old are you, Randy?" David took a step closer and placed his hand on the boy's shoulder.

"I'm sixteen." Cassy saw Randy straighten his shoulders as though trying to measure up beneath her husband's scrutiny.

"Sixteen. So, do you think you are ready for marriage? Are you prepared to support a wife and family?"

At Randy's shocked expression, Cassy glanced away and bit her lip to avoid chuckling.

"Uh, no, sir, I…uh…I was just asking for a date." Randy looked down, acting as if he'd like nothing more than to slink quietly from the room.

"Well, Randy, Nicole is only fourteen, and she's not ready for marriage either. That's why I don't think I should let her date; I don't want someone to win her heart and then break it down the road. Her heart is a delicate thing, and she is saving it for her future husband. It's not something to be toyed with. When you're ready for marriage, and if you are still interested, why don't you come see me again?"

"Yes, sir." Randy glanced once more at David before hurrying from the room.

"Bad idea," Cassy heard him mumble to himself as he hurried away, and she couldn't help but snicker.

She grinned at her husband. "You were pretty hard on the poor guy."

David smiled back. "Do you think he'll be back before he's at least twenty-one?"

"Not on your life!"

"Good!" David flicked off the lights, and they went in search of their kids.

5

Family Ministry

By the end of June, David and Cassy had made up their mind. They had decided to pull their kids from youth group and join the Andrews' study. Though Jeremy and Nicole were a little disappointed at first, they understood the reasoning behind their parents' decision. At the same time, they were looking forward to the study with their homeschool friends come September.

It didn't take long for the Knights to confirm that they had made the right decision. Sitting around a living room with other families, studying Scripture and praying for one another, was a wonderful experience. It drew the families together, and Cassy could see the immense benefit of seeing their children mentored by other adults within a family context. Not long into the fall, Cassy started looking for other ways their family could minister together.

"What would you think if we offered to volunteer at the Christian crisis pregnancy center in Red Deer?" she asked David as they were getting ready for bed one night.

"You mean you and I?"

"No, all of us," Cassy clarified. "I picked up a Hope for Life brochure at church, and they are looking for lots of help. They need more Christian counselors to meet with the young women who come in, and they need handymen to help with some of their renovations. I thought the girls might be able to help clean the office, or make baby blankets and bake cookies for the new mothers." She picked up the brochure from her dresser and handed it to her husband.

David leafed through it and nodded. "Sounds like a good idea. We could try to help here and there when we've got some free time. Why don't you call them and get some more information?"

Cassy smiled. She was sure the girls would enjoy helping the young mothers, and it would provide an opportunity to serve together.

The next day she made the call, and soon she had an appointment to go meet with the woman in charge. David had to work, but she decided to bring the kids with her so they could meet the staff and see what might be involved.

Cassy pulled up in front of the small, brick building shortly before her appointment. They decided to go in and have a look around while they waited.

"Will there be any babies here to play with?" Anika asked eagerly.

"I'm not sure." Cassy reached to open the door. "I don't know how often women bring their babies back in."

They entered a small reception area furnished with a few chairs, an oak coffee table, and a narrow wooden bench lined with plants along the front window. A beautiful photo of a mountain scene with the sun setting just above the rocky peaks hung in the waiting area. Against the opposite wall stood a metal rack containing magazines and brochures on pregnancy and parenting. Tucked in the corner was a plastic bin of toys. Cassy guessed they were for clients who already had children. Though the furniture was nothing fancy, Cassy found the room warm and inviting. A middle-aged woman smiled at them from behind the reception desk.

"Hi, may I help you?"

Cassy walked up to the desk and introduced herself. "We're here to meet with Stacey about some volunteer work," she explained.

"Ah yes, she is expecting you. My name is Kellie; I'll let Stacey know you're here."

Before long, Stacey came out to greet them and lead them on a tour of the facilities. Behind the receptionist's desk was a small room stuffed with a surprising amount of merchandise. Racks lined three of the walls on which hung clothes sorted by size. The fourth wall had shelving running the full length of it, stacked high with blankets, baby accessories, and toys. In one corner was a jumble of boxes and bags containing more items.

"As you can see, we try to keep a decent stock of items to help young moms get started. We really need someone who can come in on a regular basis and sort through the things people donate and get them put out. It's hard for the staff to keep up with that; it seems we are always behind."

"The girls might enjoy doing that," Cassy said.

Her girls nodded vigorously.

They continued down a short hallway. "These are our counseling rooms," Stacey said quietly. "Some are in use right now, but I'll show you an empty one."

At the end of the hall, Stacey stopped at a small room with the door open. She waited for her guests to enter. The room contained a desk and two chairs, a filing cabinet, and a shelf with an assortment of realistic models of developing babies at different stages of pregnancy. Cassy had seen similar ones at a Pro-Life booth at the homeschool conference. The girls immediately spotted them and headed over to get a closer look.

"Oh, look how tiny and cute this one is." Kimberleigh pointed to one of the soft, plastic models.

"That must be how big a baby is at fifteen weeks old," Nicole explained, pointing to the label on the model. "It may be tiny, but it's still so perfect. I don't know how anyone could kill a little baby like this!"

Stacey smiled at Cassy.

"Ever since Nicole heard about abortion, she has been horrified," Cassy explained. "She is very excited to think she may be able to volunteer here, knowing that you help prevent abortions."

"We've been able to help many young pregnant women make the right choice," Stacey said. "I wish I could say that all women who come in here and see those models felt like Nicole does, but unfortunately some still go through with it. Some just have no support and don't know how to cope. We try to give them all the information and support we can so they understand the precious gift of life they are carrying and don't feel so alone. We could use more counselors."

"What is involved in counseling?"

"We supply all the training. Counselors volunteer their time and can choose their hours, but we like to schedule them as regularly as possible so we always have counselors available. Some clients are only one-time drop-ins, but some you may work with throughout their pregnancy."

"Is it possible to come in one morning a week for now and see how that goes? My son goes to work with his dad on Wednesdays, so I thought it would work well if I brought the girls in Wednesday mornings. They could help sort clothes or clean, while I do counseling."

"That would be great. You would need to take the training first, but we have another counselor who wants to start soon so we were currently trying to schedule a training session for her. It would help a lot if you could do it together."

"How long is the training?"

"You come in for three days, and we explain all of our resources. You watch some training videos, observe several counseling sessions, and role-play for practice. Then you would work alongside another counselor for the first while until we feel you are ready to counsel on your own," Stacey explained. "Of course, you'd have to fill out an application first, and we would need references and all that."

"Sure, I'll get the paperwork from you before I go. My husband is a carpenter, and he would also like to help out when he can. Your brochure mentioned some renovation work that was needed."

"Oh that would be great." Stacey clasped her hands together. "We've been wanting to redo some of our counseling rooms and our staff room. The bathroom is also in desperate need of some fixing up and some paint." Stacey led them back down the hall to show them the rooms to the other side of the reception desk.

Jeremy had expressed interest in helping his dad with the work, and by the time Cassy left, she had a handful of applications and information regarding the ongoing projects. She promised to get the paperwork done soon, and Stacey said she would inform Cassy the minute the training schedule was in place. A very happy director waved to them from the door.

⌘⌘⌘

Over the next couple of months, the Knights settled into the routine of their new volunteer work. By December, Cassy was able to counsel on her own, and she was enjoying working with the young expectant mothers immensely. The girls were getting well acquainted with the other staff, who seemed to like having them around. They had fun sorting through all the new baby clothes and finding room for them on the racks. Occasionally a young mom would stop in with a new baby, and the girls would jump at the chance to hold it while the mom searched through the clothes and made her selections.

David and Jeremy had come into the center several Saturdays, and now the bathroom sported a new coat of paint and a new cabinet and sink. They had already started on some of the other projects as well.

"It feels good to be doing something to help others out without getting paid for it," Jeremy confessed one evening at supper.

"I'll remember that come payday." David looked over at his son.

"That doesn't mean it isn't nice to get paid sometimes," Jeremy quickly amended, bringing a laugh from his father.

One Wednesday night, Cassy started to cry as she climbed into bed.

"What's the matter?" David asked.

She sniffed and laid her head on her husband's shoulder. "Do you remember me telling you about Carli?"

"The sixteen-year-old girl you've been meeting with for the last month?"

"Yeah. She was responding so well, and I really liked working with her. She seemed so young and scared when she first came in, but I thought she was doing much better. I'd even gotten a chance to share the gospel with her last week."

"So what happened?"

It took Cassy a moment before she could answer. "Carli called to cancel her appointment today. She told me she had gone for an abortion and wouldn't be coming back."

David stroked his wife's hair. "It's not your fault, Cassy."

"I know, but a part of me wonders if I could have done something to prevent it. She didn't really want to have an abortion, but she is only a teenager and has no support at home. She said she couldn't handle raising a child alone, and her boyfriend was threatening to leave if she didn't have an abortion. She didn't feel she had any options."

"Doesn't Hope for Life put them in contact with agencies who help place the babies for adoption?"

"Yeah, but she was scared of where the baby would end up, and scared of carrying the baby to term and then giving it up. Somehow she convinced herself that at three months the baby wasn't real yet." Cassy wiped at her tears that were falling steadily now, making a path down David's chest. "I know that millions of babies are being aborted around the world, but it is so much harder to deal with when you can attach a face to the statistics."

"Unfortunately you can't make that choice for everyone, Cassy.

Imagine how God weeps too. It's a lie of Satan to convince people that babies are disposable but think of the young women you have helped to understand what a gift having a baby can be."

"But David, we bought into a lie too."

"What do you mean?" David cocked his head to gaze into his wife's face.

"I've been reading through Scripture to better understand God's perspective of children and family in order to give the girls biblical counsel, and I'm coming to realize that we've been deceived too. Children are a gift from God, and we should want as many as He chooses to give us. It's a lie that having lots of children is irresponsible. Maybe we never believed that babies were disposable; we just accepted the fact that they were preventable." Cassy turned sorrowful eyes to her husband. "I wish we had had more children, David. I wish we hadn't made the decision that four was enough…I didn't realize I had bought into a lie!" Cassy laid her head down once again and began sobbing uncontrollably. She felt her husband's chest shudder beneath her in quiet sobs of his own.

David tightened his arm around her, allowing Cassy's pent-up emotions to be released. When her sobs finally subsided, he whispered into her hair, "Maybe we can help keep others from believing the lie."

Slowly Cassy tilted her head to meet David's eyes. "All through school we were taught about overpopulation and how to limit your family size as a responsible citizen, or for your own convenience. It has become the norm, even in the church, and I never questioned it. I guess I shouldn't be surprised to see how our world can so easily take the step from preventing unwanted pregnancies to terminating them. I'm just sorry we didn't seek God's direction before making such an important decision."

"I'm sorry too. I didn't realize I had bought into the lie either," David added sadly. "I always found it so easy to criticize the Israelites in the Old Testament for so easily buying into the cultural practices around them, but I guess we are no different. Too often we let our culture define our standards instead of God's Word. I want to do better at leading our family in biblical truth—like Joshua. No matter what those around us are doing, I want to declare, 'As for me and my house, we will serve the Lord.'"

Cassy nodded and stretched to give her husband a kiss before laying her head back down against his shoulder. Emotionally exhausted, she heaved a tired sigh.

6

Standing Alone

Christmas was fast approaching, and Cassy looked forward to seeing her parents again. She and David had taken the kids to visit their grandparents in British Columbia last Easter, but she rarely saw her mom and dad more than once or twice a year. This year they would be spending Christmas Eve on the farm with David's family, and Christmas Day with her family at her brother Cory's. It seemed hard to get either family all together apart from the holidays or an occasional birthday. They only saw Anthony and Sarah on a regular basis, both because David and his younger brother owned a construction business together, and because they attended the same church.

Cassy wished she felt closer to her family, but over the last few years, they only seemed to drift further apart. Of course Debbie and Rob were still working in South Africa as missionaries, so that was understandable, and everyone was busy with their own families, but it was more than that. The more Cassy and David's perspectives had changed since they started homeschooling, the harder she found it to relate to a family whom she felt didn't understand them.

Cassy pulled a pan of Christmas cookies from the oven. "That's the last of them," she announced to the girls, who sat decorating cookies at the kitchen table. "Now, if we can just keep your brother from eating all of them before next week, we'll have enough to share with your cousins."

"Well, at the rate he's been going today, I think we'd better hide them." Kimberleigh snickered.

"I'm just trying to make sure you have room on the table so you don't have to stack them while the frosting is still wet," Jeremy called from David's study where he sat at the computer munching a cookie. He was working on designing a website for his dad's business.

"Yeah, thanks for the sacrifice," Nicole teased.

"Anytime!"

Cassy joined the girls at the table to help finish off the cookies, and they chatted together while they worked. She loved these moments when life seemed to slow down, and she could sit and enjoy her children. As her girls had grown older, Cassy had noticed her relationship with them gradually changing. It was growing deeper, and the girls seemed to love sitting one-on-one with her, talking through issues. Especially Nicole. As she transitioned from childhood into adulthood, Nicole sought her guidance more than ever. Cassy treasured the fact that she was not losing the hearts of her teenagers.

⌘⌘⌘

Christmas morning finally arrived, and though they had been out late celebrating with David's family the night before, the kids were all up early. They wanted plenty of time to open presents and have their own family Christmas together, before heading to Trish and Cory's for a turkey dinner at 1:00. As they gathered in the living room, David opened his Bible and read the Christmas story.

"What is our greatest Christmas gift?" David scanned the faces of his children.

Ready for the question, they answered in unison, "Baby Jesus."

"Jeremy, would you like to thank God this year for His Christmas gift to us?"

"Sure Dad." Jeremy led his family in prayer. When he was done, he and his sisters excitedly sorted out the presents beneath the tree into separate piles.

They each took turns opening one present at a time, thanking the person who had given it. When it was David's turn, he reached to pick up a brightly wrapped package from Cassy. She watched as he gauged the weight of the flat, rectangular item trying to guess its contents.

"It's a new air compressor," he teased as he started to rip off the paper. David looked down at the beautifully framed picture she had taken of him last spring while they were hiking in the mountains. In the photo, David stood on a rugged mountainside with one foot resting on a rock, a snowy peak looming behind him in sharp contrast to the blue sky. Cassy waited until her husband's eyes came to rest on the engraved gold plate mounted on the bottom portion of the frame:

"'Choose for yourselves this day whom you will serve...But as for me and my house, we will serve the LORD.' Joshua 24:15,'" David read aloud before giving his wife a tender smile. "Thank you. I love it!"

"Let me see," Nicole pleaded. David turned the picture around and held it up.

"Nice." Jeremy got up to take a closer look. "You're standing on the Solid Rock, Dad."

David smiled at his son. "Yeah, it suits. Good thing your mother didn't choose a picture of me at the beach on Vancouver Island." David turned the picture toward him again. "I will try to live up to it," he added more seriously.

Eventually all the presents were opened, and each one chose something to take to show their cousins. Jeremy had gotten some power tools to add to his growing collection, and he fiddled with them for quite some time—checking out all the specs. Cassy could tell he was having a difficult time choosing which item to take. Before long, it was time to gather their things and head out. It took several trips to load up the food and gifts that needed to go.

"See, there were lots of Christmas cookies," Jeremy informed his mother as he carried a large platter of baking out to the van. "I could have eaten more!"

"You had plenty," Cassy assured him.

"You can never have too many Christmas cookies," he insisted.

⌘⌘⌘

Mike and Joyce Harris greeted each of their grandchildren with a hug as they entered the house. Jeremy eagerly held up his tool case to show his grandpa.

"Wow, what do you have there?" Grandpa Harris leaned forward to get a peek.

"Some more tools to help Dad." Jeremy balanced the heavy case on one arm and opened the lid.

Mike let out a whistle. "Looks pretty fancy. Do you know how to use that?"

"Yep," Jeremy answered proudly as he held up his cordless drill for his grandpa to inspect. "It has 250 in./lbs. of torque, a spare battery, and an LED work light...see." Jeremy tipped the drill to point out the light. "I got a circular saw too, but I left that at home."

"I'll have to try that out sometime," Mike gave his grandson a pat on the back. With excitement, Jeremy closed the case and hurried off to find his cousins. "So Nicole, any boyfriends we should know about?" he teased his granddaughter as she hung up her coat.

"No, Grandpa, I'm not dating," Nicole stated simply.

"That won't last long," Kathy called from the kitchen. "Believe me, I know what it's like to have a teenage girl in the house." Kathy eyed her daughter, Christy, who was setting the table. Christy was almost seventeen, and Don and Kathy's son, Connor, was in his second year of university. Connor was the eldest grandchild.

"Actually, she's waiting until she is seriously ready for marriage, and then she will court, not date," David said as he set down the box of presents he was carrying.

"You're kidding, right?" Kathy looked incredulous.

Cassy could hear Christy snicker and her heart sank. *Here we go again*, she thought. *Why do we even try to explain ourselves?*

Kathy glanced at her brother-in-law. "Okay, you're not kidding," she mumbled and dropped the subject.

Cassy hung up her coat and greeted both her parents with a hug before continuing on to the kitchen. "What can I do to help?" she asked Trish.

"You want to mash those potatoes?"

"Sure." Cassy set to work, and before long dinner was ready.

Everyone crowded around the two tables, and during the meal, Cassy felt she got somewhat caught up on what her nieces and nephews were doing. As usual, most of the talk revolved around school and youth events, the kids' latest boyfriends or girlfriends, professional sports, and TV. Cassy sat back and quietly listened as everyone analyzed the contestants on several different reality shows.

She knew that, at times like this, her children felt as alienated as she did. It was difficult to interact in conversations that revolved around things everyone else had in common, but they were not part of. Not that it was intentional; Cassy doubted the others even realized how she felt. She knew it had been their choice as a family to step away from those things. And no matter how different it made them, she did not regret that decision. Besides, it was only natural that the others would talk about the things they enjoyed. What Cassy struggled with was the feeling of being on the outside. As though her family stood alone. At times Cassy thought it would help if she could just sit down and explain the biblical basis behind some of their choices, but maybe it wouldn't. The very nature of their family's choices stood in opposition to what the others were doing, which would only appear as confrontational. Instead Cassy listened and did her best to enter into the conversation when she could.

When dinner was over and cleaned up, the whole family squeezed into the living room to open presents. Afterwards, they played a few games and snacked on the many Christmas goodies, before having a late supper of turkey buns.

Eventually everyone started packing up their things to head home. Before she left, Cassy made arrangements to meet back at Trish's in a couple of days. The kids had all gotten money from their grandparents for Christmas, and Cassy had suggested they get together to go shopping on Saturday while her mom was still here to go along. The guys opted to pass on the shopping trip, deciding to go to a local Rebels hockey game instead.

It was late by the time the Knights arrived home, but David still called everyone together before bed. Cassy felt tired, but she was thankful her husband had taken the lead in establishing a family devotional time. Though they missed evenings here and there, he tried to be consistent. The kids hurried to get into their pajamas and join their parents in the living room.

David read a passage from Scripture about thankfulness and then turned to the kids. "So, what is one thing you have each been thankful for this past year?"

Kimberleigh was the first to respond. "I'm thankful for my friends."

"I'm thankful for all my new presents when some kids don't have very much." Anika turned toward her pile of gifts tucked under the tree from the morning celebration. "And I'm thankful that Jesus came as a baby to save us," she quickly added, pointing toward the manger scene peeking out from amidst the gifts.

"I'm thankful for the new babies we get to see at Hope for Life, and I'm thankful that I could make a baby blanket for one of the new moms," stated Nicole.

Everyone turned to Jeremy, awaiting his response. "I'm thankful that I get a chance to work with Dad and that he is such a good example for me."

David smiled at his son. "You're learning to work hard and to do your best when you're given a task. I appreciate that."

"I'm thankful for my family, and for the blessing each one of you are to me," Cassy said sincerely.

"I guess I am thankful for God's Word, that it helps us to know God more and teaches us how to live for Him." David gestured toward the Bible in his hands. "I don't think I fully appreciated it as I should have until more recently."

"Dad, if we are all trying to live by God's Word, why do Christian families have so many different standards?" Nicole asked. "I feel like we are so different; it's hard when people don't understand why we homeschool, or why we don't do a lot of the things they do."

"Like why you don't go to the youth group, or why you don't watch TV or listen to the same music they do?"

"Or why you don't date?" Cassy added, thinking of the question put to Nicole earlier that day.

Nicole's face fell as she shook her head. "I believe we are honoring God in waiting, but it's hard when our own family thinks we're weird."

David nodded sympathetically toward his daughter. "I know it's tough sometimes, sweetie, and unfortunately you get the brunt of some of the questions because you're the oldest. Sometimes it's hard for your mom and me too, because we are trying to do things differently than how we were raised. It's not so much that they think you're weird; they merely don't understand. Everyone needs to search these issues out for themselves in Scripture, but we feel the Bible supports our decisions. That means that no matter what everyone else is doing, we will follow the principles we find in God's Word."

"Hey, just like the verse on the picture Mom gave you!"

"That's right, Anika, 'Choose for yourselves this day whom you will serve...But as for me and my house..." David paused expectantly.

"We will serve the LORD," Nicole started and the others joined in.

⌘⌘⌘

Early Saturday morning, Cassy glanced out the window to see feathery snowflakes drifting lazily to the ground. Thankfully they didn't have far to drive, but she hoped the weather wouldn't keep Kathy from joining them for their day of shopping. Even though the hockey game didn't start until evening, David and Jeremy drove into the city with the girls. They had agreed to help Cory install some new kitchen cabinets he'd bought for Trish for Christmas. They had their work cut out to get it accomplished while the women were gone. By the time they arrived, Trish had the contents of her cupboards boxed and piled in the living room.

Eighteen-year-old Kiera met her cousins at the door, her coat on and ready to go. "They're here, Grandma," she yelled down the hallway.

"I'm coming." Joyce Harris hurried to join them. "Somebody has sure been anxious to get going this morning." She eyed Kiera and then turned to her younger brothers. "You sure you boys don't want to join us?"

Daniel, who was a year older than Jeremy, and Justin, a year younger, responded with expressions of horror. "No way! I'd rather have my toenails ripped out one by one than to go shopping all day with a bunch of girls!" Justin declared. "I'm saving my money for the hockey game tonight."

"Jeremy?"

"No thanks, Grandma, I'm going to help Dad and Uncle Cory."

"Okay, I guess we're off then."

"Aren't Kathy and Christy coming?" Cassy asked.

"Yeah, but Kathy called this morning, and they were running a bit late. She said they'd meet us at the mall around 11:00," Trish explained.

"We'll all fit in my van then," Cassy offered as they headed out.

Upon reaching the mall, Kiera headed directly to a teen clothing store and the others followed along. Cassy noticed Nicole leafing through the racks of clothes, so she came alongside to help her look. After checking out at least a dozen shirts, Cassy shook her head in dismay.

"These shirts are all very low-cut, and almost see through, Nicole. Why don't you check a different rack?"

"That's how they're supposed to be, Mom. They're supposed to be layered with other shirts."

"So you have to buy two or three shirts instead of one? That makes sense! I'm looking over there." Cassy headed to a table piled high with sweaters. Kimberleigh and Anika meandered around the store looking, even though the clothes were all too big for them.

Joyce soon joined her daughter. "The kids are all growing up so fast. I wish we could see them more often."

"I know. Have you and Dad ever thought about moving back to Alberta now that you're retired?"

"Actually, we have been discussing that possibility. It would be hard to leave our church after your dad has pastored there for so long, but we are not getting any younger. It would be good to be closer to family. We've been checking some of the real-estate listings around Red Deer and may go look at a couple houses before we head home."

Cassy smiled. "That would be great, Mom."

Joyce set down the sweater she was admiring and looked up at Cassy. "I don't think I've ever told you before, but you're doing a great job with your kids."

Cassy fought back a sudden rush of tears. "Thanks, Mom. You don't know how much it means to hear you say that. Sometimes it's hard when we are the only ones in the family who are homeschooling. It can feel pretty lonely."

"It must be difficult to keep up with all their schooling, especially with Nicole in high school now."

"Well, yes and no. The kids are a lot of help around the house, and as they get older, they work more independently. For sure some days I get tired and don't feel up to it, but I am really enjoying this stage."

"Isn't it harder to monitor all of Nicole's credits to make sure she can graduate?"

"Not really, because she's not pursuing credits; we're putting together our own program of studies." Cassy watched her mother's eyebrows shoot up and held her breath, awaiting her response.

"You mean she's not going to graduate?" Joyce stared at her daughter.

"She'll finish the studies we put together for her, but she won't get a government diploma." As she spoke, Cassy fiddled with the sweater in her hands, afraid to meet her mother's eyes.

"I guess I didn't realize you could do that, but why don't you want her to get a diploma?"

Cassy tried to relax. She could tell that her mother was surprised, but her tone was not condemning. "It's not that we're against our kids getting diplomas. It's just that a government diploma is based on following man's standards. We don't really care to win man's approval if it means using all the government textbooks, even though they banish God from the picture and teach worldly philosophies. We could take all the government tests and strive to meet government standards for education, but we feel it is more important to seek God's approval and follow His standards. We want the freedom to choose what is in the best interest of each of our children, and to teach them using books from a biblical perspective."

"Wow, I can't argue with that. I guess I don't know anyone who really questioned the government system when you guys were in school, including your father and I."

"I realize that, Mom, and I'm not trying to be critical of your choices for us. Homeschooling was virtually unheard of when we were growing up."

"Oh, I know." Joyce waved away Cassy's concern. "Who knows whether I would have seen the validity of it back then even if it had been an option? I wasn't sure about it when you started, but it seems to be working for you."

Just then Nicole joined them with an armload of clothes she wished to try on. Cassy excused herself to follow her daughter to the change room. She waited outside while Nicole tried on the first outfit. When Nicole opened the door, Cassy noticed her daughter tug gently on the front of her snug-fitting, cropped shirt in an attempt to make the bottom of the shirt meet the top of the low-cut jeans she was wearing. Even so, Cassy could still see her daughter's exposed belly peeking from between the articles of clothing.

Surprised, Cassy asked, "So what do you think of that outfit?"

Nicole turned to look at her reflection in the full-length mirror mounted on the wall adjacent to her change room. She smiled and shrugged. "I sorta like it."

"What do you like about it?" Cassy studied her daughter's face in the mirror.

"I don't know. I guess it feels stylish. A lot of girls I know are wearing clothes like this." Nicole spun back around to face her mother, crossing her arms in front to hug her belly.

"And do you think that outfit is modest and that it sends the right message about the kind of girl you are?" Cassy couldn't hide her disappointment in the clothes her daughter had selected.

Nicole frowned. "What about if I switch to a longer shirt?" she asked sullenly.

"No, Nicole. Those jeans are not permissible either. I know that a lot of girls wear low-cut jeans, but they are immodest and draw attention to the wrong things. Besides, most girls I've seen wearing those continually yank on their pants in an attempt to keep themselves covered, and it looks ridiculous. They can't even sit down properly without exposing themselves to everyone behind them."

Without a word, Nicole retreated to her change room and closed the door. It remained shut for some time, and Cassy figured her daughter was pouting. This wasn't the first time Cassy had felt Nicole pushing the boundaries concerning clothing styles in recent months, and though Nicole seldom fought her on the issue, Cassy felt frustrated. When Nicole finally exited again, she was wearing her own jeans and a baby pink, chenille sweater with a button-down collar.

Cassy smiled in appreciation. "I love that sweater; it looks very soft and feminine."

Nicole glanced in the mirror and nodded half-heartedly. "I didn't bother showing you any of the other clothes I tried on, because I knew you wouldn't let me get them. I like this sweater though, and it's on sale." She showed her mother the price tag.

Kimberleigh and Anika came bounding over to where they were standing. "Oooh, Nicole, that's pretty. You should buy that one so I can borrow it!" Kimberleigh rubbed her hand down the sweater's downy sleeve.

"It's too big for you," Nicole told her sister.

"Not much, I don't mind it being a little big," Kimberleigh assured her.

Soon after Nicole and Kiera made their purchases, they all went to meet Kathy and Christy, who had just called to say they had reached the mall. The rest of the morning was quite successful, and all the girls found more than enough to spend their Christmas money on. The mall was crowded, so Trish suggested going to a nearby Chinese restaurant for lunch instead of battling for tables at the food court. All in all, it was an enjoyable day together and they were all shopped out by the time they made it back to Trish's for a light supper while the men headed off to their hockey game.

Trish was ecstatic over her new cupboards, which were complete except for a few final touches. The women all helped her reorganize her kitchen while they waited for the men to return.

Later that night, Cassy expressed her relief to David over the fact that she had been able to explain their decision concerning high school diplomas to her mother. She had been dreading addressing that issue, as she felt sure it would confirm to everyone that their children's education was inferior.

"Mom's response was so encouraging." Cassy pulled the scrunchie from her ponytail and ran her fingers through her long blond hair. "I'm still not looking forward to explaining it to Don and Kathy, though," she admitted. "Especially since Don is a teacher in the public high school. I think he will be offended by anything we say."

"Probably, but you have to understand that he has poured his life into teaching, and in a way, our stance questions the value of his work. After all, he's striving to help kids meet the standards we say are unimportant."

"I know. I just hate feeling at odds or like people think we are purposely trying to find fault with everything. Do you think we are too critical?"

"That's something we need to be cautious of, but I believe the standards we've set for our family are honoring to God. The Bible calls us to be discerning as Christians. I would seriously have to question our walk with Him if those standards weren't in opposition to our culture." David switched out the light and climbed into bed. "You worry too much."

7

Challenge to Purity

That winter, Cassy heard about a CD series distributed through a homeschool ministry that focused on biblical femininity. It included a whole session on the topic of modesty. After reviewing it online and discussing it with David, she ordered a set. When it arrived, Cassy decided the CDs would be perfect to take along in the van. She and the girls began listening to them on the drive to and from the pregnancy crisis center each week, and the topics often triggered lively discussions that carried on through lunch once they arrived home. Cassy found the presentations very encouraging, as they reinforced so many of the biblical roles she sought to pass on to her daughters and even challenged her in some areas she hadn't considered.

However, it was the fourth week, when they listened to the message on modesty, which brought the most dramatic response. After reading 1Timothy 2:9 and 10, the speaker cautioned women seeking to live a life of purity to be discerning not only in what they wear, but in how they act both for their own sake and in consideration of the men around them. He pointed out various ways the modesty of woman has declined in our culture, causing even Christian young women to compromise. And when women cease to value modesty, they often fail to protect their inner purity. He challenged both unmarried and married women to dress in feminine attire that doesn't reveal what should be saved for their husband's eyes alone, and which is in keeping with their inner purity.

Then he went on to expound on the biblical picture of the church as the bride of Christ, which is to be pure and clothed in white robes that reflects the righteousness of Christ. In the same way, it should be every woman's desire to present herself as a pure bride to her husband. Rather than attempting to draw attention to herself, she should dress and act in a way that reflects Christ and brings glory to God.

As Cassy pulled into the garage and turned off the engine, the girls remained unusually quiet. Heading inside, Cassy turned to find Nicole following her down the hallway.

"Can I talk to you, Mom?" Tears filled Nicole's eyes.

"Sure, honey." Cassy ushered her daughter into her bedroom and closed the door.

"I'm sorry for pushing to buy clothes that I know are inappropriate." She swiped at the tears on her cheeks. "I did sorta want attention—to feel that people noticed me, especially the guys, and I know that was wrong."

Cassy enfolded her daughter in her arms. "It's natural for girls to want to seek attention; it makes them feel special. But that is the wrong kind of attention. You need to protect your purity as a treasure to be saved for one man. And when that time comes, you're going to want a godly gentleman. One who will be drawn to you for the right reasons and who sees you as a treasure worth cherishing. I don't want you to settle for less than that. You need to be patient, Nicole, and wait for God's best."

"I know." Nicole sniffed. "Those CDs have helped me see the whole picture more clearly. I want to focus on becoming the woman God wants me to be instead of trying to impress the boys. If I want to find a godly husband someday, I'd better make sure I'm prepared to be a godly wife."

"That sounds like a good attitude to have." Cassy gave her daughter a pat on the back as she released her.

"Thanks, Mom." Nicole fingered the purity ring she wore on her left hand—a present from her father on her thirteenth birthday. "I want to earn the right to wear this," she replied with conviction.

"I'm proud of you, Nicole. I couldn't ask for better daughters."

From that moment on, Cassy noticed a marked difference in the care Nicole took in her dress. A few shirts Cassy had reluctantly allowed Nicole to buy even though they were a bit snug disappeared from her wardrobe. Cassie was thankful she'd never had major battles with any of her children, and she prayed future battles would be avoided through the careful training of their hearts for God. The fact that she and David kept a firm guard on the hearts and minds of their children also helped to minimize the negative media and peer influences, which were the downfall for so many teens.

⌘⌘⌘

As the kids got older, Cassy discovered more and more the need to specialize and adjust each one's studies to suit their learning style and interests. She had seen the value of getting her children involved in the selection of their material, so they regularly set aside time to establish goals and choose curriculum each spring prior to the homeschool conference. Gathered around the kitchen table, the family would leaf through different resource catalogs, making lists of books in which they were interested.

"Do I have to do math next year?" Nicole asked as she reached the math section of her catalog.

"Yes, I think you should take some math for at least one more year. I know you don't like it, but it is good for you to learn the concepts and to challenge yourself." Cassy sympathized with her daughter's aversion to the subject. Nicole would much rather spend her time in other pursuits.

"I just don't get geometry and algebra. It makes no sense, and I don't know when I'll ever use it."

"I used to think that too," Jeremy chimed in, "until I started helping Dad. I learned real fast why it's important to be able to measure angles and make those calculations accurately after I messed up a few times. Math is very practical and does make sense if you know how to apply it."

"Yeah, well, if I wanted to be a construction worker, I might agree with you, but that occupation isn't high on my list! I want to be a homemaker, and when was the last time Mom had to calculate an algebraic equation?"

Cassy smiled. She often referred the kids to David when they had trouble with their math because it took her a lot longer to go back and figure out what to do. In truth, there were many concepts she hadn't used since her own high school math classes. It was hard to know how far to push her girls in these areas and how much to let them focus on developing skills she knew they would use. "I'll talk to Dad about it, but maybe you can take one more year of accounting or consumer math. It would be beneficial for you to know how to balance books and how to calculate interest and all that stuff."

Nicole proceeded to peruse some of the business math books. Kimberleigh and Anika shared a catalog between them, leafing through the novel and biography section and jotting down titles of books set in the time-period of the First and Second World Wars. Currently the Knights were studying the French Revolution, but as they'd already studied the founding of Canada and their country's early history, Cassy had decided to jump ahead and focus on the twentieth century for next year.

"Wow, there's lots of books to choose from dealing with Hitler and the Holocaust." Kimberleigh consulted their list.

"I know," Anika agreed. "Which ones do you think sound the best?" The two compared ideas and started checking their first choices.

"I also want to get some books on Canadian government," Cassy announced. "I think it would be good for you to learn more about our governmental process. As we are likely to be heading into an election soon, it would be nice if you understood how it all works."

"Oh, that could be sort of fun. Could we hold our own debates and vote on household rules too?" Jeremy grinned at his mother.

"The debates, maybe, but I'm sorry to inform you that our household is not a democratic system."

Jeremy laughed. "I'm not going to argue that point, or you'll have me studying Scripture to write a paper on parental authority or something."

"Hey, that's not a bad idea," Cassy teased. "I don't think you've written a paper on that topic yet."

"No, but I've written one on headship and the biblical roles of men; that comes close."

"You didn't have CDs to listen to like the girls did on biblical femininity. Those are important principles for you to understand so you can work now toward becoming the godly leader you'll need to be someday for your own home."

"I know it was good for me to study it," Jeremy acknowledged. "I just don't want to tempt you into giving me any more writing assignments than absolutely necessary!"

Cassy laughed. "So, what do you want to study next year?"

Jeremy didn't bother looking at any of the catalogs before answering. "I was talking to Dad about science; I'd like to take physics next year. It would strengthen my math skills, and I'd enjoy studying energy and motion. I could do experiments with things like electricity and gravity."

"What, like 'if I jump off the garage roof and land with this amount of force I will most likely break my leg, let me try it and see!'" Nicole smirked at her brother across the table.

"That was three years ago and I was getting *your* Frisbee off the roof. Besides, I wouldn't have broken my leg if I hadn't landed in that little hole and lost my balance."

"You wouldn't have broken your leg if you had come down the ladder either," Kimberleigh added smugly.

By the time Cassy had finished discussing plans for the upcoming year with her children, she had a lengthy list of resources. The annual conference had become a highlight for the whole family, as Nicole and Jeremy were now old enough to attend and help shop, and Kimberleigh and Anika attended the children's program.

For Cassy, the conference was also a time of encouragement as she listened to the various speakers who shared from their experiences and assisted in casting a biblical vision for the homeschooling family. This served to build a broader perspective of the homeschool movement and confirm to David and Cassy that they were doing the right thing for their family. It helped to interact with so many families who shared similar standards and with whom Cassy found it easy to relate; and now that Cassy had been homeschooling for almost six years, she found some of the moms who were just starting out coming to her for advice. She viewed these opportunities as a ministry, as she would never forget what it had meant to her to be mentored by Lauren.

⌘⌘⌘

May turned out to be cold and rainy, with a late snowstorm mid-month. Tired of the dreary weather, Cassy was relieved when the last traces of snow finally disappeared. She was going to be hard-pressed to get the yard cleaned up and the garden planted so she could focus on Kimberleigh's June 5 party. Kimberleigh was turning thirteen, and Cassy was planning a special evening with family. A delicate gold ring with a small diamond set in the center was safely nestled in David's dresser. He had picked it up just last week after having it sized at the jewelers.

The night of the party Anika and Nicole bustled around the kitchen helping Cassy put the finishing touches on the meal, while Kimberleigh finished getting ready. When the doorbell rang, Jeremy was lighting the candles on the table. Kimberleigh rushed down the hall from her bedroom to open the door for her grandparents, who were the first to arrive.

"Come on in," Cassy called to her in-laws from the corner of the kitchen.

"What a lovely dress!" Jean commented upon entering.

"Thanks. Mom helped me make it." Elegant folds of blue taffeta swirled around Kimberleigh's ankles as she spun around. "You like the black velvet sash?"

"It's very nice, and you're becoming quite the young lady."

Soon Cory and Trish arrived, followed by Anthony and Sarah, and Andrew and Laura. Each wished Kimberleigh a happy birthday. Don and Kathy would not be coming, as they had too far of a drive for one evening. Even so, with all the cousins they would have a full house.

"You look like a princess!" declared six-year-old Samantha, an ardent admirer of her older girl cousins. She followed them around after church each Sunday until either Anthony or Sarah rounded her up to go home.

"I wouldn't suggest kissing any frogs in an attempt to find a prince," Anthony teased.

"I'm not planning on it." Kimberleigh wrinkled her nose.

When supper was ready, Cassy invited the twelve kids to file through the buffet line first. After heaping their plates with Chicken Fettuccini Alfredo, they noisily crowded around the kitchen table.

"This looks fantastic." Sarah eyed her food as she made her way to a TV tray beside the couch.

"Yeah, you should have a birthday more often," Anthony told Kimberleigh as he followed his wife into the living room.

Cake and ice cream followed supper, and once the dishes were cleared away, David pulled a kitchen chair to the edge of the room for Kimberleigh to sit and open presents. The kids clamored over top of one another to find a spot on the floor. When she was finished, David came to stand beside his daughter.

"Kimberleigh, as your father, it is my duty to help protect your purity until the day I present you to your husband. In Philippians 4:8, God calls you to think on things that are noble, right, and pure. If you love Him, you must seek to be obedient to His Word and strive toward holiness. I am committed to helping you live a life of purity, because it honors God and will be a blessing to your future husband."

David reached into his shirt pocket to pull out a small velvet box. He opened it and held it down for Kimberleigh to see. "I am giving you this ring as a symbol to remind you to keep yourself pure until this ring is replaced with a wedding band. As you mature into a beautiful young lady, I want you to always remember that your beauty doesn't come from your fancy clothes and outward adornment but from your inner heart." He lifted the ring from its satin casing and handed it to his daughter.

Kimberleigh's eyes lit up as she carefully slid the ring onto her finger. "Thanks, Dad." She stood to give her father a hug.

"Let's see your ring." Samantha climbed over her cousins to get to Kimberleigh. "Ooh, that's pretty."

Her older sister, Lissy, checked it out too.

Kimberleigh thanked everyone again for her presents as she made the rounds showing her ring to her aunties and Grandma Knight. Kiera and Mandy took a peek, but the boys weren't too interested in jewelry. Timothy had started a wrestling match with his fourteen-year-old cousin, Mark, and Anthony had to tell them to settle down.

Even though she had a houseful, Cassy was sorry that her parents couldn't be here for the evening. She knew they missed being able to share in their grandchildren's special events. Hopefully, that would soon change. Her mom and dad had flown to Alberta last month to do some more house shopping. They had actually put an offer on a house in Red Deer, on the condition that they sell their home in B.C. It was hard to tell how long that would take with the current market.

Once the last of the company had gone, Cassy made her way to the kitchen to clean up. The girls chipped in to help. With the dishes done, they headed to their room to get ready for bed.

"Thanks for the party, Mom." Kimberleigh gave Cassy a hug.

"You're welcome." She lifted her daughter's hand to look at her ring. "This is a reminder that you don't need to get caught up in the whole dating scene, seeking relationships with lots of boys."

"I know."

"I'll tell you what I told Nicole. You only need to share your heart with one man, and not till you're ready. You need to be patient and wait for God's best!"

8

A Daughter's Protection

As Cassy started to think through their recent discussions on biblical femininity and the course she was setting for her daughters, she began to struggle with how to handle the high school years. What direction should she give Nicole regarding her future following graduation? Up until now, she had focused on setting goals each spring for the following year, but these last two years for Nicole would go quickly. Soon they would be heading into new territory, and Cassy wasn't sure how to prepare. She knew Nicole felt uncertain as well. The tension only mounted as friends and family started asking about her future plans.

Cassy sat on the edge of the bed and turned to face her husband who had entered the room. "David, what do you think we should encourage Nicole to pursue once she graduates? As far as college, I mean."

David frowned. "I don't know for sure. If her goal is to be a wife and mother, rather than training for a full-time career, the benefit and cost of having her pursue a college degree becomes questionable."

"What about Bible college?"

"I've thought about that too, but I'm not sure. For one thing, I think Nicole is way more mature spiritually than most young people heading to Bible college. I think she may find that frustrating. She loves to study on her own, and for the cost of even one year at Bible college, she could buy a library of good resources and gain more for her money."

"I think a lot of kids attend Bible school as much for the chance to get out on their own and for the social experience, but I don't think that is a good reason to go." Cassy flopped back against her pillow and ran her fingers through her hair. "Not only that, but the more I've checked out some of the local Bible college websites, the more I have to question what some of them are teaching anymore. There seems to be a lot of liberal theology and mysticism creeping into the class descriptions and book lists."

David walked over to the bed and propped up his pillows, taking a seat beside Cassy. "I know; I've seen some of that too. The bigger question I've been asking myself lately is if it is biblical to send our girls away from home, even to a good college."

Cassy turned to look at her husband. "What do you mean?"

"I'm not sure." David crossed his arms over his chest and looked deep in thought. "But the more I study it out, the more I see God's design in keeping a daughter under the headship and protection of her father until marriage. Even a widow in the Bible returned to her father's household, unless a close male relative chose to marry and provide for her. If a widow had no family, then God instructed the church to look after her, but I think God intended women to have a covering of protection. That responsibility was passed off to a husband upon marriage."

The tension Cassy had been feeling eased. "That makes sense. And it lines up with how we've been trying to prepare the girls for marriage." She sighed. "Nicole has been asking questions about how to plan; I'm not sure what to tell her. I wanted to tell her she should stay home, but I attributed that to my selfishness because I would miss her. It can be a lot of pressure for a girl to feel she is expected to get out and support herself. I realize some girls may relish the idea of having their own apartment and being independent, but that could be a negative thing to pursue. It not only makes a girl more vulnerable, but it might train her to despise being a keeper at home. And if she gets used to that independence, it could become a struggle for her to submit to her husband later. "

David nodded. "It would also be hard to be involved in Nicole's courtship if she were living away from home. I'd feel like I'd abdicated my responsibility as her father to protect her from making a poor decision." David stretched out his arm to encircle Cassy and pull her against his shoulder. "We can pray about it and talk to Nicole, but I don't see anywhere in Scripture that releases a father from looking after his daughters and protecting their purity until marriage."

"That flies in the face of today's culture." Cassy tipped her head to look into David's dark eyes.

He smiled at her. "I know, but that hasn't stopped us before. Besides, through most of history it was common practice to keep your daughters at home. The whole dating phenomenon and the practice of sending our daughters out on their own once they turn eighteen is only recent. And if you look at the huge rise in couples living together, the number of single mothers trying to support themselves, millions of abortions, and the unprecedented number of marriages ending in divorce, I'd say it hasn't worked very well."

Cassy reached her arm across David's chest to give him a hug. She felt a deep sense of peace after discussing the issue with him. Knowing he had been seeking God's direction for their family was extremely comforting.

Before climbing into bed, she and David prayed together, and she felt assured they were headed in the right direction. Tomorrow she'd talk to Nicole. For now, they would encourage her to continue her studies at home, pursuing her interests and ministering to the women at Hope for Life.

⌘⌘⌘

Not until midafternoon did Cassy find a quiet moment to sit down with Nicole. The others had finished their schoolwork for the day and disappeared to their rooms. Pouring herself a cup of coffee, Cassy called Nicole over to the table.

"I know you've been really confused about how to plan for the future, and I've been trying to sort that out myself. Your father and I talked last night, and he feels that, once you graduate, you should stay home."

Nicole's eyes widened. "For how long?"

"Well, I'd say at this point until you are married and he can hand you over to your husband to look after you."

"Really?" Nicole sat back against her chair, deep in contemplation. "You mean I don't have to think about college, or how I could make enough to support myself? What if I don't get married for a number of years? What if no one asks to court me, and I don't get married at all?" Tears filled Nicole's eyes as she voiced her fears.

Cassy reached across the table and took her daughter's hand. "I know you want to get married, Nicole, and we have to trust the Lord that He has someone special for you. But even if that didn't happen for some time, you have a place here. Your father feels that God has given him the responsibility to look after you and offer you protection and security as long as you need it. He doesn't want you to feel that you have to fend for yourself or train for a career that would conflict with your goals."

"But what would I do?"

"We're still trying to figure some of this out, but we're not asking you to stay home and do nothing. You could continue to study things you're interested in and develop your skills. With your music training, you could teach piano lessons if you wanted to, and there are always ministry opportunities—like Hope for Life or other places." Cassy fiddled with her coffee cup as she spoke, trying to think through her words.

"The Bible instructs young women to use their single years to focus on serving the Lord, and there are many ways you could do that. It becomes a lot harder to have time to minister if you are going to school full-time or working to support yourself. Even once you become a mother for that matter. This time could be a special blessing for you. Being at home would give you the time to pursue all kinds of things you may not have time for later, and you could be saving money instead of building up debt." She studied her daughter's face. Nicole had been sitting quietly while she spoke, but Cassy could tell her mind was racing. "What do you think?"

Nicole stared at her mother a moment before speaking. "I don't know. I guess, in some ways, I feel a huge sense of relief that I don't have to be planning how to support myself if I don't get married right away. I'm not dying to go to college just for the sake of going, and it's nice feeling that I have the freedom to stay home. But at the same time, I struggle with how I'm going to explain that to people and wonder if they'll think I have a lack of ambition."

Cassy nodded. "I struggle with that too, but I've come to realize that if we try to make our decisions based on what others might think, we'll never win. For one, it's more important that we try to please God, and secondly, we'll never please everyone anyway."

"I know." Nicole placed her elbows on the table and propped her chin in her hands. "But I worry that I won't get married right away, and then I'll still be at home when I'm forty!"

"We'll cross that bridge if we get to it, but you're only fifteen. That's a long way from forty. In the meantime, you can think about the things you might want to continue studying at home, and what you would like to be involved in."

⌘⌘⌘

Throughout the following weeks, Nicole came to Cassy several times with ideas she was considering. Now that she had a clear sense of direction and had some time to pray about the matter, Cassy could tell she felt more settled. Nicole was more of a homebody anyway, so college and the idea of getting out on her own had not been a big draw for her.

Kimberleigh, on the other hand, was a different story. Cassy prayed for wisdom in knowing how to direct her when the time came. At least by then they would have more experience, and Kimberleigh would have had time to adjust to the idea.

9

The Big Debate

Summer was always a busy time for the Knights, as it was peak season for construction work and required longer days for David. Jeremy would turn fifteen the end of July, and he was becoming proficient at swinging a hammer and following blueprints. This year David had asked his son to work for him full-time over the summer months, and Jeremy gladly accepted the offer. Cassy could tell her son enjoyed the work and being "one of the men." She worried at times that Jeremy might get injured—the terror of her husband's construction accident was still fresh in her mind—but David assured her that he and Anthony were watching out for him.

For Cassy, summer meant many hours working in the garden and tending flowerbeds, but she loved the outdoors. After the long winter, she always welcomed the chance to get out and enjoy her yard and the warm sunshine. The girls were a great help, and Cassy enjoyed sitting on the back porch shelling peas together.

"Too bad we can't grow these peas without having to do all the weeding that goes along with them!" Nicole scooped a row of fresh peas from the pod she had just opened and plopped them all in her mouth.

"I don't know anyone who enjoys weeding, but weeds are part of the curse. Just think of them as a reminder that sin always has consequences." Cassy smiled at her daughter.

"Yeah, but weren't the weeds part of *Adam's* curse?" Kimberleigh rationalized. "The Bible says that women were cursed with pain in child birth, and that men were cursed with weeds and painful toil. How come we end up with both curses?"

Cassy laughed. "You'll have to tell your dad the Bible says he's supposed to weed all the gardens and see what he says."

"He'd probably point out that Eve was created to be Adam's helper, and say that he's training us to be good helpers for our husbands some day." Nicole popped more peas into her mouth.

Anika nudged her sister. "We're not going to have any peas left for the freezer if you keep eating them all. You hardly have any in your bowl."

"Yes I do," Nicole insisted, "but they are so much better right out of the garden."

Anika held her bowl beside Nicole's to compare the two. "See, I have almost twice as many as you."

"I can fix that." Nicole grabbed Anika's bowl and dumped some of her sister's peas in with her own.

"Hey!" Anika took her bowl back and set it down out of Nicole's reach. "That doesn't count."

Cassy always found it rewarding to watch the freezer fill up with fresh produce and to see the shelves in her cold room lined with canning. Sacks of potatoes, onions, and carrots soon filled the space beneath the shelves, enough to carry them through the winter.

Once the produce was all in and her canner tucked away for another year, Cassy pulled out the schoolbooks once again. It didn't matter if most kids had already been in school for a couple of weeks. The Knights had come to view all of life as the context in which education took place, so they did not calculate "school time" in terms of set schedules and academic studies. It encompassed much more than that. The academic studies merely blended into the mix of daily chores and family activities in an almost seamless way, so that an onlooker would have a difficult time distinguishing any definite start or end to the "school" day.

⌘⌘⌘

At the fall start-up meeting for the homeschool group, Cassy noticed a few new families attending. After the meeting, she introduced herself to the woman who had been sitting directly behind her.

"Hi, I'm Sandi Bronson, and this is my son, Colby." The woman indicated the tall, slim boy standing beside her with shaggy, brown hair that hung nearly to his shoulders. "My husband just got transferred here from Calgary. We were glad to find out that Red Deer has such an active homeschool group, because Colby is an only child and needs that interaction."

"How long have you been homeschooling?" Cassy inquired.

"Four years now, since he was thirteen. He was so advanced in school that he was bored, and then he'd start getting in trouble for disrupting the class. You know how that goes." Sandi gave a short chuckle and nudged her son with her elbow. "We decided it was best to get him out of the classroom and have him do his studies online. That way he can work at his own pace."

Cassy smiled and introduced Colby to Jeremy and Nicole. Kimberleigh and Anika had already disappeared with some of their buddies.

"It looks like there are a lot of activities to choose from. Which ones are you planning to go to?" Colby directed his question more to Nicole than to her brother.

Nicole glanced at Jeremy before answering. "Uh, I'm not sure. We used to go to the skating on Fridays, but now that we're doing a bit of volunteer work, we only get there occasionally. I'd like to go to the writing workshop, though. I love to write, and it would be neat to go to a workshop with a published author."

"Sounds interesting. So, where do you volunteer?"

Nicole briefly explained about their work at Hope for Life, while Cassy continued her conversation with Sandi. "Jeremy works in construction with my dad, and they helped with some renovations at the center."

"That's nice." Colby threw Jeremy a cursory glance before directing his attention back to Nicole. "Hey, do you have your driver's license yet?"

Nicole shifted awkwardly under the boy's steady gaze. "Not yet. I turn sixteen next week. I'm hoping to get it soon." She threw her brother a desperate look.

"Why don't you come and let me introduce you to some of the others," Jeremy offered before Colby could ask any more questions.

"Sure." He paused. "You coming too, Nicole?"

She nodded and the three made their way to a group of homeschoolers chatting noisily at the back of the room.

⌘⌘⌘

Shortly after Nicole celebrated her sixteenth birthday, she asked if she could book her driver's test. It was nerve-wracking for Cassy to think of turning Nicole loose with the car keys, but her daughter was growing up. If Cassy could get past her tendency to worry, she had to admit that having another driver in the house would come in handy.

Cassy accompanied Nicole as she drove into Red Deer for the scheduled road test. They arrived early, and Cassy watched sympathetically as Nicole fidgeted nervously in her chair while she waited for her turn.

"Try to relax, Nicole. You've done a lot of driving, and you should have no trouble with the test. Just pretend you are practicing with your driving instructor."

Nicole simply nodded, but Cassy noticed that her foot did not slow its agitated bobbing. Cassy said a silent prayer for her daughter. Moments later, a huskily built man carrying a clipboard stepped around the counter and called Nicole's name. He wore his hair in a brush-cut, and Cassy studied his rugged features. Though she had never met an army commander before, this man fit her image of one perfectly. Nicole threw Cassy a frantic glance before shakily rising from her chair.

"I'm Nicole," her voice wavered as she spoke.

"Are you ready for your test?" The man crossed the room toward where Nicole stood. One corner of his mouth turned up slightly, and Cassy guessed that was as close to a smile as his stern countenance would permit.

"Yes, sir," Nicole answered meekly as she followed the man out the door to her waiting vehicle.

Cassy's heart sank, and she began to pray in earnest for her daughter. She could tell the man intimidated Nicole, and she could hardly blame her. The minutes ticked slowly for Cassy as she waited. When Nicole finally reentered the room, the tears in her eyes were immediately evident. Cassy didn't need to ask how it had gone.

"You okay?" She rose to give Nicole a hug.

Nicole nodded and handed her mother the keys. Cassy quickly went to the counter to pay for the exam before returning to usher her daughter out to the vehicle. The minute Nicole was seated in the van, she burst into tears. "He made me so nervous," she sobbed.

Cassy started the vehicle and backed out of the parking stall. "So what happened?"

"I went through a red light," Nicole choked out through her tears. "He told me to turn, and I was so flustered, I turned without checking to see if the light was green." Cassy burst out laughing, causing Nicole to stare at her mother in astonishment. "It's not funny!"

"I know; I'm sorry, sweetie. But if that man had ordered me to turn, I think I would have gone through a red light too."

Nicole snickered despite her tears. "I think they hired him to give driver's tests just to make more money by scaring kids to death so they fail and have to retake the test."

When they reached home, everyone was duly sympathetic for Nicole's disappointing experience. Jeremy offered to sit beside her in the vehicle with a clipboard in his hand and bark out orders while she was driving so she could practice, but Nicole told him that wasn't necessary. Two weeks later she rebooked her test with another licensing agency and passed with flying colors. Cassy felt relieved that they would not have to go through the process again, and Nicole had no trouble smiling as they snapped her picture to put on her official license.

⌘⌘⌘

Early in the fall, Cassy started working through the new books she had purchased on Canadian Government. One day, following an explanation of the process a bill had to go through before being ratified by the Governor General, Cassy pulled out a paper she had printed off the internet. She looked around the living room at her children. "I searched on the government website to see what bills are before the house right now, and I found a private member's bill that, if passed, would make it a criminal offense for parents to spank their children." Cassy proceeded to read the bill, which clearly classified spanking as a form of child abuse.

"They should have passed that bill about fifteen years ago." Jeremy smirked at his mother.

"Is that right?" Cassy eyed her son. "Well, you guys are all beyond spankings, but do you want the government to dictate how you should discipline *your* children someday?"

Jeremy shook his head. "I was just kidding."

"I want each of you to write one page on whether this bill is biblical, and then tell me why or why not. Anika and Kimberleigh, you can work together on yours if you want to."

"Good." Ten-year-old Anika let out a sigh of relief.

"Mom, what happens if they do pass this bill, and we feel that it is wrong?" Nicole turned worried eyes to her mother.

"That's a tough one, Nicole. The Bible says we are to honor those in authority over us, but we are never to place man's law over God's. If our government makes a ruling that goes against Scripture, then we must choose to follow God first. We shouldn't be disrespectful about it, but we still might have to face the consequences for going against the law."

"Like Daniel, when he was thrown into the lion's den for praying! Or Shadrach, Meshach and Abednego, who were thrown into the fiery furnace!"

"You don't have to make it sound so exciting, Kimberleigh." Nicole frowned at her sister. "Do you think it would be fun to go to jail, or to have your children taken away just because you spanked them?"

"No, but maybe God would send his angels to rescue us from prison." Kimberleigh shrugged. "It always sounded so exciting when people were dramatically rescued in the Bible for doing what was right."

"Just remember, they weren't all rescued. Most of the disciples were killed for preaching the Gospel!" Nicole frowned again as she turned back to her mother. "Do you think the government will really pass this bill?"

"I don't know. The government has debated similar bills in the past, which have been defeated. However, I never thought we would see same-sex marriage legalized and that passed, despite the flood of letters the government received against it. It's hard to predict; it seems like the family is really coming under attack." Cassy sighed.

"What can we do to make a difference?" Jeremy wanted to know.

Cassy contemplated her answer. "I think we have to consistently stand up for the truth where we can and be a light for God in our community. I feel like our work at Hope for Life has allowed us to share the truth with many women considering abortion, and we've been able to make a difference on a small scale. That's where it starts. We still need to write letters and pray for our government, but ultimately we need to lead people to Christ and let Him change their hearts. It doesn't do much good to focus on people's behavior, if they are still lost."

That night after supper, Jeremy approached his father while he was reading the newspaper. "Hey Dad, can I ask you a question?" He stood poised beside David's chair, pen and paper in hand.

David lowered his paper to look at his son. "Sure."

"What do you think is the biblical perspective regarding spanking your children?"

"That's cheating, Jeremy." Nicole peeked over her book at her brother.

"I'm doing a formal interview to get good quotes to support my work," Jeremy reasoned. "Dad's an authority on Scripture and a pro at spanking, so he is a good source for research."

David laughed. "Sorry, but your mom already told me about your assignment, so I'll give my comments *after* you write your paper."

"Not even any hints?"

"Try reading the book of Proverbs, and looking up the word *discipline* in a concordance."

Jeremy dragged his feet as he headed down the hall toward his room.

Throughout the week, the kids worked on their assignment, handing in their papers once they were complete.

It wasn't until Saturday night, after the kids had gone to bed, that Cassy finally found the time to sit down and read them.

"What's so funny?" David asked when Cassy broke into laughter.

"Jeremy's paper." She started to read from the paper in her hand.

> I am living proof that spankings do not kill a child. I should know; I received lots of them! Some people think that spanking a child is abusive. When I was six, I may have agreed with them. But that is not what the Bible says. The Bible says that Jesus disciplines those He loves. It also says in Proverbs 13:24: "He who spares his rod hates his son, But he who loves him disciplines him promptly." My dad must love me lots!
>
> I'm glad that my dad cared enough about how I turned out, that he wanted to discipline me. Sometimes he told me that it hurt him more than me when he had to spank me, but I'm not sure about that part because his spankings hurt a lot. I used to think that it was because it hurt his hand. Not anymore. I guess when you love someone, it hurts to see them doing bad things. I know it hurt Jesus, because He had to die for all the bad things we've done. He did that because He loved us.
>
> God also loved us enough to give us parents, so they can teach us about Him and teach us to obey. That is why God commands parents to discipline their children just like He disciplines us. Proverbs 23:13-14

says, "Do not withhold correction from a child, For *if* you beat him with a rod, he will not die. You shall beat him with a rod, And deliver his soul from hell."

So you see, spankings didn't kill me, they saved me from hell by teaching me how to follow Jesus. I sure hope that the government doesn't pass this bill about spanking, because someday I want to be able to discipline my children just like my dad disciplined me.

Cassy stared at the paper in her hand. "Not bad for a boy who still doesn't like to write."

David brushed a hand over his eyes. "I'm glad he had to think that through for himself instead of me telling him what I thought. The kids need to study these issues out so they know for themselves what Scripture teaches."

Cassy nodded. "I think we should pick other topics for them to study from a biblical perspective. Jeremy wanted to do some debating; maybe we could have them study out an issue and then take sides to debate it from both a secular and Christian point-of-view. That way they could try defending their beliefs orally as well as in writing."

"Sounds like a good idea," David agreed.

Together they discussed different issues that would be relevant to their children, and Cassy compiled a list. She would let the kids pick their next topic.

⌘⌘⌘

Early the following week, she called the kids into the living room to explain her idea. Jeremy sprawled on the floor beside Shasta, their aging cocker spaniel, while she read off the topics on her list. "Which issue would you like to debate?" she asked when she was finished.

"The one about good vs. evil," Jeremy promptly answered.

"No, I'd like to debate the inerrancy of Scripture," Nicole argued.

"I already know I can believe the Bible, so I agree with Jeremy. Defining good and evil sounds more interesting." Kimberleigh placed her vote.

"Anika?" Cassy waited for her youngest to reply.

“I don’t care; they both sound okay.” She shrugged.

“Then how about we start with defining good and evil, and if you guys like debating this way, we can do it again.” When they all agreed, Cassy explained how the debate would work. “Let’s put Kimberleigh with Jeremy, and Anika with Nicole. You can work together in teams, and I’ll give you two weeks to study out the topic. Nicole and Anika, do you want to argue from a biblical perspective, or a worldly perspective?”

Nicole conferred with her little sister before answering. “We want the biblical perspective.”

“Good!” Jeremy said. “I want to try arguing the other side.”

“Well, you’ll still need to know the scriptural arguments if you want to try and defeat them, and same for you two,” Cassy turned to Nicole and Anika. “You’ll want to think through how Jeremy and Kimberleigh might present their side so you can make a strong case for your position. I suggest you take notes on index cards, list key arguments, Bible verses, or other quotes that support your position.” She gave them a few more pointers on where to look for information and how to organize their research, before sending them off to get started.

Nicole and Anika headed to Nicole’s room to work, while Jeremy and Kimberleigh settled on the couch. “You can be the secretary and write down our ideas.” Jeremy handed his sister a notebook and pen.

Cassy headed into the kitchen to bake some cookies while the kids were busy. A short while later she noticed Anika sneak quietly down the hallway and peek around the corner into the living room. She stood listening to her opponents’ scheme for several minutes until a stifled giggle gave her away.

“Hey, no spying!” Kimberleigh called, causing her sister to dart back down the hall.

⌘⌘⌘

Over the next two weeks, the teams got together numerous times to work through their arguments. Occasionally they would come to Cassy with questions, and she would give them a few suggestions to help them along.

The day of the debate was set for Saturday afternoon, so that David could be home to help monitor and give input. They were not following the strict rules of debate but would be following a similar procedure. Each team would have three minutes to present their opening arguments, then they would take turns countering the other team's position before giving their closing remarks. When it was time to begin, Cassy called for the kids to collect their notes and come to the kitchen table.

Kimberleigh grinned suspiciously at Jeremy, and the two disappeared to his room. Moments later, they came out wearing suit jackets, ties, and dark sunglasses. Jeremy toted a black leather briefcase in one hand, which he deposited on the table and opened to retrieve their notes. Kimberleigh had to hike up her sleeves to keep her hands from disappearing in her brother's black jacket.

Cassy laughed. "Where did you get that briefcase?"

"We borrowed it from Mr. Andrews." Kimberleigh took her seat and clasped her hands over her notes in a dignified fashion.

Nicole and Anika took their seats on the opposite side of the table, while David and Cassy sat at one end.

"Any questions before we begin?" Cassy asked.

"Yes." Kimberleigh's hand went up. "Do we get extra points for dressing up?"

"No, but nice try." Cassy handed David some paper and a pen for jotting down notes to comment on when they were finished. Jeremy's team would present first, so when they were ready, David looked at his watch and motioned for them to begin.

Jeremy stood and cleared his throat. "Ladies and gentleman, we are here today to define the concepts of good and evil. *Webster's Online Dictionary* defines the word *good* as 'Moral excellence or admirableness. That which is good or valuable or useful.'[1] However, what is valuable or useful to me may not be valuable or useful to you. So how can we come up with one universal answer to define what is good? We will not all agree. We think each person must decide for themselves what is good for them. Good is relative and based on individual circumstances and opinions." Jeremy turned to Kimberleigh, who picked up the paper she had been studying and stood beside her brother.

"I'm going to give you the dictionary definition of the word *evil*, but I am sure you will conclude, as we have, that no one can truly define evil."

[1] http://www.websters-online-dictionary.com

Kimberleigh stated with all the confidence of a defense lawyer making his closing statements before the jury. She straightened the tie at her neck and lowered her sunglasses to the tip of her nose so that she might read over the top of them more easily. " *Webster's Online Dictionary* states that *evil* is: 'Morally objectionable behavior. That which causes harm or destruction or misfortune.'[2]

"But, what exactly *is* morally objectionable behavior?" Kimberleigh peered over the top of her glasses, studying each one seated around the table with intense scrutiny. "What is objectionable to you," she pointed at Nicole, "might not be objectionable to me. And, is it evil to cause harm to some, if it benefits others? If it is always evil to cause harm or destruction, then it was evil to go to war against Hitler, because in war you have to shoot people and bomb cities. I would say that causes harm *and* destruction! However, many would claim that it was *good* to go to war against Hitler. So you see, defining good and evil isn't so easy, is it?" She grasped her chin and stared at her opponents triumphantly before turning it back over to Jeremy.

"Our society tries to make laws to define good and evil by voting on what would benefit the society as a whole. However, these laws are always changing, and they differ from one country to the next. Many countries used to say that it was evil to abort babies; now they say it is good. How we define evil changes because our society changes. Everything is relative and depends on circumstances. Even a judge will look at the motives and circumstances to decide a case when someone breaks the law, because judging good and evil is not cut-and-dried." Jeremy scanned his notes one more time before nodding and taking his seat. He and Kimberleigh exchanged looks of satisfaction.

Nicole had been jotting down a few notes while her siblings spoke, but she now collected her notecards and looked at her father. David nodded, and she stood to begin their side of the presentation.

"If we look to man to determine good and evil, then we will never find answers. However, we have a higher standard, and that is God. We can know what good is because God is good, and He tells us in His Word what good and evil are. He tells us in Romans 12:9 that we are to 'Abhor what is evil. Cling to what is good.'

[2] http://www.websters-online-dictionary.com

"How can we do that if we can't know what is good and what is evil? God also says in 3 John verse 11, 'Beloved, do not imitate what is evil, but what is good. He who does good is of God, but he who does evil has not seen God.' We do what is good when we act according to God's character, but if we refuse to look to God for our example, we cannot know what good is. In the same way, evil is anything that goes against God's character." Nicole paused. "You want to read yours now?" Anika asked quietly.

Anika nodded and began to read. " *Webster's Dictionary* defines good as: 'Moral works; actions which are just and in conformity to the moral law or divine precepts.' He also says that 'Moral evil is any deviation of a moral agent from the rules of conduct prescribe to him by God, or by legitimate human authority; or it is any violation of the plain principles of justice and rectitude.'"[3]

"What's *rectitude*?" Kimberleigh mumbled.

Anika grinned at her sister across the table. "*Rectitude* means 'righteousness,' and we got our definitions from the *real* Webster's Dictionary from 1828. Noah Webster knew how to define good and evil, because he believed in God, so there!" Anika looked back at her notes and continued. "We were created good, because we were created in God's image. But we decided to rebel against God and do evil things. Now we can never be perfectly good again, like God is. It's simple. If we act like God and obey Him, that is good. If we don't act like God or we disobey Him, that is evil. But we need God's help to be good."

Nicole nodded at her sister and finished their presentation. "John 3: 19-22 states, 'And this is the condemnation, that the light has come into the world, and men loved darkness rather than light, because their deeds were evil. For everyone practicing evil hates the light and does not come to the light, lest his deeds should be exposed. But he who does the truth comes to the light, that his deeds may be clearly seen, that they have been done in God.' People are confused about good and evil because they have rejected God from whom goodness comes. But we *can* know the truth. Good and evil is based on God's truth, and God does not change. Truth is not relative!"

[3] *American Dictionary of the English Language*, Noah Webster 1828. Foundation for American Christian Education (San Francisco, CA: 1967, 1995).

David agreed to give both teams a five-minute break to discuss how they wanted to refute the other's arguments, so they grabbed their notes and quickly headed to their rooms. When he called them back, he instructed Jeremy to go first.

"You say you can define good and evil based on God, but what if we don't believe in God? What if we believe in a different god with a different standard for good and evil than your God? There are many different cultures in the world with many different beliefs. No one group has the right to say that they are right and everyone else is wrong. Even those who claim to be Bible believing Christians do not all agree on what the Bible says, so it is not so black and white. Some even argue that what Paul said was good for New Testament Christians to do is not relevant for our culture. You claim that God and the Bible is your source of truth regarding good and evil, but you cannot prove that God is real, or that the Bible is relevant to today."

"I knew we should have debated the authority of Scripture first," Nicole commented while Kimberleigh was preparing to speak.

"Anika claimed that *Webster's Dictionary* of 1828 gave a different definition of good and evil than our modern *Webster's Dictionary*, but that only proves people's ideas of good and evil change with time. In Noah Webster's day, his definition may have fit his culture, but it doesn't fit today. Just like the Bible. The Bible was written thousands of years ago, so it couldn't possibly fit our world today. People have learned a lot more since then and are a lot smarter. Um—" Kimberleigh scanned her notes—"Oh yeah, science has proven that we were not created in God's image like the Bible says; we evolved. And *everyone* knows that evolution is true, so the Bible has to be wrong!"

When Kimberleigh sat down, Nicole picked up several of her notecards and slowly stood. "You say that man can decide for himself what is good and what is evil based on his own opinions and circumstances. What if one person decides that it is good to kill another; can his opinion be wrong? And what about abortion? In our society there are strong opinions on both sides of the issue, but abortion can't be good and evil at the same time. There has to be an absolute standard, and we will all be judged according to that standard whether we believe in it or not.

"Isaiah 5:20-21 states, 'Woe to those who call evil good, and good evil; Who put darkness for light, and light for darkness; Who put bitter for sweet, and sweet for bitter! Woe to *those who are* wise in their own eyes, And prudent in their own sight!' We can't trust man to decide what is good or evil, because people are fallible. Some think we can vote on truth, or change it to suit our desires, but that doesn't work. We must follow God's standard. Just because some people don't agree on what the Bible says or think it is irrelevant doesn't mean the Bible can't be trusted. It simply means some people are wrong or have compromised the truth."

Finally, Anika stood and looked at the paper in her hand. "Just because you don't believe in God doesn't mean He is not real. If you don't believe in gravity and jump off a cliff, you will still fall. Truth does not change depending on whether you believe it or not. Psalm 53:1 says, 'The fool has said in his heart, "*There is* no God." They are corrupt, and have done abominable iniquity; *There is* none who does good.'" Anika glanced up from her notes. "I guess there is lots of evidence all around us that God is real. Some people refuse to look for it because they don't want to believe. That is why they make up silly stories about evolution too. It says somewhere in the Bible that anyone who doesn't believe in God is without excuse, or something like that. I guess I wouldn't want to be in their shoes when they die and find out that they were wrong. That's all."

David gave them one more break and then each group had a couple minutes to give any closing comments. They each did their best to sum up their positions before the debate was finished. David and Cassy praised them for preparing such good arguments and for challenging their opponents' main points as they'd been instructed. They discussed their debate awhile longer, and all agreed they would like to try another one.

"That was a lot of fun," Jeremy declared, "even though we were fighting on the losing side. It's challenging to argue something you don't believe is true."

"For sure it is," David agreed. "But it can also help you to defend the truth better if you try to understand the arguments against it so that you can be prepared with answers. It's hard to share the Gospel with someone if you don't know how to defend it. We all need to learn to do that better."

10

Sibling Rivalry

The day of the scheduled writing seminar, Nicole excitedly asked her mother for the van keys. Cassy almost regretted having told her that she could drive into the city by herself. A light snow was falling, and though Cassy knew that Nicole had a lot of practice driving, this would be her first trip without an adult in the car.

"You make sure you watch the traffic, and don't let Kimberleigh distract you," she cautioned as she pulled the keys from her purse and handed them to her delighted daughter.

"I know, Mom, I'll be careful."

"You call me and let me know when you get there, and remember that the roads might get slippery if this snow starts to freeze."

"I know, Mom. C'mon, Kimberleigh."

"Call me when you're leaving Red Deer too, so I'll know you're headed home," Cassy yelled after them.

"I will."

The back door closed, and Cassy looked at the clock. They should be there in about twenty minutes. She tried to calm her tight nerves and busy herself with straightening up the kitchen, but it wasn't until the phone finally rang and she heard Nicole's cheerful voice on the other end that she could fully relax and get on with her day.

Later that afternoon, when the girls arrived safely home, she breathed a sigh of relief. *That wasn't so bad,* she told herself. *Until the next time she wants to go somewhere and I have to worry all over again.*

"Did you have any trouble?" she asked when Nicole had gotten her coat off and entered the kitchen.

"Not except for the car I backed into in the parking lot."

"What!" Cassy looked up in alarm.

"I'm kidding, Mom. Relax." Nicole smirked.

"That wasn't funny!" Cassy shook her finger at her daughter. "So how was the workshop?"

"It was really good; I learned a lot. The only bad part was having Colby there." She grabbed a cookie and perched on a tall stool at the counter.

"Nicole, that doesn't sound very nice." Cassy set down the potato she had finished peeling and frowned at her daughter.

"I'm sorry, but it's the truth. He sat beside me all day and constantly tried to get my attention. It was clear he wasn't interested in the workshop at all. When we paired off to do some writing exercises, he insisted I be his partner since he didn't know anyone else very well, and Kimberleigh had already paired off with Brianne. He made me feel so uncomfortable."

"You should have politely told him no." Cassy went back to peeling potatoes.

"I tried, but he wouldn't listen, and by then everyone else already had a partner. I was stuck. I tried to pick a different seat after the lunch break, but he followed me."

"Don't do anything to encourage him, and he'll leave you alone."

"I wasn't encouraging him, believe me! He followed me all around the ice at skating a couple of weeks ago too, and I had to latch on to Melissa and make her promise not to leave my side. Too bad Melissa was sick and didn't make it to the workshop today."

"He's new to the group and probably looking for friends. Be patient. Once he gets to know some of the other kids better, he'll settle down."

"He's looking for more than friendship," Nicole muttered under her breath as she headed to her room.

⌘⌘⌘

Besides the study on Canadian government, Cassy had chosen to spend some time this year focusing on improving their geography skills. She had discovered a large, blank map of the world at the last homeschool conference and had bought it on impulse. Now she was trying to decide how best to use it. The map had been laminated so you could write on it with white board markers and rub it off, but now she needed to get the kids interested in learning the different countries. When she'd bought the map, she had planned to have the kids work individually to try filling it in. Then an idea came to her. *Why not have them work together and make a game out of it?*

Excited now, she collected her pack of white board markers and called the kids into the living room. She had placed the large map in the middle of the floor, and instructed them to all take a seat around it. "I've come up with a way to help us all learn our geography," she announced, "and I think you'll enjoy it." She proceeded to hand each one a different colored marker. "You are going to take turns labeling one country on the map until you can't name any more. Whoever stays in the longest, wins. We'll keep doing this once a week until the end of the year and see how many countries you can name by then." They had discussed different countries here and there throughout their studies, but she knew there were many countries they had never touched on.

Nicole wiggled her marker and grinned at her siblings. She had been studying a lot about Europe lately, and she was ready to begin. "Who starts?"

"We'll go youngest to oldest," Cassy picked up her atlas of the world and pulled up a chair so she could clearly see the map to double check their answers.

"Okay." Anika pulled the cap off her green marker and wrote *Canada* through the middle of her own country. "That one's easy."

Kimberleigh quickly labeled the *United States* in blue, and Jeremy followed suit by labeling *Mexico* in Red. Nicole labeled *England* in black, and they went around again. Anika was the first to fall out of the race, and the others finally admitted defeat while Nicole was still working away on the more obscure European countries. In all, Cassy counted forty-one correctly labeled countries when she declared Nicole the winner. She observed that South America had hardly been touched, as well as Africa—except for Egypt and South Africa where Debbie and Rob were working as missionaries. Most of Asia had also been left blank.

During that week, Cassy noticed Anika and Kimberleigh sneaking down the hall with the atlas. She smiled and went to peek at what they were doing. When she cracked open their bedroom door, Kimberleigh scrambled to hide the atlas under their bed.

"Oh, it's just Mom." She pulled the book back out again. "Don't tell

Nicole," she whispered, "but we're studying Europe so that next week we can steal all the countries Nicole knows first and try to beat her!" The two grinned conspiratorially.

"Okay." Cassy nodded. "But don't forget to learn a few she doesn't know so you can stay in the game."

"Aw, good plan," Anika agreed. "Thanks Mom."

The following Tuesday Cassy once again pulled out the map. It had been wiped clean from the week before, and each of the kids quickly selected the same markers they had used previously. Again Anika started the game, only this time she immediately wrote *Romania* in tiny green letters.

Nicole looked at her little sister in surprise. "Hey, that's my country."

"Not anymore!"

Kimberleigh threw her sister a triumphant grin and proceeded to write *Poland* in blue.

Jeremy slapped his knee and laughed. Taking his red marker he followed his sisters' lead and wrote *England* in the appropriate blank. "I know that one."

"That's not fair, but I'll still beat you." Nicole immediately started to label the easier countries, obviously hoping her sisters would not be able to keep up with labeling all the European countries and she would have some left.

The battle grew more intense as Anika and Kimberleigh continued to fill in Europe with each turn, and eventually Jeremy was the first to call it quits. Nicole hung in a while longer, but after frantically studying all the empty countries, she finally had to guess. She tried labeling *Turkey*, but guessed wrong. Anika proudly took her marker and labeled *Paraguay*, and Kimberleigh went to the middle of Africa and labeled *Zaire*. Neither one could label any further, so Cassy declared the game a tie. Anika and Kimberleigh had both labeled the same number of countries. They turned to one another and gave a big high-five.

"Good job you two," Nicole congratulated her younger sisters, "but I'll have you know that the battle is on!"

Soon all four of the kids were studying the atlas each week in an attempt to learn the more obscure countries they thought none of the others would know to save for the end. Cassy was surprised at how quickly the map started to fill up. She never knew which countries were going to be added each week, and it kept her busy double-checking what they labeled to make sure they were getting them right.

"There's nothing like a little healthy sibling rivalry to build incentive to learn geography," Cassy remarked to David one evening.

"Oh yeah? So how many countries are they up to now?"

Cassy went to retrieve the map from its place tucked behind a bookcase in the corner of the computer room. The small shelf in the kitchen, which had held all their school books their first year of homeschooling, had long ago disappeared. Now three large bookcases loaded with books and school supplies concealed one whole wall in the small room that doubled as David's study. Cassy hadn't yet wiped off all the colorful marker from earlier that day, so she brought it over to David's chair to show him.

"They've been at it for four weeks now, and they labeled 132 countries today. Jeremy finally beat his sisters."

"That's pretty good. I don't think I could label that many."

"I don't think I could either, without the help of my atlas, although I am learning them as I check what the kids label each week." Cassy got a wet paper towel and wiped off the map before putting it away.

⌘⌘⌘

The next day at the pregnancy crisis center Anika hurried up to Kellie's desk to fill her in on their geography game. She had told the receptionist about their competition, and each week she had let her know who had won the day before and how many countries they had named.

Kellie stopped what she was doing to listen to Anika. "What! You let your brother win? How'd he do that?"

"Well," Anika leaned her elbows on the corner of Kellie's desk, "he studied Africa a whole bunch, and Africa has a lot of countries in it. They're really hard to remember, but he knew most of them. Of course Mom said he didn't spell them all right, but he was close so she gave them to him anyway. Did you know that there is a country in Africa called Burkina Faso?"

"No, I sure didn't." Kellie smiled at her young helper.

"Me neither, but I do now. I think that's a funny name for a country."

"Maybe the people who live in Burkina Faso think that Canada is a funny name."

Anika smiled and shrugged. "Maybe. So what do you want us to do today?"

"I thought Nicole could check and see if the bathroom needs to be cleaned first; then she can help the two of you put out some new clothes that got dropped off. We got three big boxes since you were here last week."

"Oh good." Kimberleigh headed toward the room behind Kellie's desk. "We haven't had any new clothes to go through for a couple of weeks."

"Wait for me." Anika hurried to catch up with her sister.

Kellie looked up at Cassy and laughed. "It sure is more lively around here with your girls helping. I love having such enthusiastic volunteers."

"They love being here." Cassy hung up her coat and came back to Kellie's desk. "Do I have any messages?"

Kellie handed her a couple slips of pink paper from the corner of her desk. "Here you go. Brenda called and was hoping to get an appointment with you today. You're supposed to call her first thing."

"Thanks." Cassy headed down the hall to her counseling office.

It was a busy morning, and she had already met with two expectant mothers when Kellie came to her office once again to announce a drop-in. Cassy looked at her watch. She had forty-five minutes before Brenda's appointment, so she told Kellie to bring her back.

A moment later a young girl, whom Cassy guessed to be about sixteen, walked hesitantly into the room. "This is Wendy," Kellie introduced before she quietly left and closed the door.

"Hi Wendy, my name is Cassy. Would you like to have a seat?" She indicated the padded vinyl chair close to her own.

Wendy eyed her speculatively before reluctantly slumping into the chair. "I'm only here to get my mom off my back. I already have an abortion scheduled for next week, so there's no need for you to waste your breath."

Cassy's heart sank. She took in the girl's torn jeans, dyed hair, and pierced lip. Her T-shirt read *You're entitled to my opinion.* The motto seemed to suit the cockiness in the girl's eyes. This one was going to be a challenge. "It's clear you don't want to be here, so can you tell me why your mother wanted you to come?"

The girl stared at the wall rather than at Cassy. "She doesn't want me to have an abortion, but it's too late. I've made up my mind."

"Then can you tell me why you want an abortion?"

"That should be obvious!" Wendy rolled her eyes. "I'm only fifteen; I'm not ready to be a mother."

"Hope for Life can help you with that, Wendy. We offer all sorts of support services throughout pregnancy and after the baby's born. There are many other girls your age who have kept their babies and are doing okay."

"No, my mom and dad said they would help with all that too, but it's not for me," she said adamantly.

"There's always the option of giving the baby up for adoption. Our agencies have a long list of parents who are waiting to adopt a baby. Have you considered that?" Cassy, not feeling she was making any headway with this girl, offered a silent plea to God for help.

"And why would I want to go through nine months of pregnancy for nothing?"

"How far along are you?" Cassy tried to keep her voice as gentle as possible.

"About three months...I'm not really sure." Wendy shrugged.

"Then you are a third of the way there already."

"But I'm not showing yet. None of my friends know, but they'd all sure know if I was nine months' pregnant." Wendy shifted in her chair and glanced toward the door. "I should be going."

"Please, wait for a moment." Cassy held up her hand, and Wendy leaned back in her chair with a look of impatience. "If you are going to get an abortion, you should be making an informed decision. You need to know the facts. Would you like me to show you what your baby looks like at this stage and explain some of the risks?"

"It's just a blob of tissue, what's there to see?" Wendy started to rise again.

"Are you sure that's all it is? What if you are wrong? You might regret your decision," Cassy challenged. She had counseled a number of young women who had come to her office in tears following an abortion. It was heartbreaking.

Wendy paused, then plopped down into her chair once more. "Fine, I'll look. Then I'm outta here."

Cassy reached to retrieve two fetal models from a shelf behind her desk. "You aren't sure just how far along you are, so I'll show you two life-size models. This first one is eight weeks—you are way past this stage. And the second one is fifteen weeks, which is probably closer to the stage your baby will be next week." Cassy set the models on the corner of her desk, close to Wendy's chair.

"Why do you keep calling it a baby?" The disgruntled teen leaned toward the models and cast a glance at the first one Cassy had indicated. Cassy saw a momentary shock flicker in the girl's eyes before she glanced at the second model. As her eyes took in the details of the small fetal body, her brows wrinkled in confusion. When she turned away and leaned back in her chair, her characteristic expression of defiance was shaken.

Cassy grasped at this small window into the girl's heart and quietly began to speak. "They look like a baby, don't they? By eight weeks, all the baby's body parts, systems, and organs are in place. They are very small, but the heart has been beating since it was three weeks old. By twelve weeks, you should be able to tell whether your baby is a boy or a girl."

"That's enough! I don't have to sit here and listen to all this. You're making it up." The angry teen fled from her chair and out the door, letting it slam loudly behind her.

⌘⌘⌘

When Wendy reached the end of the hall, she almost ran into Anika, who was standing beside Kellie's desk, waiting for the receptionist to return from a quick errand. Anika had heard the door slam and watched the girl rush down the hall with concern.

"Aren't you a little young to be here?" Wendy demanded with derision.

Anika grinned at her would-be assailant. "I'm not a visitor; I work here. My name's Anika."

Wendy stared at Anika skeptically. "What do you do?"

"My sisters and I clean and help organize the clothes and things for the new moms. Sometimes we even get to hold their babies. My mom works here too," she explained.

"Is that your mom's desk?" Wendy pointed to the receptionist's desk

Anika was leaning against.

"No, that's Mrs. Wallace's desk. My mom works down there." She pointed tentatively down the hall to the room the girl had just exited. "What's your name?"

"What business is it of yours?"

Taken aback by the girl's abruptness, Anika said, "You don't have to tell me, I guess. My family just likes to pray for all the moms we meet here."

Wendy's brows furrowed. "What do you pray about?"

"Oh, that the moms would be able to get the help they need, that they wouldn't be sad or afraid, and that God would protect their babies, things like that. I thought if you were having a hard time, I could pray for you." Anika tried once more to break through the girl's hard exterior with a gentle smile. What could have happened in her short life to make her so angry?

"Well, I'm *not* a mom, so you don't need to pray for me. My mom and dad do enough of that already!" Wendy shoved her arms into her coat.

Anika flushed awkwardly. "I'm sorry. Most visitors who come here are pregnant, so I just assumed. Have a nice day," she called after the girl who was making a hasty retreat out the front door.

⌘⌘⌘

Down the hall, Cassy was already fervently praying for the young client who had left her office. "Please God, between now and next week, help Wendy to see the truth. Help her parents and others around her to be able to give her the support she needs and that they would be able to convince her not to go through with an abortion. Please protect this little baby, Lord!" She grabbed a tissue from the box on her desk and hastily wiped her eyes. Drained, Cassy glanced at her watch. Brenda would be here shortly.

Over the following weeks, Cassy anxiously quizzed her coworkers to see if any of them had heard from Wendy, but none had. After two months, Cassy gave up asking, but she still prayed on occasion for the young girl she was sure was in the area somewhere going through the grief of her abortion. Her own heart ached at the thought.

11

Elections

Shortly after Christmas, the government called an election, which they set for February 20. As members of the party, the Knights had been receiving regular updates and had known an election was imminent. David decided to contact the local Conservative Party office to see if there were ways for their family to help during the campaign. It would be a chance for the kids to get firsthand experience and apply the information they had been learning through the fall. Len Anderson, the local Conservative candidate for MP, was a Christian man with a good reputation in the community. He seemed more than glad to take advantage of their offer of help.

Soon David was filling the back of his truck with large blue signs sporting Len's name on them to place in strategic spots along the highway. Grabbing his sledgehammer, he conscripted Jeremy to help him. Pounding the spikes to anchor the signs into frozen ground was tough work, and after two hours of working in the frigid temperatures, David climbed thankfully into the cab of his truck. Jeremy slid in beside him and whisked off his gloves to blow on his fingers.

"There should be a law against calling an election during the coldest month of the year," he huffed.

"You don't stop to think about all the work that goes into running a campaign until you get more involved," David admitted, cranking the heat on high.

When they reached home, he and Jeremy stomped the snow from their boots and hurried into the house to warm up. Cassy made them some hot chocolate, and Anika offered fresh cookies she had baked that afternoon, which the men gratefully consumed.

"There are several debates being scheduled for the local candidates, and the first one will be next Friday evening in Red Deer. I think we should take the whole family." David set his empty mug on the table. "It starts at 7:00, but it might be nice to be there early to meet the candidates."

Cassy grabbed a pen and wrote the event on her calendar posted in the kitchen. "We should watch the leaders' debate too. They usually broadcast it over the internet, don't they?"

"They have before. I could even hook the computer up to the TV so we could watch them on a larger screen if you want."

"Are the government debates like our debates?" Nicole asked.

Cassy laughed. "Not quite! The leaders' debate can get pretty crazy with the candidates all trying to talk at once and doing their best to make their opponents look bad."

"Really?" Kimberleigh reached to grab one of the cookies from the plate on the table before they all disappeared.

"Not so much at the local level, but for the leaders' debate, yes." David nodded, wondering what his kids would think of the heated exchanges that often dominated the events. "And instead of one topic to debate, the candidates are each given a chance to explain their platform; then they are asked a number of questions about different issues. If you can get past all the name calling, the debates can help you learn the different party positions on things."

"It could be interesting," Jeremy decided.

"Which—the name-calling part or the question part?" Kimberleigh eyed her brother across the table.

"The question part," he clarified. "What kinds of issues will they be discussing?"

"Things like healthcare, the economy, social programs, and government spending. Each party makes all kinds of promises about what they will accomplish if they get into power. But if it's another minority government, it becomes a lot more difficult to keep those promises." David rose from the table. "You'll get a taste of it next Friday."

⌘⌘⌘

That week Cassy tried to search out some of the key issues in the news that were bound to come up in the debates. Sometimes she would read pertinent parts of the articles aloud, and other times she would briefly explain the different sides of certain issues to help the kids understand the positions each party supported. One issue that surfaced regularly was the push by some parties for government-funded daycare.

"You mean that the government is trying to encourage mothers to put their children into daycare instead of staying home with them?" Nicole wrinkled her brows.

Cassy folded the newspaper she had been reading and dropped it on the floor beside her chair. "In a way, they are. But many people assume that most women either want to work, or feel they have to work, making daycares necessary. However, our families would be much better off if the government would lower taxes and encourage mothers to look after their own children instead of placing them in government institutions."

"I can't imagine having a complete stranger raise my children so I could go to work." Nicole shook her head. "I feel sorry for some moms who may *have* to do that, but I don't know why anyone would *choose* to do it."

"Why do so many women feel they need to pursue a career anyway?" Kimberleigh asked.

"I think it is expected in our culture. I know I felt a lot of pressure growing up that I should choose a career, but I never really desired one. Luckily, your father came along and saved me from my dilemma. I think it is even more difficult today for girls who want to be a full-time wife and mother to feel like that is acceptable. From the time they are little, they are asked what they want to be when they grow up. The more elite of a career they name, the more admiration they're apt to receive."

"It wasn't always that way, was it?" Anika inquired.

"Nope," Cassy said. "It wasn't all that long ago that most women would have stayed at home."

"So what changed things?" Kimberleigh was sprawled on the living room floor, but the book she had been reading lay forgotten.

"There are probably numerous factors, but I think the biggest factor was probably the feminist movement—women's quest for equality and independence and to break free from their traditional roles. Now we are reaping the results of that, and too many women have forgotten the value of being a keeper at home." Cassy grew thoughtful. "I almost forgot that for a while too. I had been planning to get a job once Anika was in school."

"I didn't know that." Nicole looked surprised.

"That was before we decided to homeschool you guys. I'm not saying it's always wrong for a woman to work, but if it interferes with her being able to look after her family or takes her focus away from the home, you have to question it. Even though I hadn't chosen a career, after ten years of housework and looking after small children, I was looking forward to getting out of the home and having more time to pursue other things. It was a hard decision at first for me to give that up to stay home and homeschool. I have a different perspective now, and I'm glad I made the choice that I did."

"I guess if ladies' husbands are gone to work, and their kids are in school all day, they probably don't feel much need to stay home," Nicole reasoned.

"That may be true, though for years many women stayed home even after public education became mandatory. Just because your kids are in school doesn't mean it's easy to juggle looking after a home, keeping up with laundry and groceries and everything, when you are working full-time. I think families simply started pursuing a higher standard of living—wanting bigger homes, new cars, and more stuff—and that is much harder to attain on a single income. People used to be content with a simpler life-style. Now they don't think they can do without all the extras."

Jeremy paused from his work on the computer and came to the doorway of the study. "It's hard not wanting all those extras when so many people around you have them."

"You have lots of stuff, Jeremy," Kimberleigh rebuked.

"Oh, I know. I'm only saying that it's hard not getting caught up in all the latest gadgets and cool things out there when you are surrounded by them. I think people would learn to be more content and thankful if they lived in a poor country where the people didn't have so much."

"Good point," Cassy said as she got up from her chair. "And if we lived in a poor country, you would be content with a piece of bread for lunch because nobody else around you would have much to eat."

"I'm still thankful for my food," Jeremy quickly amended. "No point in not using what God has blessed us with!"

Cassy laughed as she headed to the kitchen to prepare something to eat while the kids went back to their studies. When the tuna casserole was almost ready, she called Anika to come set the table.

⌘⌘⌘

By Friday evening, Cassy felt the kids had a pretty good handle on the different federal parties, and they were ready for the debate. David had come home early from work so they could drive into the city for a quick bite to eat before heading to the conference hall. They arrived half an hour before the debate was to start, so they toured the display booths and greeted each of the candidates. As the room started to fill up, Cassy suggested they'd better find some seats.

They settled in a spot along the center aisle, a few rows from the front. The Andrews were just coming in the door, so Cassy stood and waved to Lauren. They had been discussing the election after Bible study earlier in the week, speculating on the outcome, and the Andrews had decided to meet them at the debate. Richard and Lauren ushered their five children over to find seats a few rows behind the Knights. So far, their two families were the only young people in the room.

Soon the debate got underway. When different issues arose that they had discussed during the week, Cassy noticed Nicole and Jeremy jotting down comments from each candidate in their notebooks. Kimberleigh's paper looked like it had as many doodles as words, but she seemed to be listening. Throughout the evening, Anika's notebook rested idly in her lap. However, she was sitting beside David, and Cassy could see her occasionally tug on his arm and quietly ask him a question.

When it was over, they stuck around for a short while to visit with the Andrews. David also stopped by the Conservative booth before leaving, to see if Len Anderson needed help with anything more during the election. Len's campaign manager took his information and promised to get back to him regarding a mailing that was almost ready to go out. The office staff was looking for volunteers to come in to help stuff and seal thousands of envelopes.

"That sounds like a painful undertaking," Cassy said when David told her about the prospect of helping in the office.

David stopped midstride across the parking lot to their van. He looked at his wife with confusion. "I said we'd be *stuffing envelopes.*"

"I know. Don't you remember how many paper cuts I got stuffing all those envelopes for the homeschool conference that one year?"

"No I don't," David continued in the direction of the van. "What was I thinking, to subject my family to an activity that might put them at such risk," he added sarcastically.

Cassy nudged him with her shoulder. "Paper cuts hurt, especially when you get so many!"

David laughed. "You're not supposed to be running your fingers up and down the edge of the envelopes."

"Oh thanks! I'll keep that in mind."

On the way home, the kids all had a chance to share their opinions of the debate and to discuss the different candidates. They tried to list the strengths and weaknesses of each presentation. By the time they reached home, they were all ready for bed.

Monday evening the Knights headed into Red Deer once again to help at the constituency office. They joined half a dozen staff and worked for three hours stuffing an endless supply of flyers into addressed envelopes to go out across the riding. At one point, Cassy couldn't help but snicker when she saw David jerk his hand back from the envelope he'd been stuffing to look at his thumb, before sticking it into his mouth.

"So, it's only funny when someone *else* gets hurt." He glared at his wife across the table.

"Of course!" She smirked. "You know you shouldn't run your thumb down the edge of the envelope," she advised.

The kids enjoyed chatting with the other staff and learning about what all is involved in managing a campaign. Len Anderson stopped in toward the end of the evening on his way home from another engagement. He seemed pleased to see his young volunteers busy at work and shared with them some stories from his campaign. They all received a hearty thank you when they left. Though two bins of envelopes needed to be finished off yet, the bulk of the mailing was sealed and ready to go.

Throughout the six weeks of campaigning, the Knights kept up with election news at both the local and national levels. They watched the leaders' debate and cheered on the Conservative Party leader from their living room. When Election Day finally arrived, David hooked up the computer to the TV. Once the polling stations closed, they anxiously gathered to watch as the tallied votes started scrolling across the screen.

Len Anderson won his riding by a wide margin as expected, but there were tight battles in many ridings across the country. Though the

Conservatives were clearly ahead, it was hard to tell whether they would attain their coveted majority status. The whole family stayed up late watching the results. Anika petered out before the end, falling asleep on the couch, and David carried her up to bed. When the final counts were in, everyone felt disappointed that the Conservative Party had missed their majority by a slim margin. However, it had been a well-fought race and they had gained many seats since the last election. That was good news.

With the extra focus Cassy had been placing on the elections, she decided to allow the kids a week to recoup. She gave them as much time as they wanted to read and concentrate on activities of their choice, while she caught up on some of her own projects around the house.

Jeremy had been working on teaching himself guitar, so he spent several afternoons in his room strumming away. Finally Nicole convinced him to accompany her in the living room while she played her favorite songs on the piano. They sounded nice together. Before long, Kimberleigh and Anika squeezed onto each end of the piano bench so they could sing along. Cassy sat at the kitchen table updating her photo albums, and as she listened, she made a mental note to talk to David about the possibility of voice lessons for Kimberleigh. Though Kimberleigh had never really enjoyed her piano lessons, she loved to sing. Cassy felt sure her daughter would be thrilled by the prospect of pursuing training in voice.

"Can we have some more time off?" Jeremy pleaded when the week was over. "I haven't finished the shelf I was building for my room."

"Just because you are working on your studies doesn't mean you can't finish your other projects in your spare time. Besides, you'll be getting more time off soon enough. Remember, we're going to be helping Grandma and Grandpa pack."

Earlier in the week Cassy had gotten a call from her mother to inform her that her parents' house had finally sold. The home they had put an offer on was still available, so they were in the process of closing the deal. Her parents planned to rent a moving truck the last weekend of March, and the people from their church had promised to help them load it. David had suggested they drive out over Easter to help her parents prepare.

In the meantime, they were back to their regular schedule. By now, Cassy had adjusted their weekly geography competition to every other week for review. Once they had managed to fill in all the countries big enough to label, the kids had resorted to drawing in small, island countries not found on their map in order to win. They were regularly labeling over 175 countries. Cassy declared the geography experiment a huge success.

⌘⌘⌘

One afternoon early in March, Cassy sat at the kitchen table checking off the entries on her bank statement as she balanced the checkbook. Nicole was stationed across the table from her. She nibbled on the end of her pencil as she labored over her Consumer Math text. Jeremy had gone to his room to work on his science, and music from his favorite CD drifted faintly down the hall. Kimberleigh lay sprawled in her customary position on the living room floor, working on a writing assignment, and Anika snuggled under a blanket on the couch reading.

"I'm finished!" Nicole thumped her book closed with a loud smack, causing Cassy to jerk violently in her chair.

"You could finish a little more quietly," Cassy admonished.

"No, I mean I'm *finished.* No more math!"

"You finished your whole book?" Kimberleigh called from the other room.

"Yes, and Mom and Dad said I don't have to do any more math next year!" Nicole slapped her book with the palm of her hand, causing Cassy to glare at her once again. "I'm sorry." Nicole clasped her hands quietly in her lap. "I'm just excited to have finished early."

"Well, you can be excited *after* I'm done figuring this check book and taking care of the bills."

Nicole smiled and headed down the hall to her bedroom. A moment later, she was back with a book she had been reading. She sat sideways in the recliner and curled her knees up to rest against the arm of the chair.

"You know your character is going to suffer next year without any math to help you learn how to deal with frustration." Kimberleigh eyed her sister from her spot on the floor.

"Without math, I won't have any frustrations to deal with, and my character has been challenged enough—thank you very much." Nicole opened her book and lost herself in its pages.

12

The Target

The trip to B.C. came all too quickly, and Cassy felt rushed getting things packed to go. At least the weather had been nice the last week, so the road through the mountains should be clear. David had only booked three days off work, not wanting to leave Anthony short-handed on such late notice, but with the weekend, they would have five days altogether. Still, it would be a quick trip.

The kids brought along some audio book CDs to listen to, a favorite pastime whenever they had a long drive. Cassy figured she would have to look for more CDs at the upcoming homeschool conference, so they would have some for their summer holidays. They were getting quite the collection of stories, but she enjoyed them as much as the kids.

The days at her parents were full of activity as everyone pitched in to help sort and pack. Cassy helped her mom dig through drawers and closets full of belongings collected over the years. Joyce separated out items she planned to get rid of, while Cassy packed the things she wished to keep. David and Jeremy helped Mike pack up the garage, and the girls worked together to pack their grandfather's library of books, the bathrooms, and linen closets. Together the women packed most of the kitchen. They left a few dishes and cooking utensils in the cupboard for immediate use over the remaining days before the move. Each evening Grandma and Grandpa Harris treated their helpers to supper at a nearby restaurant.

"You kids have sure worked hard; we appreciate all you've done," Grandma Harris told them as they sat around the living room their last evening. Stacks of boxes filled every spare corner. "It's amazing how much stuff you can hide in a house."

"It's been fun hearing some of the stories about when you were little." Anika sat on the couch and snuggled against Cassy's shoulder. The long days had worn her out.

"Yeah, and about how you and Grandpa met," Kimberleigh added.

"She told you what a dashing young man I was and how I swept her off her feet, did she?"

Kimberleigh giggled at her grandfather's words. "She told us you had to sell some of your seminary books to buy her an engagement ring, and that you proposed to her on Canada Day, while you were watching fireworks."

"That's because I wanted to make sure it was good and dark, so that if she said no, she wouldn't be able to see me cry."

"Oh, Mike, it was not!" Joyce gave her husband's shoulder a playful slap. "You knew I'd say yes."

Cassy stretched. "We have a long drive tomorrow; you guys should head to bed." She patted Anika's knee. The kids slowly roused from their places and said good night before trudging to their rooms downstairs.

"Are you sure you have enough help rounded up to load everything on the truck next weekend?" David asked his father-in-law.

"We have more than enough volunteers from the church; that won't be a problem," Mike assured him. "And Cory will be flying out to help drive the moving truck, so don't worry. Your family has done more than enough."

"Be sure to give us a call when you are getting into Red Deer, so we can come help unload." David looked at Cassy. "You ready for bed too?"

Cassy nodded. "Yeah, I'm really tired." It was going to feel weird spending Easter Sunday on the road, but David needed to be back to work on Monday.

⌘⌘⌘

The following Friday afternoon, Jeremy bounded out to the van. The homeschool group had planned a special event that he'd been looking forward to all week. Between music lessons, their work at Hope for Life, and the Bible study at the Andrews, his mom had felt they had enough running every week, so she had limited their involvement in other activities. She allowed them to choose a couple of events each month to attend, and they had chosen laser tag. Their group had booked the whole facility for an hour.

When they arrived at Laser Emporium, a small crowd of homeschoolers had already gathered. Mrs. Thomas had organized the event, so she assigned each participant to a team, while the mothers found a spot in a corner of the lobby to sit and visit during the game. Once all forty students were accounted for, the attendant issued their vests and laser guns, then explained the rules before allowing them to begin. The vests contained sensors and the equipment was programmed to keep track of how many times each player was hit by an infrared laser beam, as well as who hit them. Each time a laser struck the target on someone's vest, that person would not be able to fire his laser or be tagged again for five seconds. The group chose to play two games back-to-back, at the end of which, the teams would receive a printout itemizing each player's individual scores, as well as the team scores.

"Hey, Nicole." Colby made his way to Nicole's side as the staff person opened the doors into the arena. "I see we're on the same team; let's stick together."

Jeremy heard his comment and strained to catch his sister's response over the heads of the noisy students. Nicole gritted her teeth and tried to smile. "Uh, that's okay. I'll probably slow you down too much."

"No, you won't. I'll be your bodyguard." He threw her a wide grin.

Jeremy frowned and turned to find Kimberleigh, who was on his team. "You'll never guess who is trailing Nicole again," he whispered.

"Colby?"

Jeremy nodded. "He wants to be her 'bodyguard.' That guy won't take no for an answer, and he's driving Nicole crazy. Let's nail him with lasers every chance we get. Maybe he'll get the hint," he said with a grin.

"Okay." Kimberleigh snickered.

Together they entered the large, dark arena. It only took a moment for their eyes to adjust to the black-light, which illuminated the room with its ultraviolet glow. Jeremy spotted Colby following close on Nicole's heels and pointed them out. The two dashed after their intended target and ducked behind a black barrier. Once everyone had entered the room, a buzzer gave the signal to begin.

Cautiously, Jeremy eased himself to the edge of his hiding place and peered around the corner. He could just make out Colby's lanky form as he worked his way around an obstacle. Taking careful aim at the target on the boy's chest, Jeremy fired several shots in succession. Colby's vest flashed, signaling a hit. Jeremy pulled back and turned to give Kimberleigh a high-five.

As the brother and sister duo maneuvered quickly around the room, they opened fire on any opponents they came in contact with, all the while keeping Colby in close range. Whenever the opportunity arose, they would take aim and fire until they saw the telltale flash.

"Not again!" Colby turned to Nicole, clearly frustrated. "I've never been hit this much when I've played before. It doesn't matter where I go; someone always gets me!"

"Maybe you'd do better on your own," Nicole suggested as she scanned the room for an easy target.

"No, at least I'm blocking you. You've hardly been hit." He pointed to a web of barriers in the corner of the room. "Let's head over there."

Jeremy chuckled to himself as he watched Colby grip Nicole's arm and urge her forward. The boy's vest flashed once more before reaching cover.

At the end of the first session, they had a short break to regroup before the game began again. Jeremy turned to his comrade-in-arms. "I've lost count of how many times we've gotten him."

"Me too," Kimberleigh acknowledged. "Do you think we should let up on him?"

"Nah. Only if he quits following Nicole." Jeremy surveyed the room before choosing a strategic spot to hide and wait for the signal to begin.

Throughout the second game, Jeremy and Kimberleigh managed to keep up their hot pursuit. Early in the game, Nicole started darting from barricade to barricade, but Colby was always close behind her. This only made him an easier target.

"Nicole, stop that! We need to use better strategy; we're getting hit every time you do that," Colby complained.

"What do you mean? I've only gotten hit twice. I think you should quit following me, Colby. I'd like to play by myself." She peered around the edge of her barricade and fired a number of shots. "Got you, Jeremy."

He ducked for cover, and Kimberleigh followed. "If only Nicole knew you were trying to help her, she wouldn't have shot you," she whispered.

"Oh, well, it's worth it; I think he's ready to give up," Jeremy told her.

Sure enough, Colby finally left and allowed Nicole to finish the remainder of the game on her own. When it was over, everyone returned to the lobby to rehash the game and await the scores. Jeremy and Kimberleigh turned in their equipment and came to wait beside Nicole.

"You finally lost your shadow, did you?" Kimberleigh asked her sister.

"Oh, you noticed? I've tried to tell him I'm not interested in him, but he never gives up." She rolled her eyes. "I don't like to be rude, but I don't know what else to do."

Kimberleigh smiled at her sister. "We tried to take care of that for you."

"What do you mean?"

"You'll see."

By the time they got a copy of the printout, Anika had joined them. They all huddled around the paper. "We won the first game, and you won the second." Jeremy pointed to the team scores. He quickly ran his finger along the individual scores until he got to Colby's. He nudged Kimberleigh. "He was hit sixty-two times, more than anyone else!" Jeremy ran his finger across the row showing all the players who had hit Colby. "Over half those shots were from us."

Surprised, Nicole looked at her brother. Then she smiled at Kimberleigh. "So that's what you meant. It was so funny. He couldn't figure out why he was getting hit so many more times than I was."

Kimberleigh scanned the figures again. "Wait a minute. Anika, you shot Colby five times." Anika gave her a mischievous grin. "But you were on his team!"

"I know."

Jeremy burst out laughing. "I guess we weren't the only ones looking out for you," he told Nicole.

They stayed to compare scores with some of their friends, checking to see who received the least number of hits, and who had scored the most shots on others.

At one point, Jeremy caught Colby staring at him from across the room. Jeremy held his gaze without flinching, and Colby slowly made his way over to meet him.

"What's the deal hounding me like that?" he demanded.

"You're smart enough; you figure it out. In case you didn't notice, we stopped near the end." An unmistakable challenge resonated from Jeremy's eyes.

After a few seconds, Colby glanced in Nicole's direction and back again. Jeremy just nodded and walked away.

⌘⌘⌘

Finally, the mothers started rounding up their kids, and the Knights headed for home. Cassy wondered if David would beat them there, but there was no sign of his truck when she pulled in the drive. She hurried into the house to get supper started. The beep of the answering machine greeted her as she entered the kitchen. She punched the play button en route to the pantry.

"We're finished loading the truck." Cassy immediately recognized Cory's voice. "As soon as the cleaning is done and Dad drops off the keys with the realtor, we'll be heading out. Still planning to stop somewhere tonight, and reach Red Deer midmorning tomorrow. See ya."

Cassy rummaged through the pantry until she found some cans of brown beans. Grasping two cans, she deposited them on the counter and went to work forming hamburger patties. After supper, she would conscript the girls to bake some cookies to take along for all those helping to unload. Moving was a big job, and she would be relieved to get her parents settled.

"Can I help with anything?" Nicole joined her mother in the kitchen.

"Sure. Why don't you slice some tomatoes and wash some lettuce?"

David arrived home before supper was ready, but the kids entertained him with their laser tag escapades while he waited. "I can't say that I would normally recommend ganging up on a guy like that, but it sounds like Colby had it coming. He needs to learn to respect Nicole's wishes." He turned to his daughter. "If he bothers you again, let me know, and I'll speak to him myself."

⌘⌘⌘

By the following evening, Cassy's parents had all of their furniture in place and the kitchen sufficiently unpacked to be navigable. The Knights had spent most of the day helping with the move, and Cassy felt exhausted.

Heading straight for her bedroom, she collapsed on her bed. She'd packed and unpacked enough boxes in the last week and a half to last her a good long while.

"Now that we're all practiced up moving, I thought maybe we should look for a larger acreage and build a new home," David said as he entered the bedroom and closed the door. He turned around just in time to catch a pillow square in the face. He laughed. "I thought you'd like that suggestion."

13

Answered Prayer

"We're going to be late." Cassy, coat on, waited by the back door.

The girls collected their gifts for the pregnancy crisis center and hurried to join their mother. They had each completed the baby afghans they'd been crocheting through the month of April and were anxious for a chance to give them away. Grabbing their jackets, they scurried outside to the van. David and Jeremy had already headed to work half-an-hour ago.

Once at the center, Anika headed straight for Kellie's desk. Setting her bag on the corner, she lifted out the delicate pink blanket. "This is my first afghan." She held it out to the receptionist.

Kellie lifted the afghan from Anika's hands and held it up to inspect. "It's very soft, and you did a great job on it." She carefully folded the blanket and handed it back to her young helper. "So have you chosen someone to give it to?"

"Not yet, but Nicole and Kimberleigh have. Nicole is giving hers to Tracy, and Kimberleigh's is for Lisa." The other girls came over to show Kellie their afghans as well.

"Very nice; that blue one will be perfect for Tracy's little boy, and I'm sure Lisa will love the purple one. Do you want me to call them and see if they will be out today? If they are, they might be able to stop in later so you can give your gifts in person."

"That would be great, thank you," Nicole said softly.

"Yes, please." Kimberleigh shook her head enthusiastically.

"I'll let you know if I get ahold of them. In the meantime, do you guys mind straightening up the staff room? Then the toys in the corner need to be washed, and some of the brochures should be restocked. I noticed that the rack is running low." The girls headed off, and Kellie turned to catch Cassy before she could disappear down the hall. "Someone called for you this morning, but she didn't leave her name. She just wanted to know if you would be in. Whoever it was, she seemed anxious to see you."

Cassy knit her eyebrows and tried to think who it might be. She had counseled several new girls lately. It was unusual for a client not to leave a name if she planned to come in, but Cassy shrugged it off. "I guess I'll find out who it is if she shows up. My morning is pretty open so far." She headed down the hallway to her office. As there were no clients waiting, she would straighten her desk and make a few phone calls.

Half an hour later, there were still no clients, so Cassy meandered back down the hall. She stopped in the kitchen for a drink of water before making her way to the reception area. The girls were busy wiping down the toys.

"It's quiet today." Cassy leaned against the wall beside Kellie's desk.

"Yeah, we're just making up for yesterday. It gives me a chance to catch up on all my paperwork."

"It's hard to believe we've been helping out here for a year and a half already," Cassy mused. "Last week Sandra brought Rosa in for a visit. Sandra was one of my first clients, and she seems to be doing well. Rosa's so cute; she's just starting to walk."

"It's a rewarding feeling, isn't it? Even though we all have our difficult days."

Cassy smiled and nodded.

"We've sure appreciated all the work David and Jeremy have done around here to fix things up. It's neat seeing a family minister together." Kellie glanced over at the girls sitting on the floor in the corner, chatting as they worked. "You have a great family."

"Thank you." Cassy had never met Kellie's two grown children.

Just then the front door opened and Cassy turned to see who might be coming in. A well-dressed woman entered, followed by a young girl carrying a small baby. Something about the girl triggered a memory in Cassy's mind, but it took her a moment to place who she was.

"Wendy?" Tears stung Cassy's eyes as she looked from the smile on the girl's face to the bundle in her arms.

The girl nodded and held out her baby as she approached Cassy. "I had to come back and thank you. I know I was mad at you when I stormed out of here six months ago, but I couldn't forget those models you showed me and what you'd said about the heart beating and all." Tears streamed down Wendy's face, and she swiped at them with her hand. "I couldn't go through with it."

Cassy reached to take the precious newborn girl in her arms. She looked back at the young mom before her. The ring had disappeared from her lip, but that wasn't the greatest change she saw. The countenance of her face had been completely transformed, the hardness and anger erased.

Cassy had almost forgotten the woman who had entered with Wendy until she stepped forward. "I'm Wendy's mother, Carmen, and I want to offer my gratitude as well for your part in saving my granddaughter. It has been a rough year, but I finally have my daughter back, and she has recommitted her life to the Lord." Carmen held out a gift to Cassy.

"Thank you." She took the gift and set it on Kellie's desk. "That's so good to hear. I've often prayed for Wendy and wondered what happened to her when she never came back." Cassy regarded the teen girl with tender eyes. "So, what did you name her?"

Wendy glanced at the girls who had sneaked closer for a glimpse at the baby. Her gaze locked on the youngest of the three. "I named her Anika," she said simply.

Anika's face lit up in surprise. "Really? That's my name."

"I know. You told me when you asked if you could pray for me. I refused to give you my name."

"I prayed for you anyway, even if you didn't want me to," Anika said sheepishly. "Even though I didn't know your name, I prayed that God would take away your hurt, and that He would help you." Anika peeked at her tiny namesake. The baby was starting to wake up, and her rosy lips puckered as she scrunched up her face and arched her back in a stretch. "Can I hold her?"

"Sure." Wendy smiled.

"Wait." Anika's face brightened in excitement. "I have something for you first." She darted behind Kellie's desk and retrieved the bag she had deposited there earlier. She held the present out to Wendy, who took it in surprise. "I made it, but I didn't know who to give it to. I want Anika to have it."

Wendy reached into the bag and pulled out the baby afghan. "Oh, how sweet! You made this?" She unfolded it and held it up for her mother to see. "Thank you so much." She reached hesitantly to give Anika a hug. "I hope my little girl grows up to be as kind and caring as you are."

Anika smiled and turned once again to take the baby from her mother. "She's so tiny," Anika said in amazement as she gently caressed the baby's cheek with the back of her fingers. The baby turned her head toward the touch and her mouth started pumping in a sucking motion. Anika laughed.

Nicole and Kimberleigh crowded around their sister, eager to get a better look. "That's so cool she has your name," Nicole said softly. She reached out a finger to touch the baby's curled fist. The little one rewarded them by opening her eyes to gaze at her admirers. "When was she born?" Nicole asked the baby's mother.

"April fourteenth, two weeks ago."

"You need to pick out some clothes and things for her." Kimberleigh pointed to the room behind her.

"I have a few things already." Wendy appeared hesitant.

"That's okay; babies need lots of stuff, and our shelves are overflowing right now. Come on." Kimberleigh reached for Wendy's hand. "I know where all the cutest girl clothes are; I'll help you. By the way, I'm Kimberleigh, and that is my sister, Nicole." She pointed over her shoulder as she dragged Wendy into the room behind Kellie's desk.

Kellie laughed. "You'd better go with them; they won't be happy until you leave with a bag full of clothes."

"We have strollers too; do you need a stroller?" Anika offered as she and Nicole followed the young mother into the room.

Soon the girls were all talking at once as they enthusiastically helped Wendy find what she needed. Nicole and Kimberleigh each took a turn holding baby Anika while the others "shopped." Cassy offered Wendy's mother a seat in the empty reception area, and they were able to visit together while they waited.

Carmen shared a little more of Wendy's story. The teenage girl had been fighting her parents' standards for some time, but in the last year, she had taken to lying in order to pursue a secret relationship with an older boy at school. His influence had gotten Wendy into the party scene, but the boy quickly deserted her once he discovered she was pregnant.

"The whole ordeal nearly destroyed Wendy, and it broke her father's and my hearts. She totally turned her back on us, and we thought we'd lost her."

"So what happened to change things?" Cassy gazed sympathetically at the mother so close to her own age. She had heard too many similar stories over the last year and a half.

"I finally convinced her to come here, hoping she would listen to someone else. When she came home, she shut herself in her room for days and wouldn't talk to anyone. However, she didn't get the abortion, and I started to feel some hope again. It was a difficult few months, but she slowly started to open up to us. It was tough for her to face her friends at school and to show herself at church again. She said she kept seeing the face of the young girl who worked here who wanted to pray for her. She couldn't understand why your daughter would care what happened to her, and she wished she could believe God still loved her. One day she broke down in tears and said she was tired of being angry and needed God's help."

"It's great to see her doing so well; I'm glad you came," Cassie said. "I thought she had gone through with the abortion. It's a relief to know that little Anika's life was spared, and that Wendy won't have to deal with the incredible guilt and regret I've seen other women go through." Cassy stopped when she noticed the girls headed toward them. Wendy carried her daughter against her shoulder, gently patting her back to calm her fussing.

"We should be going, Mom. Anika's getting hungry."

Carmen nodded and rose from her chair.

Anika handed the woman a bag stuffed with baby clothes and a couple of toys, as well as the bag with her afghan. "Wendy can still come back and get some more items as she needs them. She said that a lady at your church had already offered her a stroller."

"Thanks so much, all of you," Carmen said warmly.

It wasn't until they had all said good-bye and their visitors were gone that Cassy remembered the gift she had set on Kellie's desk. She picked up the small package. Reaching into the tissue-lined bag, she pulled out a square, plaster plaque. The surface revealed two tiny foot imprints, labeled with Anika's name and birthday. Mounted along the bottom was an engraved gold plate which read: *For You formed my inward parts; You covered me in my mother's womb. I will praise You, for I am fearfully* and *wonderfully made. Psalm 139:13-14.*

"Oh, look." Cassy turned the plaque so Kellie and the girls could see it.

"What a special gift." Nicole ran her fingers over the tiny footprints.

They each admired the plaque before heading back to work. Cassy made her way down the hall. "Thank You, Lord, for answering our prayers and saving little Anika," she whispered as she took a seat at her desk. Her heart was almost too full to speak. *I must make sure to tell Anika later how much her concern had meant to Wendy*, she thought. *One never knows what effect our words and actions might have on those around us.*

⌘⌘⌘

When David and Jeremy walked in the door that evening, the girls bombarded them as they raced to share the news of their special visitor. Cassy stood at the corner of the kitchen watching. David held up both his hands as he looked at each of his daughters with the stare of a deer caught in the headlights.

"Hold it!" he yelled above the commotion. "One at a time please, and slow down."

The girls halted. "Let Anika tell them," Nicole suggested.

"Are we allowed to come into the house first, or do we have to stand in the entranceway for this?" Jeremy was still holding his coat, waiting for his sisters to move so he could hang it up.

"Okay, come into the kitchen and Anika will tell you who came to visit us at Hope for Life today." Kimberleigh grabbed her sisters' arms and dragged them backwards into the kitchen.

The minute the men made it into the room, Anika started telling them about Wendy and her baby who had almost been aborted. "I gave her the afghan I made, and we got to hold her today. Her name is Anika!"

"That's because Anika stopped to talk to her when she was in a hurry to leave and get her abortion," Kimberleigh cut in. "Anika offered to pray for her, and now Wendy has turned back to God."

"She is so cute and tiny, only two weeks old," Anika continued. "I'm so glad God saved her."

"Wait until you see what they gave to Mom," Nicole said.

Cassy picked up the plaque from the kitchen counter and handed it to David. He smiled as he read the words below the footprints before passing the plaque to Jeremy.

"That *is* an exciting story," he said as he gave each of his girls a hug. "I'm glad you can have a part in ministering to the moms who come to the center."

"Hey, do you think anybody will name their baby after me because I painted the bathroom and helped with renovations?" Jeremy teased.

Cassy chuckled. "Probably not, but they appreciate it anyway."

"This world can only handle *one* Jeremy." Kimberleigh gave her brother a playful punch.

"Yeah, too much of a good thing can be overwhelming."

14

Road Trip

A large, blue suitcase lay open on Cassy's bed surrounded by mounds of clothes waiting to be packed. Cassy started selecting items and organizing them into her luggage as snuggly as possible. Swimwear, towels, and hiking gear needed to fit alongside a week's worth of clothes. Over recent years, they had taken few vacations during the summer months, as summer was typically the busiest time in the construction business. But this year would be an exception, and Cassy had been looking forward to this vacation for months.

She knew the kids were equally excited, in part because this trip they would be accompanied by the Andrews. The families had grown quite close over the years of homeschooling together, and that relationship had deepened the last couple of years as they met for weekly Bible study. Just last weekend, they had celebrated Melissa's homeschool graduation, making Nicole and Brianne anxious for their own graduation next June. Jeremy was a year older than Christian, but he got along well with all three boys. Eleven-year-old James and ten-year-old Kegan tried their best to imitate the older boys. The two families were going to spend a whole week together on a large houseboat out on the Shuswap, a multi-armed lake located in the Okanogan Valley of British Columbia.

After the busy spring getting her parents moved and settled, and the recent push to get the garden planted and the yard in shape, Cassy was looking forward to the break. No music lessons or activities to be running to, and no schedules to keep. She and Lauren would be sharing the meal responsibilities, so there would be less preparation for both of them. She paused to eye her suitcase with speculation. It would be impossible to get everything piled on her bed into her suitcase. She would have to pack some of the extra gear in a smaller bag.

"Mom, are you packing all the shampoo and toothpaste and stuff?" Kimberleigh yelled down the hall from her room.

"Yes," Cassy shouted back, "but you all need to pack your own towels and extra things you want." Cassy poked her head around the corner of her door. "Nicole, can I put you in charge of packing some games?"

"Sure."

Once the suitcases were packed and ready, Cassy headed to the kitchen to organize as much of the food as possible. The cooler would have to wait until first thing in the morning, just before they headed out. She rounded up two plastic storage bins for packing the cans and dry goods and headed to her pantry. Taking her list she had written out, Cassy checked off each item as she deposited it in one of the bins. It didn't take long before the bins were full. The baking, which the girls had completed the previous day, had already been carefully stored in a box on the counter.

"I've got all the sleeping bags stacked by the back door. Is there anything else that needs to be packed?" Kimberleigh asked as she entered the kitchen.

Cassy paused to think. "I'm about done here for now. Did you guys pack your cameras and the new CDs for the car?"

"Forgot the CDs." Kimberleigh bounded off once again.

"The hardest part about vacations is getting everything ready to go," Cassy muttered to herself as she went over her list once again. She still needed to get Shasta to the kennel.

⌘⌘⌘

The next morning, the kids began carting everything out and stacking it beside the van. David carried out the cooler and placed it in the back of the vehicle. He turned to eye the growing mountain of belongings that somehow needed to fit inside.

"We're only going to be gone a little over a week." He raised his eyebrows at Cassy, who had just added an armload of pillows to the pile.

"I know. But unless you plan to go without either food or bedding, I can't help it."

David started loading, sandwiching in suitcases as tightly as possible. The pillows he tossed into the backseat. The kids would have to either sit on them, or tuck them in the cracks. Finally, by fitting smaller items between the front seats and in any available floor space, he managed to get it all in. "Nobody open the back hatch!" he admonished when the kids came out to watch for their friends.

When the Andrews arrived, Christian suggested that Jeremy join the boys in their van, and they could send Melissa and Brianne with the girls. Cassy made one last check to make sure she hadn't forgotten anything, before everyone squished into the snuggly packed vehicles. It would be a seven-hour drive to Sicamous. Noisy chatter soon filled the air, as the girls eagerly discussed their upcoming adventure.

"Did you see the pictures of our houseboat online?" Melissa shifted in her seat so she could see the three girls seated in the back.

"Yeah! I can't believe it has a hot tub on top and a gas fireplace; it looks pretty cool," Kimberleigh squirmed with excitement.

"I can't wait to find a cozy chair on the top deck and relax with my book in the sun," Nicole added.

"What book did you bring?" Melissa peered over the stack of pillows at her friend.

"You mean books; I couldn't decide so I brought three." She proceeded to list off the titles.

"Oh, I've read all of those; they're really good. That G.A. Henty book is one of my favorites."

"I can't wait to go swimming in the lake and go down the slide off the top of the boat," Anika declared. "I'm going to be too busy swimming and hiking and playing games to read."

"Hey, let's take a picture for the start of our trip. We need lots of pictures for scrapbooking." Brianne dug her camera out of its bag and handed it to her sister. "Here, you see if you can get all of us in one picture from up there."

Melissa turned on the camera and held it out at arm's length. Leaning towards Nicole, she aimed the camera and pressed the button. After it flashed, she turned the camera around to view the screen. "You need to squish in tighter; I cut off half of Anika and Brianne."

Melissa repeated the process multiple times, and the girls laughed as they took turns viewing the results. They tried all different angles and facial expressions until they were satisfied that they had a sufficient number of shots for the first half hour of their journey.

"I want some copies of those; we'll have to swap pictures when we get home," Nicole suggested.

About an hour down the road, Kimberleigh remembered the CDs she had packed. "Do you guys want to listen to a story? We have three new audio books. One's from Lamplighter, one's a G.A. Henty, and one's a Bethlehem book."

"Sure," Brianne agreed.

They soon decided on *Sir Malcolm and the Missing Prince*, and Cassy stuck the first CD into the player. The next two hours a hush fell over the van as the girls listened intently to the story of the selfish young prince unfold. The story had just ended when David pulled into a fast-food parking lot behind the Andrews' van.

"What good timing; I'm hungry." Anika unbuckled her seatbelt.

The girls climbed from their cramped positions and began all talking at once as they discussed the highlights of the story. Cassy had to quiet them long enough to get their orders and direct them to find some seats. After lunch, the kids decided to swap vans, so the four boys shoved and tussled their way into the Knight's vehicle to claim the spots vacated by the girls.

"Hey Mom, do you have any of those cookies packed where you can get at them?" Jeremy asked less than ten minutes down the road.

Cassy glanced back at her son. "We just finished lunch."

"I know, but I'm still hungry. I need some dessert."

Cassy dug through the pile of things jammed between the front seats and managed to pull out a plastic container of chocolate-chip cookies. She handed them back, and Jeremy passed them around. Greedy hands snatched at the cookies.

"What's the most number of cookies you've eaten at one time?" Christian asked with his mouth full.

Jeremy glanced at his mother and whispered, "I think eight, and they were big ones."

Cassy swung her head toward her son. "I heard that, and we're not having a competition right now, so you can pass those cookies back up. We only have so many to last the week." She had long ago given up trying to regulate how much her son ate, as long as he acted within reason.

Jeremy just snickered and passed her the cookies. "What about you?"

"Ten, and I could have eaten more, but Mom caught me and made me quit."

"I ate three loaded hamburgers once, plus a bunch of other stuff," James bragged.

"I ate two whole platefuls of macaroni and cheese." Kegan entered his bid for recognition.

"What's the grossest thing you've ever eaten?" Jeremy eyed his friends. "I've tried Shasta's dog food before, just to see what it tasted like."

"Oh, that's nothing. I ate a clump of dirt from the garden," Kegan countered.

"Christian dared me to eat four worms, and I did," James declared loudly.

"You threw them up afterwards," Christian reminded him.

"So, I still ate them. You never ate worms!"

Cassy turned to her husband with a grimace. "Okay, I want the girls back."

David laughed. "Time to change the subject, boys," he called over his shoulder.

From there, the boys settled on looking for sports cars along the highway, competing to see who could identify the model first. That kept them busy for a while, but they eventually tired of watching out the window and grew restless. Turning sideways in the back seat, James placed his feet against his brother's leg and gave a shove. This succeeded in rousing Kegan to push back with his feet, battling to see who could claim the largest portion of the seat.

Counting down the miles to Sicamous, Cassy breathed a sigh of relief when they pulled into the hotel parking lot and the boys could get out and run around. They would be spending one night here before boarding the houseboat the next morning. She opened her door and stood up to stretch while David went inside to check in.

"You survived?" Lauren asked as she circled her vehicle to join Cassy.

"Barely. It was informative, though. I learned that James has eaten worms, Christian tried snowboarding off the roof of your house, and I might even be able to identify a car model or two."

Lauren chuckled. "Yes, I didn't appreciate the snowboarding incident too much. Luckily, I caught him before he broke his neck, and he had to pay for the eaves trough he broke."

Soon the men were back with the keys, and everyone began hauling in their things. At least the bedding could stay in the vehicles for now. Once settled in the rooms, they decided to wander down the street to a nearby restaurant. The weather forecast looked promising for the next week. Over supper, the men plotted out some of the hiking trails along the lake they would like to aim for, marking them on the map they had picked up in the hotel lobby.

With all the excitement, it proved difficult getting the kids settled down to sleep that night. Even so, they straggled from bed early the next morning, anxious to head to the marina.

15

Family Vacation

Finally, after the men sat in on the orientation explaining how to maneuver the boat and how to anchor it each night along the shore, someone directed them to their fifty-four-foot houseboat. The kids hopped aboard and scattered as they investigated each room and climbed the stairs to peek in the penthouse loft. Anika and Kimberleigh raced up the stairs off the back deck, to check out the view from the top, as well as the hot tub.

"C'mon, you guys," David called. "We need to go collect all our stuff and haul it down here."

The girls quickly claimed the penthouse for their room, and carted their sleeping bags and suitcases up to their cozy hide-away. It would be a tight fit, but they could all be together. Once the adults chose their rooms, they assigned Jeremy to the extra bedroom at the end of the hall, Christian to the little room off the kitchen, and the younger boys to the hide-a-bed in the living room.

"Wow, look at all the supplies in the kitchen," Cassy marveled as she and Lauren stashed the groceries away and unloaded their coolers into the fridge.

"They sure design these boats to utilize every square inch of space." Lauren stopped to glance around the interior. "Nice décor too."

"I like having the barbecue out on the deck. It will save on dirty pans to wash."

Just after noon, when everything had been loaded onto the boat, one of the marina crewmen directed them out of the narrow harbor and into the first arm of the lake. The kids all scrambled to the top deck to get a good view. Spread along the rail, they pointed out interesting landmarks and watched as their boat slowly churned its way through the deep blue water beneath them.

"There's stuff for sandwiches on the table if anyone's hungry," Cassy called up the stairs.

"Can we bring our food back up here?" Nicole asked as she headed to the back of the boat.

"Sure. Just don't eat by the hot tub."

For the next while, David and Richard took turns driving the boat leisurely across the lake. They could easily visit with the others from their captain's chair located by the big front window in the corner of the dining area. The warm July sun beat down on those sunning themselves on the top of the boat. Finally, Anika came down to see if they could stop and go swimming. David turned off the motor and allowed the boat to drift gently in the middle of the lake. In no time, the kids were taking turns shooting down the slide to drop into the cool water. Cassy and Lauren ventured to the top rail to watch and take pictures as their kids splashed below.

Even David and Richard donned their suits and came to try out the slide.

"Whew, that's enough to wake a person up," David said when he emerged from his first plunge.

"Just the first shock feels cold; it's fine once you're in." Jeremy shot a spray of water in his dad's face.

David dove for his son; Jeremy turned to flee but was too slow. David grabbed his shoulder and placing his other hand atop Jeremy's head, shoved him below the surface.

"I think I'll stay right here where it's nice and warm," Cassy declared as she watched from her cozy deck chair. "That sun feels wonderful!"

It was late afternoon by the time the swimmers climbed the stairs to warm up in the hot tub. The men dried off and resumed their path across the lake. Spotting the floating store anchored in the center where the spiderlike arms of the lake met, the men made their way to the dock and tied down the boat. Everyone hopped off to check it out, while David and Richard went to the rental counter to reserve a couple of Sea Doos for later in the week.

"What did you find out?" Jeremy asked eagerly when he joined his dad at the counter. "We were able to get two Sea Doos, a tube, and a pair of water skis for a few hours tomorrow afternoon, and again on Thursday."

"All right!" Jeremy raced to tell the other boys, who were checking out the store's ice cream selection.

Once back on the boat, the men decided to head down the shorter Anstey Arm of the lake. That way they could do some exploring, hike one of the trails in the morning, and make it back to the boat rental in time for the afternoon.

"Sounds good to me." Lauren stretched out on the couch. "I can handle this for a while."

It was Cassy's day to get meals, and they had agreed beforehand to allow the one who wasn't cooking the freedom to relax and stay out of the kitchen. Cassy smiled at her friend as she headed through the open glass doors onto the front deck, carrying several packages of chicken for the barbecue. "That will be me sprawled on the couch tomorrow!"

After supper that night, the guys started looking for a nice quiet beach to tie anchor. Richard carefully maneuvered the boat toward a sandy bank, while David and the two older boys waited on the front deck—lead ropes, stakes and sledgehammer in hand. Richard pushed the throttle forward to hold the boat against the beach; and the others jumped ashore. Cassy and Lauren watched the process from the bow, waiting to see if they needed help.

"Christian, you pull your rope towards that side of the beach. Jeremy, you follow me." David walked up the beach at an angle from the starboard side of the boat. Stopping about twenty-five feet from the water's edge, he dropped one long metal stake at his feet. With the sledgehammer, he drove the other stake firmly into the beach. Together, David and Jeremy stretched the rope attached to that side of the boat around the stake and pulled it taut, looping the rope several times.

"We'll have to do this every night, so let me show you how to tie it off so that it holds tight." David demonstrated how to knot the rope for his son. Picking up the other stake, they crossed the beach to where Christian stood waiting. Once the stake was in the ground, David stood back. "You guys try that one." He watched as the boys worked together, bracing themselves to pull the rope as tight as possible before looping it around the stake.

"Here, let me show you," Jeremy said as he tied the rope off as his father had done.

David checked to make sure it felt secure and then waved to Richard to let off the throttle. The boat held its position, keeping the bow perpendicular to the beach so the boat could not turn sideways, possibly damaging the propeller against the shore.

"Good job you two."

Cassy turned from the rail, regarding her friend with a smile. "So much for the warning about building your house upon the sand. I hope we aren't adrift tonight."

Lauren glanced up at the clear evening sky. "Don't worry; there's no rain in the forecast. We should be fine."

When they headed back inside, some of the kids were already playing a rowdy game of Dutch Blitz on the coffee table in the living room. Cassy arranged some snacks on the counter, and soon the rest crowded around the kitchen table to play another game. The boat bobbed in rhythm, carried by the gentle waves as they broke against the sand. It was late by the time the games wound up and everyone shuffled off to bed. Lauren helped Kegan and James make up their bed on the pullout couch.

"You want to take a quick peek at the stars?" David asked as they headed down the hall.

Though Cassy felt tired, she nodded. Following her husband onto the back deck, they ascended the stairs to the top of the boat. A few lights twinkled here and there along the curving shoreline. Standing against the rail, David wrapped his arm around her as they gazed at the heavens. Countless stars sparkled like diamonds against a velvety backdrop.

"Have I told you recently how much I love you?"

Cassy stared into her husband's eyes, dark pools glistening in the moonlight. "I think so, but you can always tell me again," she whispered.

David pulled her into a hug and brushed her lips with a kiss. "I love you, Cassy. You're a wonderful wife and mother, and you're doing an awesome job teaching the kids."

"Thanks; that means a lot coming from the principal of our school. Does that mean I get a raise?" She eyed David with a mischievous smile.

"Sure. I'll double your salary, starting next year. It's not hard to double zero."

Cassy laid her head against David's shoulder. "The salary may not be great, but the benefits are worth it. I'm so glad we began homeschooling when we did. I didn't think I could handle it at the time, and it hasn't always been easy, but it's been a good thing for our family."

"It sure has. I've enjoyed working with Jeremy and being able to build into his life as well. He's learning skills he'll be able to use even if he doesn't pursue construction as a career." They stood together for a while longer in the darkness. "You ready to head in?"

"Yeah." Cassy took one more look at the night sky as she followed David down the stairs. All was quiet except the muffled laughter of the girls in the penthouse.

⌘⌘⌘

After breakfast the next morning, the guys untied the boat and headed toward a nearby bay where they could anchor once again to go hiking. There were several trails to pick from, but they had chosen one that followed a small stream that fed into the lake. As soon as the men secured the boat, they were off. The narrow path wound its way through dense brush, and Cassy could see the boys bounding over fallen logs far in front of the rest of the group. Occasionally, they would stop to hop across smooth rocks submerged in the foamy stream, allowing time for everyone to catch up before they raced down the path once more.

"Here's a cool spot for a picture." Nicole pointed to a gnarly Douglas Maple tree along the edge of the water. "Can you guys all peek out from around those branches?"

The other girls quickly set down their own cameras beside the trail and circled the tree. Kimberleigh climbed onto a twisted branch and Anika hid behind the trunk, bending to peer around it.

"That's good. Melissa and Brianne, can you peek through the branches on that side?"

Cassy paused to watch the girls take yet another picture. Now that they all owned digital cameras, going on a hike took on a whole new dimension. Glancing up the trail to check on what the boys were up to, she noticed they had disappeared around the bend. She had never learned to totally relax when hiking in bear country, her mental images of one day meeting an angry grizzly on the path too vivid to ignore.

"David," she called to her husband, who had stopped a little further down the path. He stood chatting with Richard, but he turned his head. "Do you think we should tell the boys to stay within sight of the rest of the group?"

David just cocked his head. "They're fine; there are enough of them together. Besides, they're making plenty of noise. If there were any bears in the area, they would be long gone by now."

Cassy sighed and turned to Lauren, who was walking back to join her. "He knows me too well."

Lauren smiled. "Jeremy is almost sixteen; he's not a little boy anymore. But I know it's hard to let them grow up."

"You spend so many years looking after your kids, trying to keep them safe. How do you just quit? Especially when you have an overactive imagination?"

"I don't know if a mother ever stops being concerned for her kids," Lauren said as she stood watching their girls. "We simply have to learn to trust God more and leave them in His hands. When I master that one, I'll let you know."

The girls were collecting their cameras again, so Cassy and Lauren made their way over to join their husbands. As they all continued down the path, Cassy enjoyed listening to the gurgling stream as it tumbled down its rocky bed to the lake. Sunlight filtered through the fluttering leaves overhead and danced upon the green foliage bordering the trail, and Cassy relaxed as she took in the beauty around her. Eventually they caught up with the boys, who were by now nearly soaked from splashing one another in the stream while they waited for the others.

"It's time to head back to the boat," David announced. "We need to grab some lunch and head to the rental store to pick up our Sea Doos."

"Yeah!" Jeremy yelled.

The boys were off on a run, and Cassy didn't see them again until she boarded the houseboat. Clad in their swim trunks, they were rummaging through the cupboards looking for something to eat.

"Hold on, you guys," Lauren called. "I'll have lunch ready in a bit."

"Aw, we're starved!" Christian complained.

"Have a couple cookies to hold you over." Lauren opened a tin and held it out to them.

David took the captain's chair and started the boat. "If you boys are in such a hurry, you can go help untie the ropes and pull up the stakes."

Soon they were on their way. The store was in sight by the time Lauren had lunch ready. Turning off the motor, they floated out in the middle of the lake while they filled up on tacos and nacho chips. The minute their plates were emptied, the kids started clamoring to get going. Finally, David maneuvered the boat up to the dock. Once they had paid for the rentals, David volunteered to drive the boat out into the lake while Richard and the boys drove the Sea Doos.

Each Sea Doo could hold three riders, so Richard took James and Kegan on the back of his Sea Doo, while Christian and Kimberleigh hopped on with Jeremy. Richard eased away from the dock and an attendant hooked a large tube to the towrope on his Sea Doo. The girls nominated Brianne to be the first to ride in the tube, so she hopped on. They would wait to try the water skis once they were in open water.

Cassy and Lauren joined the rest of the girls on the top deck of the houseboat where they could watch as the Sea Doos zigged and zagged, following the slower moving "mother ship" out into the mouth of the Seymour Arm of the Shuswap Lake. When David turned off the motor, Richard and Jeremy brought their Sea Doos alongside the back deck of the houseboat to trade positions and pick up the water skis. For the next hour, Cassy and Lauren watched from their deck chairs on the top of the boat, as the kids took turns driving the Sea Doos, riding in the tube, and making attempts at water skiing. They laughed as Jeremy plunged headfirst into the water over and over again, before finally gaining his feet on the water skis long enough to make a loop around the boat. When David dropped him off on the back deck, he bounded up the stairs to the top.

"That was awesome!" He grabbed a beach towel and wiped his face.

"How much of the lake did you swallow before you made it up?" Cassy teased her son.

"A little," he admitted with a laugh. He stood at the rail for a while as he watched some of the girls take a shot on the skis. Melissa and Nicole each made it up for a short stretch, before somersaulting into the water, skis flying in opposite directions.

"Whoa, that is a lot harder than it looks," Nicole said as she came dripping up the stairs and took a seat beside her mom. She flexed her arms. "My muscles are going to be sore tomorrow."

"I don't know whether to try it or not," Cassy admitted. She watched as Jeremy accelerated away from the boat and David rose effortlessly on the skis. "Now if I could make it look that easy, it might be fun. But something tells me I wouldn't look that graceful."

"Yeah, I didn't know water could feel so hard when you wipe out."

Nicole propped her feet on the rail and leaned back in her chair. "That sun feels so good."

"The tube looks like fun. I'll have to try that." Lauren pointed as Christian cut a tight turn on his Sea Doo. James and Kegan were both on the tube, and they clung to the handle grips as the tube skimmed quickly across the wake of the Sea Doo, giving them a rough ride. Their shouts and laughter could be heard across the lake. Richard sat backwards on the Sea Doo, watching in case they fell off.

Nicole sat up in her chair. "You both need to take a turn at the tube and skiing."

"Okay." Cassy stood up from her comfortable position in the sun. "But I hate to show you up." When Nicole burst out laughing, Cassy gave her shoulder a slap. "No laughing! C'mon, Lauren." The two made their way down to the lower deck to wait for the Sea Doos to come back.

Anika smiled when she saw her mother coming. "You gonna give it a try?"

"Yep."

Jeremy was the first one back, and David let go of the towrope and swam to the rail. "Who's next?" He held up the skis.

"Cassy is," Lauren quickly nudged her forward. "I'm waiting for the tube. I want to see how you do on skis first."

"Oh no, you don't," Cassy turned back. "If I try them, you have to too."

"Okay, go," Lauren agreed.

"Do you want me to drive or spot you?" David asked as he handed his wife the skis.

"You can spot me, but take it easy driving, Jeremy." She sat on the back of the boat to put on the skis and ease herself into the water. Brianne climbed off the back of the Sea Doo and David took her seat. He handed Cassy the towrope.

"Now, we'll ease out until the rope is taut, then we'll accelerate fast."

"Not too fast," Cassy said nervously.

"We have to go fast, or you can't get up. Just keep your legs together in front of you, the tips of your skis tilted up, and lean back against the pull on the rope or you'll just flip forward."

David motioned for Jeremy to pull forward and Cassy gripped the tow bar so tightly her knuckles turned white. The tips of her skis were sticking out of the water in front of her. Once she felt the slack in the rope pull tight, David signaled Jeremy to go and Cassy braced herself. Immediately she felt her arms jerked forward, and she fought to keep them from being pulled ahead of her skis. The force of the water against the bottom of her skis surprised her, as it drove her legs apart. She strained her muscles, willing them to cooperate and bring her legs back together, but they only continued to spread."

"Keep your legs together," David called back to her.

"I'm trying," she yelled in exasperation. "As if I'm trying to do the splits on purpose!" she muttered. Cassy was now nearly bent in half, and her arms felt like they were being pulled from their sockets as the Sea Doo continued to pick up speed. Suddenly she felt herself plunge face first into the water, her skis flying off her feet as her legs swung around behind her. Water flew in her face and up her nose as she tried to lift her head against the spray. The Sea Doo dragged her another fifty feet before Jeremy got it stopped, and she finally loosened her grip.

"You're supposed to let go of the tow bar when you wipe out," David said. "If you let go, we'll circle around and pick up your skis for you."

Cassy nodded and flung the offending rope away from her. She lay back in the water and tried to relax her tense muscles. When Jeremy pulled up beside her, David handed her the skis, and she struggled to get them back on her feet. Once again, David tossed her the towrope and Cassy felt her muscles tense as the Sea Doo edged forward. This time, she pushed with her legs against the force of the water beneath her feet, straining to keep her legs together and lift her body out of the water. She felt her skis level out somewhat, but try as she might, she couldn't straighten her legs. Hugging her knees, she rose half out of the water in a squatting position, before the tug on her arms got the better of her once more and she somersaulted forward. This time she remembered to let go of the rope and managed to keep her skis, but Nicole was right. Hitting water at that speed hurt.

By the fifth try, Cassy managed to rise completely out of the water for a short stretch, though she still couldn't straighten up all the way. However, her muscles were starting to feel like jell-o, and she'd had enough. David swapped places with her, skiing his way back to the boat. Her arms rebelled as she reached to pull herself up the ladder.

When Lauren got back from her tube ride, Richard took her out to try the skis. Cassy and David sat watching at the rail. After one particularly awkward tumble, Cassy glanced at her husband.

"Did I look that ridiculous?" she whispered.

David burst out laughing. "I refuse to answer that one on the grounds that it might be held against me."

Cassy smirked in spite of herself. "That's what I thought."

The kids groaned when it was time to take back the rentals, but they would have another afternoon yet to try them again. After scrounging the kitchen for snacks, they disappeared to the top deck to enjoy the hot tub.

Cassy settled on the couch with a can of pop. "I'm glad it's your turn to fix supper," she said to Lauren. "My legs are still shaky. I don't think I could stand up long enough to cook anything."

Lauren plopped down on a chair beside her and stretched out her legs. "That's okay; we'll be stiffer tomorrow when it's your turn."

"You're such a great encouragement."

"Thanks, I try to be."

By the end of the week, they had managed to explore most of the lake and had ventured out on a number of hikes. Everyone exhibited a healthy glow from their days in the sun and water. It had been a great holiday, interacting as families, and Cassy reluctantly packed their things in preparation for leaving the houseboat.

"This is one holiday I'd love to repeat," Cassy told Lauren, who was emptying the remains of their food from the fridge.

"Yeah, me too. The right balance of adventure and relaxation. Though I think the kids would have gladly lived on the Sea Doos all week, and we could have saved the rental of the houseboat."

Cassy laughed. "No, they still would have wanted some food and a place to sleep. The Sea Doos were fun, but I think I'll leave the water skiing to someone who knows what they're doing." Cassy eyed her almost empty boxes and looked through the cupboards once more to make sure she wasn't forgetting anything. "At least we'll be a little lighter going home. We've managed to eat just about everything we brought."

She crossed to the window and looked out. David skillfully maneuvered their boat up to the dock back at the marina. Whether she felt ready or not, it was time to head home.

16

Bedtime Shenanigans

"Nicole, do you want to sleep in our room tonight?" Anika begged her big sister as they were getting ready for bed one night late that summer. "It's been awhile since you've joined us, and I'm sure we can talk Kimberleigh into entertaining us with one of her stories."

Nicole reached to take the toothpaste from Anika. "Sure," she agreed readily. "None of us have to be up too early tomorrow."

Over the years, the three sisters had often squished into Anika and Kimberleigh's double bed, where they would each vie for the middle spot so as not to be the one to be shoved out on the floor when the tussling matches started. They had built many memories as they invented silly games, wrestled for the covers, and told stories, trying futilely to keep the noise down to avoid having Mom or Dad come to settle them. Even though she was almost seventeen, and it had become a snug fit, Nicole still enjoyed this time together too much to give it up.

When she had gotten into her pajamas, Nicole ran into her sisters' room and dove for the middle of the bed, landing on top of Kimberleigh who had already claimed that spot. "I get the middle, because I'm the guest." She tried to shove her younger sister to the side.

"Nope, I'm the storyteller, so I have to be in the middle so you can both hear me," Kimberleigh insisted.

"Oh, all right." Nicole climbed under the covers on the side of the bed closest to the wall. "So, what's the story for tonight?"

"I thought I would tell the tale of the many princes who come seeking to court the noble Lady Nicole," Kimberleigh declared in her best Scottish accent.

Anika giggled as she flipped out the light and scurried to climb into the only vacant spot on the bed. "This should be good."

"Did you say there were *many* princes who wanted Lady Nicole's hand in marriage?" Nicole asked eagerly. She loved to dream about the day some young man would come and ask her father to court her.

"Yes, many." Kimberleigh cleared her throat in preparation to begin. She snuggled further under the covers. "Once upon a time there lived a family of noble Knights who had three daughters. Lady Nicole, the eldest daughter, was a virtuous young woman who was known for her fine intellect and kind heart. She was much admired throughout the land." Kimberleigh stopped to nudge her younger sister. "No giggling, Anika; this is a serious story."

"I'm sorry, Kimberleigh, but your accent makes it sound so funny." She tried to stifle her giggles.

Kimberleigh cleared her throat once again. "The second eldest daughter, Lady Kimberleigh, was a raving beauty and was said to have the voice of an angel."

"Oh, right!" Nicole smacked her sister. "I thought this story was about me."

"I can't tell this story with so many interruptions!" Kimberleigh said in exasperation.

"Okay, okay, we'll be quiet," Anika promised. "What about the third daughter?"

"Well, the third daughter was a gentle young lady, who was well known throughout the villages for her service to others and for the excellent cinnamon buns she made and delivered to all the sick. As Lady Nicole was nearing marriageable age, a young prince came calling. His name was Sir Haughty. The girl's father, Sir Knight, went out to meet Sir Haughty, and ask the purpose of his visit.

"'I have come to offer Lady Nicole the highest honor by asking for her hand in marriage,'" Kimberleigh gushed in a pompous tone.

"'And why, pray tell, do you think I would consent to give one of my dear daughters in marriage to you?' Sir Knight inquired. 'What noble character hath you to show me that would convince me that you deserve her?'

"'Why sir, doest thou not know who I am?' Sir Haughty cried with indignity. My father is the King; I have charm beyond measure and admirers aplenty.' The prince puffed out his chest and tilted his nose in the air. 'See for yourself if I am not the most handsome prince in the land!'"

At Anika and Nicole's giggles, Kimberleigh jabbed her sisters with her elbows. "I said, no laughing."

"I can't help it," Anika giggled. "You sound so snobby."

"It's not me, it is Sir Haughty, and he *is* snobby."

"Finish your story." Nicole elbowed Kimberleigh.

"Well..." Kimberleigh paused to collect her thoughts. "Sir Knight surveyed the man before him. 'I see a prince who prizes looks and popularity more than true character, which I doubt you have ever found it necessary to develop. Noble character comes from a humble heart, which honors God more than self. I am sorry, Sir Haughty, but you are not a man worthy to court my daughter.'"

"Farewell, Sir Haughty, you are not the prince I am looking for," Nicole interjected.

"Who's next?" Anika asked anxiously.

"Next came a prince dressed in fine robes and adorned with many jewels. His name was Sir Spend A Lot."

"Sir Spend A Lot?" Nicole laughed. "How about Sir Wealthy, or Sir Richie?"

"Or Sir Buy More," Anika quipped.

"Whose story is this?" Kimberleigh huffed. "No, instead of Sir Lancelot, it's Sir Spend A Lot. Anyways, Sir Spend A Lot knocked on the castle door."

"Ooh, we live in a castle!" Anika reached across Kimberleigh to poke her eldest sister.

Just then a knock sounded on the door and the girls hushed instantly. "Will you guys be quiet and go to sleep!"

"It's just Jeremy." Nicole giggled quietly. "Keep going."

"When Sir Knight opened the door, he eyed the gaudy prince before him. 'What brings you calling to my door?' he asked.

"'I come to buy Lady Nicole as my wife,' Sir Spend A Lot declared.

"'And why thinkest thou that my daughters are for sale?' Sir Knight questioned, too taken aback to even inquire after the man's character.

"'I have more money than I know what to do with and there is nothing which I desire that I cannot buy.' The wealthy prince pulled a bag of gold from his belt and dangled it before Sir Knight.

"'I'm sorry to disappoint you, but you appear to be a very spoiled young man who needs to learn the discipline which comes from hardship and self-denial. You must learn that there are some things which money cannot buy. I would not sell my daughter for all the money in the world.'

"Over the next year, one prince after another came to Sir Knight in hopes of winning Lady Nicole as a bride. One after another, Sir Knight sent them away when he found them lacking. He was insistent that he would not give his precious daughters away to any man unless he was proven to be a man of noble character."

Nicole thought of her father and smiled. That part of the story at least was true.

"Finally, when Lady Nicole was about to give up all hope of ever finding her prince, along came a handsome but humble young man. He was not dressed in fine clothes and wore no jewels. His name was Sir Faithful, and he carried a Bible in one hand, and a beautiful bouquet of red roses in the other. Sir Knight had heard many good things about Sir Faithful, and when he saw him coming from an upstairs window, he ran to greet his visitor before the man even reached the door.

"Sir Faithful bowed low before his host. 'I come humbly before you in the hopes that I might find favor in your eyes.'

"'Arise, what is it you seek?' asked Sir Knight.

"'I have watched your daughters from afar and know of their great virtue. I have come in the hopes that I might earn the right to court Lady Kimberleigh.'"

Nicole punched her sister's shoulder. "Oh no you don't; this is my story. He came to see me!"

Kimberleigh and Anika burst out laughing. "It's my story, and I get to tell it any way I want!" Kimberleigh punched Nicole back. Nicole grabbed her sister's pillow out from under her head and started to pelt her with it. "Fine," Kimberleigh gasped, "you get the pillow, and I get the prince."

⌘⌘⌘

Jeremy listened to his sisters' laughter and swung back his covers again. *Why do they always have to make such a racket when I'm trying to get to sleep?* he fumed. Then an idea struck him. Climbing out of bed, Jeremy sneaked down the dark hall to the kitchen. He searched the cupboards until he found a straw and then returned quietly to his room. There he rummaged through his closet until he found the small tin box he was after. Cranking his window as far as it would go, he squeezed through the tight opening. It was a hot evening, and he was sure Anika and Kimberleigh would have their window open.

⌘⌘⌘

Meanwhile, the antics continued in the girls' room down the hall. "Let her finish." Anika grabbed Kimberleigh's pillow and gave it back to her sister.

"Finish it right!" Nicole insisted.

"Okay, so Sir Faithful asked to court Lady Nicole," Kimberleigh replied with exasperation. "'What noble character hath thou to show me that I might consent to your wish?' Sir Knight asked once again.

"'I am a man of integrity, Sir Knight, and I will admit that I have many faults. However, I am a child of the King of Kings, and depend upon His Word in all matters. I strive to honor the Lord in all I do, and I would strive to honor and cherish your daughter and protect her with my life.'

"'You have answered well, Sir Faithful, I will take you in to meet my daughters. I think you may find Lady Kimberleigh more to your liking.'"

"Sure!" Nicole started to tickle Kimberleigh.

⌘⌘⌘

By now, Jeremy had crept around the corner of the house and sat crouched below his sisters' window. Just as he had expected, the window was cocked open, and he flattened himself against the side of the house. It was a dark night, but he didn't want to take any chances that the girls would see him. Jeremy pulled the tin container from his pocket and opened it, careful not to spill its contents. He felt inside and selected one of the rubbery beetles from within. Gently he stuffed a portion of the beetle into the end of his straw and aimed it through the crack in the window. The starlight was just bright enough to allow him to make out the moving shadows of his sisters as they wiggled in the bed. Jeremy placed the free end of the straw between his lips and gave a firm blow. The beetle shot out the end. He waited expectantly to see if he'd hit his mark. The girls were still giggling, so he selected another beetle and reloaded his straw. This time he got a response.

⌘⌘⌘

"Eew, what was that?" Nicole demanded.

"What was what?" Kimberleigh giggled.

"Oh right, act all innocent. What was that slimy thing you threw at me?" Nicole brushed at her arm and involuntarily shivered.

"What slimy thing?"

"The slimy thing that hit me in the arm!" Nicole sat up in bed. "Was that you, Anika?"

"I didn't throw anything. I was too busy trying to keep the two of you from shoving me out of bed!"

"Kimberleigh…"

Just then something landed on Kimberleigh's shoulder. She reached her hand up to grab it, but when her fingers gripped the squishy bug, she screamed and brushed it off.

"Sure, flick it at me!" Anika shrieked and jumped out of bed. "That hit me in the face!"

"What was it?" Kimberleigh was standing on the end of the bed now. "That felt gross!"

"Okay you guys." Nicole bolted from the bed and hurried across the room. "You're freaking me out!" She flipped on the light switch, and the three of them stared at the bed. When they saw the ugly bugs lying in the space they had just vacated, they started to scream. A shadow moved across their window, and Nicole pointed with a shaky finger. "What was that outside?"

Kimberleigh jumped off the bed and raced to the window, but her brother had already darted around the corner of the house. "Jeremy, you're dead!" she yelled.

Nicole turned and spotted her parents standing in the doorway of the room.

"What's going on in here?" David demanded.

"Jeremy was throwing his bugs through the window and into our bed." Kimberleigh pointed at the evidence.

David walked over to the bed and collected the offending insects. "Okay, back to bed and settle down. I'll have a talk with Jeremy."

⌘⌘⌘

David ushered Cassy back into the hall and closed the girls' door. "I'll take care of this." He watched as Cassy headed back to bed before turning toward his son's room. Without bothering to knock, David opened the door and flicked on the light. Jeremy lay curled in bed, his eyes closed, looking convincingly as if he were asleep.

"Okay, son, what's the deal scaring the living daylights out of your sisters?"

A smirk tugged at the corners of Jeremy's mouth, and he opened his eyes. "It's just a few harmless beetles; they aren't even real."

"Real or not, they frightened your sisters."

"Well, they've been gabbing and giggling for over an hour and wouldn't be quiet," Jeremy declared in his defense.

David gave an understanding nod. "I'll talk to your sisters, but you owe them an apology." He motioned for his son to follow him back down the hall. Jeremy reluctantly climbed from bed.

After apologies had been offered on both sides, and David felt the situation had been adequately dealt with, he headed back to his room. A quiet chuckle escaped him in the dark hallway. He couldn't be too tough on his son. After all, Jeremy reminded him too much of himself at that age. If he'd had giggling sisters keeping him up at night, he probably would have retaliated in a similar fashion.

17

Auditions

Just before the fall start-up for the homeschool group, Teresa Henderson mentioned to Cassy at church that she had decided to direct a homeschool drama. Teresa explained she had always loved theater and felt that the homeschoolers should have more opportunities to take part in a full drama production.

When Cassy told the kids during lunch, Kimberleigh could hardly contain herself. "Do you know what the play is going to be about?" Her face was bright with excitement.

Cassy paused to relish the suspense as she watched her daughter. "She's ordered scripts for *Anne of Green Gables*." She smiled as Kimberleigh nearly choked on a mouthful of water. It was no secret that *Anne of Green Gables* was Kimberleigh's favorite movie.

The fourteen-year-old plopped her glass down beside her plate, sloshing its contents onto the table. "Are you kidding?"

Cassy laughed. "No, I'm not. Auditions are in two weeks." She looked around the table. "Are any of the rest of you interested in trying out?"

"I might like a small part," Anika said tentatively.

Nicole screwed up her face in thought. "I think I would rather help sew costumes and help out behind the scenes if I could."

"Same here." Jeremy nodded. "Not the sewing part," he quickly amended, "but I could help make some props and stuff."

"Teresa's planning practices for Friday mornings at the church, so it will mean more driving." Cassy looked at David and let out a sigh. "We haven't been going to skating real regularly on Fridays, because we're already in the city on Mondays for music lessons and Wednesdays for volunteering." She guessed she'd have to resign herself to the extra time commitment.

"Is it possible to switch the music lessons to Friday?" David asked simply.

Cassy brightened. "I don't know. I just booked Kimberleigh's voice lessons for Monday to coincide with Anika and Nicole's piano lessons, but it might be possible to switch them all. I'll call first thing tomorrow."

Immediately after dinner, Kimberleigh dug out her *Anne of Green Gables* movie and popped it in the DVD player. "I have to get a feel for all the characters so I'm ready for auditions."

Over the next two weeks, the family witnessed various renditions of Anne as Kimberleigh paraded around the house, her long brown hair tied back in braids, quoting Anne's lines from memory. Cassy had to laugh when she came to the table for lunch one day with freckles sprinkled across her cheeks and nose, compliments of a brown marker.

"Oh, isn't this simply splendid having grilled cheese sandwiches to eat." Kimberleigh slid onto her chair at the table. "I can just imagine they are delightful bits of fruitcake with cherry preserves, and that my milk is raspberry cordial."

"As long as you don't get drunk on your milk, you can imagine all you want. I'm happy with grilled cheese sandwiches." Jeremy rolled his eyes as he sat down. "Is she going to sound like this all year?"

"Only until March, when we perform the play," Anika consoled her brother.

"Great!"

"I have to practice so I'm ready for auditions." Kimberleigh glared at Jeremy.

⌘⌘⌘

Finally, the day of auditions came. Thankfully, Cassy had managed to switch the girls' music lessons, so she packed a lunch for them to eat in their break between. The sandwiches barely made it into the bag with the fruit and cookies before Kimberleigh started herding her sisters out to the van. Jeremy opted to stay home.

There were close to a dozen other homeschool students already milling about the church foyer when they arrived. Teresa came to greet them and handed the girls a sheet of paper, instructing Kimberleigh and

Anika to read over the sample lines from the script. Turning to Cassy, she explained that auditions would start as soon as Lynn Morris arrived. The girls spotted Brianne and Christian sitting on the floor just outside the sanctuary doors, so they headed over to join them. Cassy found a chair and pulled it over beside Lauren. While they waited, Kimberleigh paced back and forth, quietly reading some of the audition lines Teresa had given her.

"Quit that, Kimberleigh. You're making me nervous." Anika sat cross-legged on the floor, gripping her paper. Closing her eyes, she leaned her head against the wall for a moment before bending over her script again.

Kimberleigh took a seat beside the others and started to fidget.

"She's so excited she just can't sit still," Cassy whispered to Lauren.

"Let me guess which part she's hoping to get."

"You mean the braids?" Cassy asked her friend.

Lauren nodded.

"That's become her new hairstyle of late. I'm surprised she didn't beg to dye her hair red. She says she'd be happy to get any of the larger roles, but I know she's hoping for Anne. What about Brianne?"

"She's wants to be one of the schoolgirls. She doesn't think she can be dramatic enough for Anne."

When Lynn arrived, Teresa ushered her into the sanctuary and called in the first student. About every five minutes the door would open, and the student who had just completed an audition would choose another to go in. When Brianne finished her turn, she held the door and motioned for Kimberleigh.

"How'd it go?" Kimberleigh ducked under her friend's arm and into the sanctuary.

"Pretty good. A little nerve-wracking standing up on the stage, but I thought it was fun."

Cassy watched as her daughter disappeared inside with a wide grin. Even if it meant a little more time commitment on her part, it was worth it for Kimberleigh's sake. The minute Brianne sat back down, Anika began pelting her with questions concerning her audition, so she quickly explained what Teresa had asked her to do. Cassy could see the tension leave Anika's face. By the time Kimberleigh bounded out the door and called for her sister, Anika seemed ready.

"Mrs. Henderson wanted me to audition for one of the bigger roles!" Kimberleigh plopped down beside Cassy's chair and beamed up at her.

"She had me read the lines for Marilla, Diana, and Anne several times."

"When will you find out which part you get?" Cassy knew the suspense would drive her daughter crazy.

"She's going to call everyone tonight, after she and Mrs. Morris have a chance to discuss the auditions and get all the parts figured out." Kimberleigh held up a thick folder and fanned through the pages for Cassy to see. "We owe Mrs. Henderson ten dollars for the script."

The door opened once again and Anika returned, smiling. The four friends huddled together and pored over their scripts, skimming through some of the lines. Nicole set down the book she'd been reading and scooted over for a peek. As soon as the auditions were finished, Cassy went in search of Teresa to pay for their scripts.

"This was such a good idea; the kids are really excited."

Teresa smiled. "I could tell. I'm glad we have enough parts to go around, because I'd hate to have to turn anyone away. There aren't very many boys roles, so I was a little worried about that. Only a few boys showed up, though, so we should be all right. If we get any more kids now, they'll have to join the prop and stage crew."

Cassy reminded Teresa that Nicole and Jeremy wanted to help in that area and left to join her girls for lunch. They chose a quiet corner of the foyer to sit and eat before heading to their lessons. After dropping them off, Cassy ran to the store to pick up a few groceries. At least she could accomplish some of her other errands while she was in town. She decided to get a couple of pizzas for supper while she was at it, since she had forgotten to get something out of the freezer this morning.

As soon as they got home, Kimberleigh grabbed the phone and carried it around with her everywhere she went. Twice it rang, and she answered it immediately, only to hand it over to Cassy with disappointment.

"Relax, Kimberleigh," Cassy set the phone down and her daughter snatched it back up. "Teresa probably won't call right at supper time, so just be patient."

"Other people always call at supper time." Kimberleigh stuck the phone in her pocket and began to set the table.

"Yeah—usually they're telemarketers though."

The girls discussed the play all through supper, trying to guess who would play each part. Finally, at about seven-thirty, the phone rang again. Kimberleigh hit the talk button and held it to her ear.

"Hello, Kimberleigh speaking," she said eagerly.

Cassy glanced up from her book and was relieved to see Kimberleigh's face light up.

Kimberleigh sat without moving as she listened for a moment. "Really? Yes!" She jumped up from the couch. "What about Anika?" By now, Anika was plastered to her sister's side, straining to listen in. "Okay, I'll tell her." Kimberleigh turned to mouth something to her sister, but Anika held up a hand to stop her.

"I heard. I got the part of Ruby Gillis." She grabbed her script from the end table by the couch and sat down to look through it once more.

When Kimberleigh hung up, she did a little dance around the living room. "I got the part of Anne!" she announced, as though everyone hadn't already figured that out. "Anika is Ruby, Brianne is Diana, and Christian is Gilbert Blythe."

Nicole stuck out her arm to stop Kimberleigh as she came near her chair. "Who's playing Marilla and Matthew?"

"Josh Henderson is playing Matthew, and I think she said that Katie Bennet is Marilla."

"Oh, good. I told you Josh would make a great Matthew."

"It's too bad you didn't get the part you wanted." David had been working on his expenses in his study, but he had gotten up when Kimberleigh started making such a commotion.

"What?" She spun around to stare at her father and David laughed. "Oh, you're kidding." Kimberleigh finally took her seat back on the couch.

"Are you happy with your part, Anika?" Cassy cocked her head toward her youngest.

Anika lifted her eyes from her script. "What? Oh, yeah, I wanted to be one of the school girls. I didn't care which one, although I'm kind of glad I'm not Josie Pye. She's more snobby."

Jeremy was out in the garage working on one of his wood projects. *Wait until he finds out he's going to be living with Anne for another six months.* Cassy smiled and went back to reading her book.

Fridays quickly became the highlight of the week for the girls as play practice started in earnest. Even though Nicole wasn't in the play, she didn't seem to mind being at the practice while she waited for her piano lesson. She often brought a crocheting project along to work on while she watched. Cassy usually brought a book to read, or joined some of the other ladies, who settled in the fireside room to sit and wait.

Since the Friday activities didn't involve Jeremy, David decided to bring him to work two days a week for the next while, which didn't hurt Jeremy's feelings a bit. Cassy knew how much Jeremy enjoyed working construction with his father, and he was gaining good experience. The arrangement kept him from spending every Friday home alone.

One day after rehearsal, Teresa approached Nicole with some of the patterns and material she had picked out for costumes. Explaining what she had planned for each character, Teresa offered Nicole first choice of which outfits she wanted to sew. The rest would be divvied up among some of the mothers who had offered to help. Nicole immediately selected the emerald green fabric and pattern for Anne's dress, as well as the pale blue fabric for Ruby.

"Can I take this white material you got for all the aprons as well?" Nicole pointed to the thick bundle of white, cotton fabric. "I can cut out the aprons for both the girls' dresses and bring the rest back next week."

"Sure." Teresa put all the cloth Nicole had chosen into a bag, along with the thread and zippers she would need. "Thanks, this helps a lot. Can you give this list of props to your brother and tell him to let me know which ones he would like to make?"

"Yep." Nicole took the paper and added it to her bag.

As they ate a hurried lunch, Nicole showed her sisters their fabric. "Look at the big, puffed sleeves on your dress." She held up a pattern for Anika to see.

"Cool."

Kimberleigh leaned over to look. "No fair. I want puffed sleeves on my dress."

Cassy smiled. "Is that Kimberleigh talking or Anne?"

Glancing up at her mother, Kimberleigh grinned. "Both."

⌘⌘⌘

That fall, Jeremy puttered away in the garage, working on some of the props in his spare time. One item he had chosen to design was the slate Anne would need to break over Gilbert's head during the performance. He had purchased a small chalkboard with a narrow wooden frame, which he had found at a craft store. Using his dad's scroll saw, Jeremy carefully made a thin, jagged cut all the way across the middle, slicing the board in two. Then he stained the wood edge, giving it an antique finish. The trick would be keeping the slate in one piece until Anne would crack Gilbert over the head with it. To accomplish this, Jeremy screwed two flat, sliding hooks onto the back of the frame, which could be unlatched just before impact to give the impression that the slate was being broken. He tried it out over his knee and was happy with the effect.

"Hey Kimberleigh, check this out." Jeremy said later that evening, as he entered the living room clutching his slate.

Nicole had just finished sewing Anne's dress, and Kimberleigh stood posing in the middle of the room, modeling it for everyone. She turned to face her brother. "You finished it! So how does it work?"

Jeremy flipped over the slate and showed her the hooks. "You'll have to make sure you pick up the slate in the right place and that you are holding it tightly together so the crack doesn't show. If you smear some chalk across the front, it should help hide it better." With a grin, Jeremy raised the slate above Kimberleigh's head. "Then, if you slide the hooks back with your fingers as you bring the slate down, you can bend it apart as you hit Christian's head. You don't actually have to hit real hard, to make it look good." He smiled when Kimberleigh winced as he brought the slate down on her head, separating it into two pieces.

She straightened with surprise. "Aw, that worked great! Let me try."

Jeremy proudly put the slate back together and guided Kimberleigh's hands in how to hold it. Kimberleigh had to stretch to lift the slate above her brother's head. Swinging her arms back, she brought it down with a whack.

"Ow, Kimberleigh!"

A horrified expression crossed Kimberleigh's face as she slowly lowered the slate, which remained intact. "Oops, sorry. I guess I didn't get it unhooked fast enough." Her words were nearly drowned out by the laughter from the others in the room who'd been watching.

Rubbing his head with one hand, Jeremy grabbed the slate and held it up to inspect it for damage. "I said you didn't have to hit very hard! I'm going to have to warn Christian not to let you try it on him until you practice on something else."

18

Confrontations

Though the weeks were busy with all the extra drama activities, Cassy felt thankful that her children had the opportunity to pursue so many of their interests. It was such a blessing to have the freedom to direct the education of each one to suit their individual needs. With her graduation fast approaching, Nicole had spent a fair bit of time over the past months thinking through and planning for her next few years at home, and Cassy knew her daughter had begun to anticipate this stage of her life. However, the route their family had chosen would not be without its challenges from those who didn't understand their goals.

One Sunday, the middle of December, Cassy stood in the foyer after the service visiting with Bonnie Sorenson. As the church started to empty, Cassy shifted impatiently. Once Bonnie had someone's full attention, she didn't let them escape easily. Finally, Nicole walked over to join her.

"Hey, Nicole." Bonnie's focus immediately shifted to her new audience. "How old are you now?"

"Seventeen."

"Boy, that's hard to believe; I remember when you were just a toddler. Does that mean you're graduating this year—or maybe you can't do that sort of thing when you're *homeschooling*?" She said the word as if mentioning some horrible disease.

Nicole smiled sweetly. "Yes, I'm graduating this year."

Cassy held her breath, hoping Nicole wouldn't go into any details about not following the government curriculum. Bonnie would get a lot of mileage out of that one. Glancing around the foyer she looked to see if David was waiting for her, but he was still talking with Anthony. Too bad.

"So, where are you going to college next year?"

"Actually, I'm not going to college."

"I suppose it is hard for homeschoolers to get into college." Bonnie eyed Nicole sympathetically.

"Homeschoolers get into college all the time, Mrs. Sorenson," Nicole answered softly. "But I'm planning to study apologetics and church history from home and continue with my music. My family has also been volunteering at Hope for Life, and I've been talking to the staff about becoming a peer counselor there several days a week. I'd love to be able to work with the teen girls who come in."

"Oh, so you're taking a year at home to make up your mind what you really want to do. Of course my Emma knew exactly what she wanted to do from the time she was in ninth grade." The woman threw Cassy a cursory glance. "My daughter just finished her degree in Behavioral Psychology, and she's landed a great job in Edmonton, you know." She turned back to Nicole before Cassy had a chance to respond. "That's okay; some kids need a little more time to figure that out."

A shadow crossed Nicole's face, and she glanced toward her mother. Cassy knew Nicole fully accepted the direction they felt God leading them but found it tough facing all the questions. With a shaky breath, Nicole made an attempt to correct Bonnie's misconceptions. "I've known for a long time what I want to do. I desire to be a full-time wife and mother. Until then, I plan to stay at home and do what I can to serve the Lord."

"Oh, that's so cute." Bonnie chuckled loudly. Turning to Cassy, she placed a hand on her arm. "Don't worry; she just needs to learn a little independence after being isolated for so long. She's not going to stay home forever."

Cassy could see Nicole's eyes fill with tears and felt her own face flush with anger. She paused long enough to take a deep breath. "I'm not worried, Bonnie. Nicole has been sheltered, but not isolated. And Scripture does not teach that women are to chase after independence. Nicole is honoring both her father and God by her decision to stay home until she has a husband to provide for her." For once, Bonnie seemed to be speechless. Out of the corner of her eye, Cassy saw David moving toward them. She turned to Nicole. "I think your dad is ready to go," she said quietly before telling Bonnie good-bye.

⌘⌘⌘

For New Year's Eve, the church planned a family games night. Cassy put together a platter of leftover Christmas baking and grabbed a couple bags of chips as they headed out into the blustery night. The temperature had dropped to minus twenty-five, and snow swirled in their headlights as they merged onto the highway. Hopefully the roads were not going to get too nasty by the time the evening was over. When they got to the church, Cassy hurried in out of the cold.

Placing her goodies on one of the tables already loaded with food, she glanced around the room. No sign of her parents yet. It wouldn't surprise her if they decided to stay home instead of going out in the bad weather. David pointed across the fellowship hall to where Anthony and Sarah sat at a table visiting. The kids had already disappeared with some friends.

"So, has Samantha gotten over her bad cough? She sounded pretty miserable at Christmas." Cassy settled into a chair beside her sister-in-law.

"Yeah, she's feeling much better, and thankfully no one else has come down with it yet. The cough didn't bother her as much as the fact that she got sick over the holidays and didn't get to miss any school." Sarah rolled her eyes. "She's not concerned that if she misses school, I have to miss work to stay home with her. Unless of course, Anthony happened to be home. I'm sure glad the guys will be starting a new job this next week. I don't know if David has been as stir crazy as Anthony, with work being so slow this past month. Anthony can't stand puttering around the house with nothing to do."

"David's glad to have the work, but they've been so busy the last few years, I thought it was kind of nice to have things slow down a little. He kept busy enough cleaning out the garage, and helping Jeremy with one of the sets for the play. It's been so cold anyways, and he enjoyed having a bit of extra time over the holidays to play some games with the kids and take them tobogganing. They like having him home more."

"How's the play coming?"

"Great. This is the first big production Kimberleigh has had a chance to be part of, and she's loving it. Anika has more lines than she was expecting, but she's getting them down. They're having a lot of fun, and the costumes Nicole made turned out really nice."

"I'm anxious to see it."

"Hey, are you two going to play a game or are you just going to gab all night?"

Cassy looked up to find Anthony impatiently shuffling a deck of cards. "Can't we play and talk?"

"Sure." Anthony smiled. "If you're distracted, it will be easier for me to win."

Cassy's parents wandered in a little later, and they came over to join in the game. There was a good turnout, despite the weather. Throughout the evening, Cassy interacted with a number of different families, sometimes playing games, and sometimes just relaxing and enjoying a sample of the many tempting goodies people brought. Her parents seemed to have settled in well since their move, and they had quickly developed some new friendships.

⌘⌘⌘

Partway through the evening, some of the boys headed to the gym to play basketball. During a break for everyone to get a snack and something to drink, Jeremy found himself sitting on the floor beside Rob Myers. He was home for the holidays from his first year of university, and Jeremy wondered if he had settled down at all in his time away.

"How's school going?" Jeremy asked between mouthfuls of chips.

"Aw, it's not bad. I like hangin' with the guys in the dorm. They can be pretty wild and crazy!" Rob gave him a cocky grin. "There are some pretty hot chicks on campus too." He smirked and nudged Jeremy with his elbow. "I've been out with a few of them."

Jeremy gritted his teeth and shook his head. No, Rob hadn't changed. He took a sip of root beer, not really interested in continuing the conversation.

"Speaking of hot chicks, your sister is looking pretty sweet. She have a boyfriend yet?"

"Nicole?" Jeremy cringed. He wanted nothing more than to keep the likes of Rob Myers as far away from his sister as possible. "No, she's not looking for a boyfriend right now. But when she's ready to find a husband, she won't be interested in someone who hops from girl to girl like you do. She's looking for a godly man who will be committed to her, so leave her alone." Jeremy stared at the older boy with steely determination.

Rob laughed. "Aren't you the protective *little* brother? Maybe you ought to let Nicole make up her own mind." He gave Jeremy a sly look. "She might like to have a little fun."

Before Jeremy could stop himself, his hand flew out and caught the other boy across the chest. Rob jerked back in surprise; his eyes narrowed. "I mean it, Rob. Stay away from my sister." Jeremy collected his plate from the floor and got up before he was tempted to punch the guy again.

Halfway across the gym, Christian grabbed his arm.

"Hey, what was up with that?" his friend whispered.

"With what?"

"With you socking Rob like that? What'd he do?"

"He was getting a little too interested in Nicole, and I thought I'd discourage him before he got any further." Jeremy glanced back to see Rob still watching him.

"Oooh." Christian whistled softly. "Good plan. I don't know him very well, he never came to church much, but I've heard he's trouble."

Once the guys had their fill of food, they resumed their game. Jeremy disposed of his plate and cup to join in. The heated competition carried past midnight, the players oblivious to the New Year being welcomed in. Drenched with sweat, Jeremy raced across the court with the basketball. Blocked along the sideline, he looked for an open player to pass to. All his teammates were heavily guarded. All except Rob, who stood gawking towards the door of the gym. Jeremy glanced over to see what had captured his attention and noticed Nicole standing in the doorway. He clamped his lips together and drilled the ball across the court into Rob's shoulder. His unsuspecting receiver staggered backward at the force of the blow. Whipping around, Rob glared at Jeremy.

With a smile, Jeremy sprinted across the floor toward the door. "Keep your eyes on the ball!" he hissed at Rob as he passed.

"Mom and Dad are ready to head home," Nicole informed him when he reached her.

"Good. I'm tired."

Nicole looked sideways at him as they walked through the foyer. "You threw that ball pretty hard at Rob, and he wasn't ready. You should have apologized."

Jeremy stopped by the coat racks and studied his sister. The thought of Rob wanting to ask her out still irked him. "He had it coming. He should have been watching the ball."

Nicole frowned at her brother. "He was distracted. You don't whip a ball at someone when they're not looking."

"He was distracted all right," Jeremy mumbled as he slipped on his coat.

"What's that supposed to mean?"

"He had his eyes on you, Nicole. I was just diverting his attention."

"Jeremy Knight! You did that on purpose?" Nicole smacked his arm and stared at him in shock.

Jeremy smirked. "Yes, I did. He's not the kind of guy I want chasing after you. I thought I'd save you the hassle of dealing with him."

Nicole frowned and shook her head at him, but Jeremy could see a sparkle in her eye. "With you around, I'll never get married. No guy will be able to get close enough to ask me."

Jeremy laughed. "You weren't too upset when we got Colby to leave you alone. Don't worry. If I find a good one, I'll let him through."

19

The Performance

The next couple of months, more focus was directed toward the coming homeschool production. Since Nicole had to wait at the church during play practice anyway, Teresa asked if she would like to be in charge of the lighting. Each week Cassy saw a few more props added to the scenes, and rehearsals ran a little smoother as scripts were set aside to practice the lines from memory. Teresa appointed a crew to paint the sets Jeremy had built, which the church allowed them to store in a small room off the gym. Cassy volunteered to help supervise the painting, laying out tarps on the gym floor for them to work on.

The main set was the kitchen at Green Gables, which Jeremy made using three sheets of plywood with braces so they would stand. In one, he cut out a window, framing it with scraps of trim and inserting lattice. It was the crew's job to paint the walls and hang some curtains over the window. One of the parents donated a couple rolls of extra wallpaper, which Cassy helped apply to the bottom third of the walls once they had been painted. She had Jeremy add some narrow trim along the top of the wallpaper, and they rounded up a couple of pictures for the wall.

The kids painted the backs of the plywood brown and hung a chalkboard on one section, so they could be flipped around for the schoolroom scenes. A few of the participating families agreed to bring in some furniture and larger props in time for the performance on the first weekend in March. Cassy hadn't realized just how much work would go into putting the production together, but she was pleased with the results of everyone's effort.

⌘⌘⌘

Finally the weekend of the performance arrived, and everyone scrambled to get last-minute details in place. Teresa had bought Kimberleigh some colored hair spray, which Cassy sprayed onto her braided hair to give it a reddish tinge.

"I sure hope this stuff washes out as easily as the can says." Cassy checked to make sure she hadn't missed any spots.

"I'm sure it will." Kimberleigh smiled as she viewed her reflection in the mirror. "Now you need to add the freckles."

While Cassy worked on Kimberleigh, Nicole helped Anika with her hair, and soon both girls were dressed and ready to head to the church. They had just enough time to pose for a few pictures.

"All set?" David asked them.

"I think so, but I'm so nervous." Anika eased into her jacket.

David put one arm around her in a quick hug. "You'll do fine. Pretend it's a dress rehearsal and forget about the audience."

Anika nodded and headed out to the van. The girls had to be at the church early, so David dropped them off and went to pick up Cassy's parents. Even so, they arrived back at the church in plenty of time to get seats in the second row. Cassy estimated there were close to two hundred people seated when the lights dimmed for the performance to begin.

Considering that most of the students had little dramatic experience, Cassy thought they were doing very well. They all seemed to have a good feel for the personalities of their characters and did their best to project their voices. Cassy let out a sigh of relief when Kimberleigh's slate broke at the perfect moment as she hit Christian over the head. When Brianne acted out the scene in which Diana got drunk on currant wine, Cassy had to nudge Jeremy to keep him from laughing too loud. However, he was not the only one laughing as a tipsy Diana continued to guzzle more of the wine she thought to be raspberry cordial, and poor Brianne had to pause in her lines until the laughter died down enough so she could be heard.

At intermission, Cassy's mom stood to stretch. "They're doing really well. That's a lot of lines to memorize."

"They've been working hard at it for months, and Teresa has done a great job directing. Now the kids are going to want her to do a play every year."

Trish and Cory, who had been sitting a couple of rows back, came over to say hi. "Kimberleigh makes a terrific Anne, and I didn't realize that

Anika was such a little actress," Trish commented.

"Yeah, even the boys said it wasn't too bad for a girl story," Cory added.

"That's good. Hopefully they'll still think so after another hour." Just then, Cassy felt someone tugging on her arm. She turned to discover Samantha and Lissy standing behind her. David had moved to the aisle and was talking to Anthony and Sarah.

"Can we get Anne and Ruby's autographs?" Samantha held up her program and a pen expectantly.

Cassy stooped to her nieces' level. "Sure you can, but you'll have to wait until the end. They're getting ready for the second half. As soon as the play is over, all the kids will come out and you can ask them then."

When the lights flickered to signal the end of the short intermission, they all took their seats once again. The second half went as smoothly as the first, with only a couple lines that Teresa quietly prompted from offstage. Josh gave such a dramatic rendition of Matthew's death that Cassy noticed Katie struggling not to smile, but she quickly covered her mouth with one hand as she fell to Josh's side. Even though Cassy had seen most of the scenes numerous times during practice, she thoroughly enjoyed watching the finished product.

As the cast came on stage to take their final bow, the audience showered them with applause. David leaned over to whisper in Cassy's ear. "The girls did a great job; Kimberleigh is beaming up there."

"I know, but it's been a long haul. I think they'll all be glad for a break."

The cast posed for some group pictures, and Cassy took a few more to add to all her pictures from the dress rehearsal the day before. The minute the cameras stopped flashing, Kimberleigh bounded off the stage to find her family.

"That was so much fun! I wish we could perform it more than once. It's hard to believe it's all over."

Anika joined them a moment later, and both girls received praise from family and friends. Samantha and Lissy squeezed through the crowd to get a close-up look at their cousins' fancy dresses, and to get their autographs.

"Is that your real hair?" Samantha reached up to touch Kimberleigh's braid.

"Yep, we sprayed it red for the play."

"Is it going to stay that way?" The little girl's eyes grew large.

Kimberleigh laughed. "Nope. The color will wash out."

"Oh good, 'cause you look kinda funny with red hair." Samantha looked relieved.

"How'd you memorize all those lines?" Lissy asked Anika.

"We practiced lots at home, but we've been working on them awhile." Anika sat down on a nearby chair.

By the time they all chipped in to clean up after the play and put the church back in order for the service the next day, Cassy felt tired. As they filed out the front door of the church, Teresa's husband locked up behind them. At least Cory had offered to take their parents home, so her mom and dad hadn't been kept waiting.

"Thanks again, Teresa; everyone seemed to really enjoy that. You did a great job." Cassy paused in the dark parking lot beside her friend.

"Thanks. I thought it went well, and there was a good turnout."

"You think you'll direct another play sometime?"

Teresa shrugged. "I'll see. I need to recoup from this one first."

"I don't blame you." Cassy laughed. "See ya bright and early tomorrow morning." She waved as she hurried to catch up to the rest of her family.

20

Graduation

There were eight homeschool students taking part in graduation this year. As June drew near, the families of the grads worked together to finalize the program for the ceremony to be held at the church. For special music, Nicole had asked if her siblings would be willing to perform one song. After some consideration, they had agreed to sing. Nicole and Jeremy would play the accompaniment on the piano and guitar. Cassy had enjoyed hearing them play together more often over the last year, but this would be their first public performance.

One evening, Cassy sat on her bed staring at the certificate she'd framed. She and David had worked on it together. He'd found a picture of an open Bible with a candle beside it, which he'd used as a watermark in the background. Cassy read the words they had written once more.

In Honor of Your Graduation

Nicole, we brought you home to train you up for God, because that is what we believe He commissioned us to do as your parents. Throughout your years of homeschooling, it has been our desire to teach you the things of the Lord and to give you a solid foundation in Scripture. We have watched you grow in knowledge and wisdom, grace and beauty.

As your parents, we are pleased with the godly woman you have become. You have learned to love the Lord with all your heart, soul and strength, and you are well equipped to serve Him wherever your future may lead. May His Word be a light unto your path.

Nicole Marie Knight

On this eighteenth day of June
we wish to recognize your faithfulness on this journey,
and ask God's blessing for the days to come.
With Love, Mom and Dad

Cassy carefully wrapped the frame in tissue paper and slid it into a large gift bag so Nicole wouldn't see it before they presented it to her. The certificate bore little resemblance to her own high school diploma, but then Nicole's education had been vastly different from her own. It was only right that the certificate reflect their vision of education. It was hard to believe Nicole would soon be eighteen. Where had the time gone? Tucking the bag beside her dresser, Cassy got ready for bed.

⌘⌘⌘

The morning of grad, Cassy rushed around the kitchen getting trays of meat and cheese, veggies and fruit, and a variety of finger foods ready. Most of Cassy's and David's family would be coming back to the house following the ceremony. The girls helped to straighten up, and Jeremy put out some extra folding chairs.

"You look like you're planning to feed an army." David eyed all the food when he came in from mowing the lawn.

"I'm sure it will feel like an army by the time we squeeze everyone in. Hey—" Cassy swatted David's hand as he sneaked a cream puff from the platter she was filling—"I already shooed the kids away from these."

"I won't tell." He shoved the pastry in his mouth in three bites.

"How come Dad gets a cream puff?" Jeremy walked into the kitchen just as the last bite disappeared.

"Because he's the boss. You can have a brownie if you want." Cassy pointed to the pan on the counter beside the stove. "There's more of those."

"I'll take what I can get." Jeremy eagerly scooped a brownie from the pan.

When Cassy completed her preparation, she made a quick lunch before everyone headed to their rooms to change. "It feels kind of strange celebrating graduation when Nicole didn't pursue credits and isn't getting a diploma. In a way, it doesn't feel like anything will be different since she'll still be at home next year." Cassy stepped in front of her mirror to brush out her hair and clip it up.

David stared at her reflection as he spoke. "It's not like we're marking an end to her time at home; we're acknowledging her faithfulness in her studies and her growth in the Lord. It's more a milestone in her transition to adulthood."

"I guess." Cassy turned to look at her husband. "I wonder what everyone else will think about it."

"Because she's not getting a government diploma? Cassy, I wish you would quit worrying about what others think."

Her shoulders slumped. "I try. Every time I think I'm past letting it bother me, something else comes up to worry about. I know we're doing the right thing, but I don't think everyone else will understand. And when the rest of our family is following the government system, it is hard to explain without sounding confrontational."

David walked over and placed his hands on her shoulders. "Jesus said to give to Caesar what belongs to Caesar and to the Lord what belongs to Him. Our children belong to the Lord, not the State, and God gave us the authority to educate them—no matter what anyone else thinks."

"I know; I totally believe that. I need to let it go." Cassy stretched to give her husband a kiss. "I'd better hurry. Anika wanted me to French braid her hair." She grabbed her things and headed to find her daughter.

A moment later Nicole walked into the kitchen. Cassy looked up from fixing Anika's hair. Her daughter wore the new dress she'd made for the occasion—an elegant gown made of rose-colored satin. It had white braided trim encircling the high waist, and a touch of white lace at the neck and capped sleeves. The skirt hung to mid-calf with a scalloped hem, revealing a lacy, white underskirt that reached to the floor. She had gathered her dark, curly hair up on the sides and secured it with decorative combs.

"You look very nice, honey. Do you have your music and the notes for your speech?"

"They're with my purse by the back door."

"Good. You want to check and see if the others are about ready?" Cassy tied a ribbon around the bottom of Anika's braid and turned to collect her camera and the bag with Nicole's certificate from the table.

A moment later, Jeremy came down the hall carrying his guitar, followed by Kimberleigh and Nicole.

"Dad's coming in a minute; he's just tying his tie," Nicole said.

Cassy surveyed her children as they stood waiting together. She placed her bag back on the table and pulled her camera from its case.

"Here, let me get a quick picture of the four of you before we go. Can you stand over by the couch?"

Jeremy set down his guitar and followed his sisters into the living room. He and Nicole stood in the center, with Kimberleigh and Anika to each side, arms encircling one another. By the time Cassy snapped several shots, David was waiting for them and they hurried out to the van.

Once at the church, Nicole greeted Brianne and the other grads with excitement. Their eight chairs already stood in a line across the platform from their practice the day before. Jeremy tuned his guitar and placed it on a stand by the piano, then went to join Christian at the doors leading into the sanctuary. They had the task of handing out the programs for the ceremony. Cassy set her camera and Nicole's certificate on a seat in the front row and returned to the foyer to wait for family members to arrive.

Finally, everyone was seated, and Cassy shifted anxiously in her chair. Richard went to the platform and opened in prayer, then turned the microphone over to another couple from the homeschool group who were emceeing the ceremony. One by one they called in the grads, reading a little about each one as they walked down the aisle and took their place on the platform. When the grads were seated, they introduced the special music by Nicole and her siblings. Huddled beside the piano, they sang the song Nicole had picked out. For one verse, Kimberleigh sang a solo, and Cassy felt a surge of pride as she listened to her children.

After the song, a short powerpoint presentation played, showing pictures of the first grad and his family. Following the slides, the grad went to the mic for his two-minute speech about his years of homeschooling. As soon as he finished, his parents came up to present the framed certificate they had made. The same process was followed for each student, broken in the middle by another special number played by two grads on the flute and violin.

When Nicole's powerpoint presentation ended, she walked gracefully to the mic and stared out into the audience, her eyes large as they scanned the room. Cassy said a quick prayer that God would calm her nerves. Nicole glanced down at her paper and began.

"First of all, I want to thank my parents for choosing to homeschool me. I realize now that it wasn't an easy decision for them. It would have taken a lot less effort to leave us in the school system. But if there's one thing I've learned from them, it's that they are committed to following

God even when it's not easy. Even when they have to go against the flow. As Christians, we are not to be conformed to the world; and my parents were not afraid to challenge the world's philosophies when it came to our education.

"The thing I value most from my years of homeschooling is the gift of being taught to be discerning—to view everything around me in light of Scripture. I've learned that everything you hear, everything you read, and everything you watch is presented within the framework of a belief system. Nothing is neutral, and I'm thankful that my parents realized that education is not neutral either. Eliminating God from education teaches that either God does not exist, or that He is not relevant. My parents wanted me to have a biblical worldview, and to achieve that, I needed to be taught within the framework of the Bible.

"I couldn't truly understand science without being introduced to the Creator—the One who put all the laws of nature into place. I needed to understand the character of the Designer. And what lasting value is there in learning math, if I learned nothing of the God of order? I could learn to write, but I wouldn't honor God and write what is biblically sound, unless I first learned to think biblically. I could study history, but what is history without the providence of God? It would be like learning the Bible stories, but leaving God out of them all. I could study about the Mede-Persian Empire, but it would not be the same if I didn't also learn about a man of prayer named Daniel. A man who remained faithful in the midst of opposition, and whom God rescued from a den of lions. God used this man to turn the heart of a mighty king. There have been many 'Daniels' throughout history, and many kingdoms have risen and fallen by the power of God's hand. I needed to learn true history."

Nicole's voice was gentle, but full of conviction as she spoke. While Cassy listened, her mind immediately went to her brother, Don. As a history teacher in the public school, she wondered how Nicole's words would affect him. Even so, she was glad that Nicole was boldly speaking the truth. Cassy suddenly remembered her camera sitting idly in her lap and quickly took a few pictures as Nicole continued her speech.

"More than anything else, my parents wanted to teach me a love for God's Word. I have learned that I must apply the Bible to all areas of my life. That includes learning to be a woman who will serve God faithfully within the roles He has given me. I still have lots to learn, but my greatest desire is to someday be a wife and mother—a keeper at home like my mom is. I don't have to go away to college to learn how to do that; the best place to learn to be a homemaker is in my home. And the best place for me to learn to submit to my future husband is to live under the headship of my father. That's not very popular in our culture, but my mom and dad taught me that I am not to be deceived by the philosophies of this world.

"I am so thankful for my family, and I'm thankful that they have chosen not to follow the way of the world. One of my dad's favorite verses is found in Joshua 24:15, which says, 'And if it seems evil to you to serve the LORD, choose for yourselves this day whom you will serve, whether the gods which your fathers served that *were* on the other side of the River, or the gods of the Amorites, in whose land you dwell. But as for me and my house, we will serve the LORD.' Thanks, Dad, for taking that stand, and thanks, Mom, for being my example and taking the time to homeschool me."

Cassy looked at her daughter through tear-blurred eyes. David nudged her and she pulled Nicole's certificate out of its bag and followed him onto the platform. They each gave Nicole a hug before Cassy handed her the frame.

"I'm proud of you," David whispered.

"Thanks," Nicole whispered back as she glanced down at the certificate. She waited a moment while her parents returned to their seats before walking quietly back to her chair.

Once seated, Cassy watched as Nicole read the words they had written. She thought how well the words coincided with her speech. When Nicole had finished reading, she looked up and smiled at her parents.

After the last speech, David made his way onto the platform once again to pray for the graduates. Then he thanked everyone for coming and dismissed them. Cassy watched as Nicole crossed the stage holding her certificate to give her father a hug, before descending the stairs to join her.

"Thanks for the certificate, Mom. It means a lot to me."

"You're welcome. I'm glad you like it."

They headed toward the foyer in search of family, but Cassy's mom met them halfway down the aisle.

"That was quite the speech, young lady." She squeezed Nicole's shoulder. "You did a very nice job, and your dress turned out lovely. I can't believe you made it."

"Thanks, Grandma. I love to sew."

"Can I see your certificate?" Joyce reached for the frame in Nicole's hand. She smiled as she read it. "That's very special, and I must say, I like it better than my old diploma," she said as she handed it back to her granddaughter.

Soon they joined the rest of the family gathered in a corner of the foyer and headed back to the house. Cassy set to work mixing up punch, while Trish and Sarah lined her counters with the trays of food she had prepared earlier. The others crowded into the living room or settled around the kitchen table. She noticed Nicole stacking the numerous presents she had been given in the corner beside the couch to open later. As she stirred the punch, Cassy glanced across to where her oldest brother sat in the recliner, arms crossed against his chest. He hadn't said a word since the ceremony, and she thought he looked sullen. Had Nicole's words about eliminating God from education gotten to him, she wondered?

"That was a nice ceremony; Nicole gave a very thought-provoking speech," Trish said quietly, as though reading her thoughts.

Cassy turned to look at her sister-in-law who began arranging cups on the counter beside her. Her youngest brother's children attended the local Christian school, so Cassy knew they agreed with the need for a Christian based education. She smiled at Trish. "Thanks. I'm not sure everyone appreciated it, though," she murmured.

Trish's eyes lifted momentarily in Don's direction before dropping once again. "I know, but what Nicole spoke was true. It was a good challenge. Even in the Christian school, we need to be careful not to forget God in the whole scheme of things."

Staring into the punch bowl, Cassy nodded. Maybe Trish understood their choices more than she had given her credit for. Though Cassy's family members had chosen different means of education, she knew that each one cared deeply about the spiritual well-being of their children. And though she had come to feel strongly that God never intended Christian parents to hand their children over to a godless state system for training, she must remember that at one time her own children had been in that system. If not for the struggles Jeremy had faced and the teacher who had challenged Nicole's belief in the Bible, her children may have remained there. Initially, she had fought the notion of homeschooling, but God, in

His grace, had changed her heart. She must show the same grace.

Throughout the evening, Nicole received several compliments on her certificate, but Cassy hadn't heard a single enquiry about a government diploma. Don remained aloof, even though she tried to draw him out. It wasn't until Cassy stood at the door as he was leaving that he finally revealed what was on his mind. Laura and the kids were already climbing into their vehicle, but Don turned back as he stood on the step.

He paused a minute before speaking in a subdued voice. "I'm not a bad Christian for teaching in a public school or because my kids went through the system." He dropped his eyes.

Cassy's heart sank. "I never said you were, Don."

Slowly Don's eyes rose to meet hers. "You've obviously taught your kids that."

Cassy joined her brother on the step and eased the door shut behind her. "David and I have tried to teach our kids to be discerning and to view everything from a biblical perspective. We want God to be relevant to their everyday life." She shifted uneasily. "I know we don't always see eye to eye on things, but that doesn't mean we can't try to understand one another."

Don nodded and glanced over his shoulder toward his waiting family. "There are some things I wish I had done differently, but Connor and Christy are out of the home now." He sighed and stared absently at the shrubs beside the front step. "I may not agree with everything you do, but I wish I could see the strength of conviction in my kids as I saw in Nicole today."

"We all have some regrets. None of us are perfect parents."

Nodding again, he backed slowly down the steps.

"Bye, Don," Cassy called after his retreating form.

21

Keepers at Home

The adjustment into Nicole's new schedule went smoothly. After all, nothing really changed all that much. Stacey was glad to have Nicole as a peer counselor at Hope for Life, and she began volunteering on Monday and Thursday mornings, besides the Wednesday mornings she shared with her family. At first she felt intimidated, trying to counsel young girls struggling with so many issues that were foreign to her. However, her gentle, quiet spirit offered hope and healing to many of the girls, especially those who had suffered abuse in childhood. Even though her position was on a volunteer basis, the work was rewarding, and Nicole found the time she spent with the girls very satisfying.

On occasion Nicole also helped do a little cleaning at her father's job sites. This not only saved her father's crew some time but gave her a little extra spending money, which came in handy. The rest of the time she spent at home, studying and practicing her piano, helping her mother, and playing music together with her siblings when they got the chance.

Her first year following graduation was pretty uneventful. Still being in her teens, most people didn't question her too much about a career, so she seldom felt the need to explain her decision to stay home.

By spring, a new opportunity presented itself. Aware of Nicole's love for music, some homeschool families in the area asked if she would consider teaching piano lessons. Nicole decided to give it a try and soon had five students lined up to start lessons in the fall. She scheduled all their lessons for Monday afternoons after her return from volunteer work, and she spent the summer preparing in anticipation of her first pupils.

⌘⌘⌘

Jeremy's final year of homeschooling, he had started a formal apprenticeship under his father, working to get his certification in carpentry. By the end of summer, he'd accumulated enough hours of work to head to Edmonton for his first eight-week stint of classes. Jeremy purchased a small secondhand car and made arrangements to stay with a couple friends from church who shared an apartment in the city. By the Sunday afternoon before his course was to start, he had everything ready to go.

"It seems odd heading off to school," Jeremy acknowledged as he collected his things and piled them by the back door.

"Yeah, you sure you're going to be able to handle eight weeks of sitting in a desk?" Nicole eyed her brother.

"Luckily only half that time is technical training in a classroom; the other half is shop work." Jeremy grinned. "But I think I can handle it better now than when I was little. Besides, I'll be studying something I enjoy, and I don't think there will be any spelling tests."

"You never know," Kimberleigh said. "You sure you know how to spell the names of all your tools?"

"I think I can manage. Hey, I even know how to spell *level* backwards! Hmm, how about that?" He gave his sisters a haughty look, and they laughed.

"I baked some cookies for you to take with you." Anika handed a metal tin to her brother.

"Ooo, thanks. I'll have to hide these."

Everyone helped Jeremy cart his things out to his waiting vehicle. When everything had been loaded, they took turns giving their brother a hug good-bye.

"Are you sure you know where you're going?"

"Yes, Mom, and I have a map with me just in case. I'll call you when I get there." He climbed into the car and waved as he backed from the drive.

"It's going to be quiet with him gone," Nicole mused as she headed into the house. She wondered fleetingly what it would be like to be the one heading away.

"He'll probably be back every weekend to restock his cookies and pick up some food," Kimberleigh reasoned.

That evening, as she was getting ready for bed, Kimberleigh let out a horrified scream. "Jeremy!" she yelled a moment later.

Racing around the corner into their room, Nicole was surprised to see Anika laughing while Kimberleigh stood fuming. Anika pointed to the bed, and Nicole spotted an assortment of Jeremy's fake beetles scattered across the sheets. She joined her younger sister in laughter.

"Ooh, I'm going to get him," Kimberleigh declared. "When I whipped back the covers, they all jumped as if they were crawling. Wouldn't he be sorry if I died of a heart attack!"

"You haven't died yet from any of his antics; I think he figures he's safe." Nicole headed for the door.

"Where are you going?" Kimberleigh grabbed her elbow. "Help me get those things out of my bed. I don't want to touch them after they jumped at me."

"It's not my bed, and I don't want to touch them either." Nicole waved as she left.

When she got to her room, she walked tentatively to her own bed and gingerly lifted her comforter to peek underneath it. Slowly she peeled the covers all the way back until she felt satisfied that no creatures were concealed. Putting her bed back in order, she flipped off the light and went to sleep.

⌘⌘⌘

When Jeremy came home for a weekend partway through his course, he seemed satisfied with how things were going. "It hasn't been too hard yet. The worst part is that none of the guys I'm staying with know how to cook. What's for supper? I'm starving for something besides macaroni and cheese."

"Told you the food would bring him home," Kimberleigh commented.

While they ate, Jeremy told them about his classes. He was in the midst of explaining his project in shop when Kimberleigh nudged Nicole. Peering over at her sister, she noticed that Kimberleigh had furtively reached around the corner of the table to curl the edge of the vinyl tablecloth into a little trough. When Nicole looked questioningly at Kimberleigh, she held one finger to her lips and motioned for Nicole to curl the tablecloth in front of her as well. With a shrug, she quietly gripped the cloth and did as her sister asked. As Kimberleigh lowered her glass of water and tilted it toward the mouth of the trough, Nicole glanced over at Jeremy who sat beside her. The curl in the tablecloth ended precisely over her brother's lap. With a smile, she leaned forward to conceal what her sister was up to and nodded. Kimberleigh casually poured the contents of her glass into the trough as she listened intently to what her brother was saying. Nicole watched Jeremy's face as the water ran past her and was deposited with a rush into his lap. Immediately she released her hold on the cloth, as Jeremy's eyes flew open and he leaped from his chair.

"Where did that come from?" he asked in astonishment as he looked down at his soaked jeans.

Anika burst out laughing. "I don't know, but it looks like you wet your pants."

"Yeah, well I didn't!" Jeremy looked in bewilderment around the table. "But I think I know who did it." He stared at Nicole and Kimberleigh, who were covering their mouths, trying unsuccessfully to keep from laughing.

"That's for the bugs in my bed that almost sent me into cardiac arrest," Kimberleigh retorted between giggles.

"Ha." Jeremy let out a laugh. "I forgot about those. That was to keep you from missing me while I was gone."

"How'd you get him from your end of the table?" Cassy asked.

"That's my little secret," Kimberleigh answered demurely.

"I think she had a little help." Jeremy grabbed a kitchen towel to wipe some water off his chair and eyed Nicole as he came back to the table.

Nicole held up her hands in defense. "I never touched the water; I just saw it coming."

"Sounds like you were asking for that." David smiled at his son.

"It's good to have you home." Nicole eyed her brother sweetly.

"Yeah, right."

⌘⌘⌘

Over the past weeks, Nicole had gradually been adjusting to her new schedule of teaching piano. One afternoon she took several minutes trying to explain to five-year-old Emily Carlson the difference between a quarter note and a half note. The little girl sat beside her on the piano bench, watching her face intently while she clapped out the beat. "Does that make sense to you, Emily?" Nicole questioned her.

"Miss Nicole, did you know that your eyes twinkle when you talk?" she asked sweetly.

Nicole smiled at the little girl who had obviously not heard a word she'd said. "And did you know that God gave you cheeks as pretty as roses?" She tapped Emily's nose.

"Really?" The little girl looked delighted. "I like you, Miss Nicole."

"I like you too. How about we try to clap out this rhythm together?" she suggested, pointing to the page of simple music.

"Okay." Emily looked at the notes and clapped along while Nicole counted.

As Nicole waved good-bye to Emily a while later, she smiled to herself. What a sweet little girl. In any given week, she had the chance to interact with so many people of all ages. She was thankful for each new experience, even though at times she felt weary. Turning from the door, she spotted her mother and Anika in the kitchen. It would be time for supper soon. She went to the cupboard to get some dishes to set the table.

"How are you enjoying teaching piano now that you've been doing it a little while?" Cassy turned to look at Nicole.

"It's pretty challenging; teaching lessons is a lot different than taking them. I'm still trying to figure out the best way to present certain concepts, so there's a lot more prep work than I thought there'd be. My students are all so different. But I think I'm going to like it."

"You sure seem to have a good rapport with your students; that goes a long way."

"Yeah, I don't remember our piano teacher's eyes twinkling. Maybe it was because I didn't practice enough." Anika laughed. "Emily is too funny."

"So do you think you'll continue teaching next year?" Cassy asked.

"I've been considering it, if you think it works for me to keep teaching in the living room. It is nice to feel like I can be saving some money for the future, but I hate making you guys tiptoe around the house all afternoon."

"Kimberleigh and I are fine with studying in our room; it doesn't bother us." Anika finished making her salad and brought it to the table.

"And I can easily work around your schedule one or two afternoons a week," Cassy added. "You volunteer so much of your time, it's nice you can be earning a little bit and still be doing something you enjoy. I think it's a good experience for you."

Nicole walked over to lean against the island. "I think so too. I just wish I knew how long I'll be around. It would help me know how to plan better. "

"You have to take one year at a time and see where God leads," Cassy said as she stirred the gravy. "None of the things you're doing have to be a long-term commitment, but they all fit with your personal goals. I like that you are investing your time in ministry and areas of interest, developing skills that are worthwhile and will benefit you after marriage. Besides, you can't just sit around doing nothing while you wait for the right man to come along."

"I know. But it would sure be nice if God showed me a bit more of the picture so I would know what to expect."

"None of us really know the future. But that's why these years are such a gift. You have so many opportunities right now that you may not have time for once you have a family. Try not to view what you are doing as merely something to pass the time until you can get on with your life—use this time wisely."

Nicole tried to take her mother's words to heart. She wanted to focus on living in the present and not wile away her days dreaming of her future. And for the most part she was successful.

22

Pressing On

By the time Nicole turned twenty, she started to get a few raised eyebrows when she told people she was living at home. Some started to question her about her goals and when she planned to get out on her own, and Nicole began dreading those encounters. It was difficult to explain in a concise manner what her goals were, and she didn't feel that people really expected the long version. Never had she felt the alienation from her culture so keenly.

Like most young adults her age, Christian Andrews had recently headed off to university, and Jeremy would be leaving soon for his second round of classes towards his certification. Thankfully Melissa and Brianne had remained at home, as they were her only link with others who held the same standards she did. Nicole felt extremely grateful for their companionship.

"I feel like I was born in the wrong era," Nicole shared with Melissa one day when she stopped by for a visit.

"I know what you mean," her friend responded ruefully. "We don't seem to fit in our culture. Though I'm sure women in other eras had their share of challenges too."

"I guess so, but it doesn't seem possible that their biblical roles as women could possibly have been challenged more than they are today." Nicole leaned back against the head of her bed and hugged her pillow to her chest. She let out a heavy sigh. "What if there are no mature, godly men around here who believe in courtship and in what we are doing?"

"Can't say I have met too many, besides our brothers and maybe Josh Henderson," Melissa acknowledged.

Nicole smiled. "Yeah, well, Josh went off to college, like most of the other guys. Last I heard, he has a girlfriend out east."

"I know, but even though he's a great guy, he wouldn't have suited you."

Nicole nodded in agreement.

"Of course that doesn't mean there aren't other men out there. I've heard of a few homeschooled girls who followed the same course we are, and they found mates through courtship."

"Which means they probably married the only decent candidates in a thousand-mile radius, and all the good men are already taken." Nicole gave her friend a sarcastic look, and Melissa swatted her arm.

"You trying to encourage me?"

"Sure, we can thank them for narrowing the field for us and making our decision easier." Nicole giggled.

"Are any of your family still asking you about college?" Melissa asked, changing the subject.

Nicole shook her head. "Nope. I think some have accepted what we are doing, and the others think our family is hopeless and have given up asking questions."

"Same here."

Nicole fiddled with the pillow in her lap as she thought for a minute. "You know, most girls head out to get their degrees and have to work to put themselves through school. They have all the pressure of living on their own and paying the bills, and then they have to come home to an empty house. I'm thankful I don't have to deal with all that and that I have my family here. I think it makes this time before marriage so much easier."

"I agree. Speaking of which, I'd better get home and help Mom with supper." Melissa scooted off the bed, and Nicole got up to walk her friend to the door.

Nicole returned to her room and opened her dresser drawer. Digging beneath her socks, she pulled out a small notepad. In anticipation of marriage, she had begun to think more seriously about what type of man she was looking for in a husband. Over the past months, she had searched the Scriptures, writing down important qualities the Bible attributed to godly men. Not that her prospective spouse would need to fulfill every item on the list, but some would be non-negotiable. Like the fact that he must have a strong relationship with the Lord. She wanted to find a man with a mature faith, who would be prepared to be the spiritual leader in their home.

Besides these qualities, Nicole hoped her future husband would be able to share her vision for raising children, and that he would support her role as a homemaker. She opened the tablet and scanned her list, which had steadily been growing. She began to wonder if she were placing her requirements too high and whether she would ever find someone who came close to meeting them. Tossing the notepad back into her drawer, she headed for the kitchen.

"Mom, do you think it's wrong to make a list of the qualities I want my future husband to exhibit?" Nicole leaned against the counter where her mother was making cookies.

"No, I think it's good to set some standards, as long as they are reasonable and you aren't expecting the man you marry to be perfect. Why, what kind of things are you putting on your list?"

"Well, number one that he has to be a Christian...that goes without saying. But I've been listing some of the qualities from 1 Timothy, that Paul gave for leaders in the church, and other godly attributes I find in Scripture. I think those are all biblical things to look for, but like you said, I know I'm not perfect and I can't expect the guy I marry to be, either. So where do I draw the line? And if I add other qualities to my list, like that he's supportive of homeschooling, am I setting my standards too narrow? I mean, it's hard enough to find guys who meet the qualifications of 1Timothy."

Cassy held up her hand to halt her daughter's barrage of questions. "Slow down and let me answer one thing at a time!" Nicole heaved a frustrated sigh. She reached over and swiped a mound of cookie dough and plopped it in her mouth. "I think you are on the right track in setting some standards," Cassy explained, "as long as you realize that people continue to mature spiritually throughout their life, and it's a process. However, you can still evaluate where a fellow is at now and determine what direction he is heading to know if he is serious about his walk with the Lord. And, if there are things you feel strongly about that he is totally against, then you'd better consider that. You can't assume that he will change or that the issue will go away after marriage."

Nicole thought about her mom's advice. "I guess I don't want to place my expectations so high that I'll never find someone to marry."

"I think you'd have more regrets if you place your expectations too low. You don't want to settle for less than God's best."

"That makes sense." Nicole discussed her list with her mom a little longer, then grabbed one more handful of cookie dough before heading back to her room. She resolved to hang onto her list for future reference in order to help her be discerning when the time came to choose a husband. In the meantime, she would continue to prepare herself to be a godly wife and mother through her pursuits at home and ministering to others.

⌘⌘⌘

Cassy was thankful that, by the time Kimberleigh graduated, she had well established plans for what she wanted to pursue. Mrs. Warner at church had a little girl with epilepsy, and she'd been desperately looking for someone to do respite for her two mornings a week. Kimberleigh often interacted with Chastity after church and jumped at the opportunity. After spending a number of days at the Warners' through the spring, Kimberleigh learned how to handle Chastity in the event of a seizure. With Cassy's permission, she arranged a schedule with Mrs. Warner to start bringing Chastity to the Knights' home two days a week so the tired mom could catch up on some sleep and chores around the house.

Kimberleigh also had spent many hours her last year working on an original play script. After showing her pet project to Teresa Henderson and getting rave reviews, Kimberleigh offered to lead the homeschool drama program in the fall. Grateful for a break in her demanding role as director, Teresa had accepted. Cassy knew it would be a huge commitment for her daughter, but she encouraged Kimberleigh in the new endeavor.

This stage of life took on a whole new dimension as Cassy tried to keep up with the busy schedules of her grown children. The dynamics of their home constantly shifted. With three of her children graduated and Anika in grade ten, Cassy felt her homeschooling years drawing to a close. However, even though she now had more time to pursue some of her own interests, her family still depended on her for regular support and advice. And between all the piano students coming and going, Kimberleigh working with Chastity, and all the preparations for the homeschool drama, Cassy found her house full of activity. No one could call her home life dull.

The months sped by, and before Cassy knew it the night of the big production was at hand. Kimberleigh's first attempt at leading her own drama production had gone fairly well. The script she'd written revolved around a pioneer family from the late 1800s who banded together to work through a series of difficult circumstances. Through their unshakable faith in God and their love for one another, they touched the lives of many in their community. Cassy felt proud of her daughter's efforts and the message of her story. The families involved seemed to appreciate it, and many people stopped to compliment the young director following the performance. Cassy thought her daughter looked exhausted, but pleased.

"Your family has a lot of talent and a real outreach within the community," Cassy's mom told her as they visited afterward in the foyer of the church.

"They're just doing what they love," Cassy responded.

"I know; it shows."

"I think Kimberleigh will sleep well tonight. She has been so busy the last few weeks getting all the final touches in place. I'm tired, and I was only helping—speaking of which, I should go help clean up."

"What can I do?" Joyce followed her daughter back into the sanctuary.

Cassy paused to scan the room. "I think Anika is collecting all the costumes to bring home and wash. You want to help her?"

An hour later, the Knights had everything packed, and they were finally ready to head home.

"You did a great job, honey." Cassy reached to hug Kimberleigh before climbing into the van.

"Thanks, Mom. It was a lot more work than I realized, but I'm glad I did it. I hope it ministered to those who came."

Cassy smiled to herself. It was such a blessing to see her family seeking to bring glory to God through their activities, rather than focusing on what they got out of it and the pursuit of pleasure. She thanked God that her children were developing a heart to serve.

⌘⌘⌘

As yet another school year drew to a close, Cassy looked forward to the change of pace for summer. The girls' schedules had slowed down somewhat, so Cassy decided to give them more responsibility at home.

Over the next months, she gave her daughters a budget and had them take turns planning meals for a week or two at a stretch. They did all the grocery shopping, kept track of expenses, and prepared all the meals for their assigned weeks. This not only gave her a welcome break from the kitchen but provided them with more experience in managing a household.

During one such week, Cassy walked into the kitchen while Anika was busy at the sink. "What's for supper?" she asked.

"Pork chops and roasted potatoes."

"After so many years of answering that question over and over, I love being the one asking it!"

Anika smiled at her mother. "This has helped me realize how much time you've put into planning and fixing meals for us over the years. I never thought about how tiring it can get always trying to think ahead to the next meal, and making sure you have everything you need." She began chopping up the potatoes she'd just washed.

"After twenty-four years of marriage, you do start to run out of new ideas." Cassy sneaked a cookie from the jar on the corner of the counter.

"Yeah, I guess. I sure appreciate all you have done for us." Anika glanced up at her mother. "And in case you're wondering, we're having lasagna tomorrow night."

"Oh, don't spoil my fun in asking." Cassy laughed as she went back to the living room to retrieve her book. She could read for another hour yet before supper would be ready. Her years of training the girls were reaping benefits. They were becoming proficient little homemakers.

23

New Prospects

One evening, David sat at his desk trying to put together a schedule for the homes he and Anthony currently had under contract. It looked like their busy season would continue right through the fall. As the business grew, he and Anthony often split up to oversee separate crews at the different sites, and it was becoming more challenging to find enough good tradesmen. The company they usually had install cabinets had recently switched hands, and David had not been pleased with their quality of work ever since. It had become a battle to get them to come back and fix things that he and Anthony both felt had been poorly done. Clearly, it was time to change companies.

David had been asking around, and several tradesmen had recommended a Christian fellow by the name of Jacob Thompson. He ran a family-based cabinet business west of Red Deer. David decided to give the fellow a call. In no time, he managed to make arrangements to meet with Jacob the following morning. He tucked the slip of paper with directions to the farm where their shop was located into his wallet.

Early the next day, after dropping Jeremy off at the job site, David headed west out of town. It didn't take long to locate the sign announcing *Thompson Family Cabinetry* beside the entrance to a quarter section farm. David followed the lane to the right, which branched off toward a large, metal-clad building, and parked his truck. A German Shepherd bounded across the yard to greet him as he opened the door of his vehicle.

"Hey, boy." David held his hand down for the dog to sniff before reaching to pat his head.

"Behave, Chomper."

David looked up to find a dark-haired young man standing in the open door of the shop. "Does that name have any significance?" David asked, pulling his hand away from the dog's head.

The fellow laughed. "No, Chomper is very friendly, but not everyone likes to be greeted by a large dog. When we got him as a puppy years ago, my brothers and I thought Chomper sounded like an intimidating name for a guard dog. Thankfully he hasn't lived up to the name."

Smiling, David reached to rest his hand on the dog's head once more. Chomper stepped a bit closer, tail wagging. "I'm David. I talked to Jacob last night about coming to see some of your cabinets. It sounds like I'm at the right building." The shrill whine of a table saw rang through the Quonset, and even from outside, he could smell the pungent aroma of fresh-cut wood.

"You sure are. My name is Josiah." He stepped forward and reached to shake David's hand. "My brothers and I all work alongside my father."

David returned the young man's hearty handshake and followed him into the shop. He seemed like a nice fellow. Once inside, David looked around the long building. Finished cabinets made from a variety of wood lined one end. Even from a distance, he could see the quality of workmanship. At the other end of the building, David counted five young men who were busy at different workstations. "Are these all your brothers?" he shouted above the steady noise. The workers definitely bore a resemblance to each other.

"Yes, though my youngest brother isn't here right now. Jesse's only ten, but he helps out sometimes." Josiah pointed to a teen boy using a power nailer. "Nathan is fifteen, so he works part-time as well. Just a moment, and I'll get my father."

The broad-shouldered young man strode across the room to where his father was feeding a sheet of oak board along the saw blade. One of the brothers grasped the freshly cut board and carried it to a workstation behind him. At Josiah's approach, the older man looked up and flipped the switch, silencing the blade. Brushing sawdust from his jeans, he followed Josiah back to where David stood waiting. The young man introduced Jacob.

"You've got quite the production crew." David grasped the hand offered to him. "That's one way to ensure you get good help—raise them and train them yourself." He could see the pride in Jacob's eyes as he glanced toward his sons and nodded.

"They're good workers."

"So you homeschooled your family?"

Jacob's eyebrows rose. He glanced at Josiah, but Josiah shook his head and shrugged. "Yes, how'd you guess?"

"It's fairly obvious to another homeschooler. All the large families I know are homeschoolers."

Jacob let out a hearty laugh. "You haven't even met them all. My oldest daughter is married, and I have twin daughters and a younger son in the house."

"Well, Josiah did mention his younger brother and the fact that Nathan is only fifteen, which helped in my deduction since he's not at school." David's eyes scanned the busy shop once again. "You have a great set-up here."

"You said on the phone that you were looking for a new supplier. Let me show you some of our work so you can see if it's what you are looking for." Jacob directed him to the far end of the building, and Josiah politely excused himself to head back to work.

As they walked along a row of cabinets waiting to be delivered and installed, David ran his hand along the smooth oak finish. He was pleased with the solid construction. The men discussed business and pricing, and by the time they were done, David felt confident that the Thompson family would be a vast improvement over their last cabinetmakers. He left some drawings of their current projects for Jacob to look over and get back to him with some quotes.

Within the week the figures came back, and David happily contracted Jacob to do all the cabinets for their next homes. It was a relief to know that they would get quality work without any delays to their building schedule.

⌘⌘⌘

The day the first set of cabinets were scheduled for installation, David and Jeremy were on site laying hardwood flooring, while Anthony and the rest of the crew worked at another location. David had just finished nailing the second board when Josiah came to the door.

"Looks like we're at the right place." Josiah waved to his brother sitting in the driver's seat of the truck, and the tall, young man hopped out of the vehicle and joined them. "This is my older brother, Seth."

"Pleased to meet you." David shook the fellow's hand. "Come on in, and I'll show you around." Leading the men to the kitchen, he stopped to introduce them to Jeremy.

Setting the board he was carrying beside the compound saw, Jeremy turned to greet them. "Hi, my dad told me about your family. I thought you might have a spare brother or two you could send my way. I'm kind of outnumbered by sisters."

"Seth's wife might object to that, and I can't say I'd like to give away any of my brothers, but I might lend a couple to you on occasion," Josiah offered with a smile.

"I'd take what I can get," Jeremy muttered as he bent over his saw once again.

David showed them the kitchen and each of the bathrooms where the cabinets needed to go, and the brothers set to work hauling in their supplies. Contemporary gospel music played over the radio in the corner of the living room where David and Jeremy worked on flooring. Throughout the morning, David glanced occasionally toward the kitchen to see how the cupboards were progressing. Josiah and Seth worked well together as they anchored the units into place. At one point, David noticed them singing along to the music, and he stopped a moment to enjoy the rich blend of their voices. He had a feeling that the Thompson family would be an interesting family to get to know. How would Cassy have handled raising seven boys? He smiled at the thought. By noon, they'd finished the living room and were ready to start on the hallway.

"I'm starving." Jeremy rose from kneeling on the floor and went to retrieve their lunch.

David stretched the kinks from his back as he wandered over to the kitchen. "The cabinets are looking great," he said, watching as Seth finished mounting a door.

"Thanks. We should have everything installed today, and we'll come back tomorrow to do the countertops." Seth turned to face him.

"Sounds good."

"Am I the only hungry one around here?" Jeremy joined the others in the kitchen, holding a large, insulated canvas bag.

"I'm ready to eat," Josiah admitted. "I just need to grab our lunch from the truck, and we'll join you."

Soon the four men took a seat on the new hardwood floor, stretching their long legs out before them.

"Do you mind if I say grace before we eat?" David eyed the young gentlemen leaning against the wall adjacent to him.

"That would be great." Seth smiled and bowed his head.

While they ate, David asked them more about their family. They explained that their father had gotten his certification for finished carpentry about ten years back, in an attempt to supplement their farm income and feed his growing family. As he trained each of his sons in the trade, their little business had grown.

"So, do you and your brothers plan to keep on in the cabinet business?" David asked.

Seth shook his head. "I've completed my degree in computer science, and I'm working on setting up my own business creating websites and doing a little computer programming. I've appreciated learning the woodworking skills, though, and I took most of my computer training through correspondence, so I was still able to work with Dad while I got my degree. Now I just work part-time, mostly doing the installations with Josiah, until I can build up my clientele."

"What about you?" David looked at Josiah.

"I plan to stay on and help Dad," Josiah replied. "But my brother Caleb is just finishing his degree in business management through correspondence, and Benjamin plans to leave next fall to train with New Tribes Missions. We'll be losing their help in the shop before long, but we're okay for now. Eventually we might have to hire more tradesmen."

"Where does your family attend church?" David asked the young man.

Josiah rested his bottle of water in his lap. "Actually, our family is involved in a local house church. We used to go to a Community church near Rocky Mountain House, but a few years ago we joined with five other homeschooling families to start a family integrated church. We take turns meeting in each other's homes, and the fathers lead the worship. It's a bit squishy at times, but we can meet outside when the weather is nice."

David was intrigued. "So what exactly does a family integrated service look like?"

"It's fairly simple. Some of us who play the piano or guitar accompany the singing, we have a sharing and prayer time, and sometimes a story or special feature geared for the younger children. Then we read a passage of Scripture and the fathers take turns leading the study. We don't have all the age-segregated programming that most churches do; we're just families ministering to families."

David liked the quiet, yet confident manner in which Josiah spoke. The church concept he described sounded a lot like their family Bible study, but on a larger scale. He and Cassy had often discussed their longing to eliminate all the segregated programming in the church in order to strengthen families, but they had never seen a church that had accomplished that feat. The questions tumbled over one another in his mind, causing the lunch hour to fly by as they discussed church issues. Reluctantly, David packed the remains of his lunch into its bag, and they all headed back to work.

By the end of the second day working with the Thompson brothers, David had come to appreciate the young men. They were both diligent and conscientious workers and had done a marvelous job installing the cabinets. However, their heart for God and the maturity of their faith is what struck David the most. Throughout the day, he had observed them and listened to their conversation while they worked. During lunch he had casually questioned them once again, systematically piecing together their core beliefs regarding issues of family and faith. They both seemed to have strong convictions solidly founded on Scripture.

Late that evening, after everyone else headed to bed, David joined Cassy on the couch. "I sure like the new cabinet makers we've contracted to do all our homes."

She glanced up from the book in her hands. "That's the big homeschool family you told me about?" David nodded. "I'm glad they worked out; I know you were getting pretty frustrated with the last workers."

David stroked his chin as he pondered his dilemma. "I wish there was some way to introduce Nicole to Josiah."

He had Cassy's full attention now. She set her book down and turned toward him. "You hardly know him."

"I know." David studied his wife with a smile. "But you'd be surprised how much I have learned in a couple of days."

"David! You didn't interrogate the poor guy, did you?"

"No, I asked him if I could interview him for the position of future son-in-law, and he agreed."

"You didn't!" Cassy threw him a horrified expression, causing him to burst out laughing.

"No, I didn't. But we did talk about doctrinal issues, and I asked about their family." David proceeded to tell her about their house church and some of the things Josiah and Seth had shared concerning their commitment to God and His Word. "I've been impressed with their character."

"You found all that out in two days? It sounds to me like you interrogated them." Cassy cocked her head and studied him.

David smirked. "Okay, maybe a little, but it was subtle. They didn't know they were being interrogated."

"So, does Josiah have a girlfriend?"

"I don't think so. Josiah didn't mention any girls. And I do know they don't believe in dating—Seth told me about courting his wife."

"I suppose the next time you see Josiah you'll just tell him, 'By the way, I have a lovely twenty-two-year-old daughter at home I thought you might like to court!'"

"Sure, why not?" He chuckled. "Actually, I think I might ask Nicole to do some clean-up for me sometime when I know he'll be around. It will give me a chance to introduce them and see what happens. Of course I wouldn't give Josiah permission to court her without asking him a lot more questions, but if he showed some interest, it would give me the chance to do that."

"That might make Nicole feel really awkward, setting up a meeting like that."

David shrugged. "Neither of them have to know I want to introduce them. It could be a casual meeting with no pressure. She's been around our work crews before."

"If you think this guy is good enough for your daughter, I'd like to meet him myself. He must be quite the fellow!" Cassy gave his knee a pat. "How soon will you be ready for them to do the next home?"

"About a month."

24

The Encounter

Over the following weeks, Cassy noticed that David made a point of running out to the Thompson farm a couple of times to drop off plans and to schedule the installation of the next set of cabinets. Usually he would have done the scheduling over the phone, but she figured her husband needed an excuse to interact with the family a bit more. Cassy smiled to herself. She had never imagined her husband as a matchmaker, but she was thankful he was taking an active role in looking for godly men for his daughters.

"Hey Nicole, would you have some time after work on Thursday to stop by and do some cleaning at one of our job sites?" David asked one evening after supper. "It could use some sweeping, and we still need the stickers scraped off the windows."

Nicole paused from helping clear the table. "Sure, Thursday should be fine."

"Anthony will have most of our crew at the new site that is ready to start framing. I thought I'd order in a pizza and you can join us for lunch. Maybe you could stop and pick up some cold drinks on your way over."

"Sounds good. Are you still working in that new development?" Nicole lifted the bowl of corn from the table and began scraping the remnants into a smaller container.

"Yeah, just down the street from the last house you helped with. You'll see my truck out front."

As she prepared to wash the dishes, Cassy couldn't help but smile to herself, fully aware of the ulterior motive behind her husband's nonchalant manner. She would love to be a mouse in the corner for the day, her curiosity to meet the man who had captured David's attention escalating. But she would have to wait and hear about it later.

⌘⌘⌘

On Thursday, Nicole remembered to collect some cleaning supplies to take with her before heading into work. At Hope for Life, she met with several teen clients, making her morning fly quickly. When she left, her mind was still on the new girl who had dropped in, a seventeen-year-old who had run away from home and was now pregnant. Only a few years younger than herself, the girl had lived a vastly different life than her own. Nicole found it hard to comprehend what some of her clients had been through.

After stopping to pick up a six-pack of cold pop, Nicole wound her way through the new development on the east side of town until she spotted her father's black, half-ton truck. Parking along the curb, she grabbed the drinks, her broom and dustpan, and the pail of supplies she had brought with her. She made her way in the front door of the new home.

"Cleaning lady's here," Nicole bellowed as she rounded a corner into the kitchen, nearly bumping into a tall, young man. She stopped short. Startlingly blue eyes stared back at her as she tilted her head to look into his face. This was not one of her dad's crew. Nicole felt her face flush as she glanced quickly around the room for someone she might recognize. The only other worker in sight was a man squatting in front of a corner cupboard unit, but he didn't look familiar either. "Am I in the wrong house?" she stammered.

The young man flashed her a disarming smile. "That depends on whose house you are supposed to be cleaning."

"I thought that was my dad's truck out front."

Flustered, Nicole spun toward the front door, accidently whacking the man behind her across the chest with the broom stick she had tucked under one arm. The impact jarred the broom from under her elbow, causing her to drop it with a clatter.

"Oh, I'm so sorry!" Nicole swung back in horror. She quickly set down her pail of cleaning supplies and stooped to pick up the broom, grasping it more securely. "Are you all right?" She noticed a glimmer in the man's eyes as if he struggled not to laugh.

"Don't worry, I'm fine." His voice was low and kind. "And if your father is David Knight, then that is his truck. He and Jeremy are putting the railing on the back deck. My name is Josiah, and this is my brother Seth." Josiah indicated the man who had come to stand beside him.

"Hi." Seth nodded.

"I'm Nicole, and I'm here to do some cleaning for my dad." She wiggled the broom in her hand.

"Yes, I got that part." Josiah smiled.

Nicole looked away as she felt her face flush again at the thought of her grand entry. Yes, he was well aware of her broom. Just then the door off the kitchen opened, and with relief she saw her father and Jeremy enter.

"Ah, Nicole, I thought I heard your voice." Her father walked across the room to join her. "So, it looks like you've already met Josiah and Seth. Remember the homeschool family I mentioned who are making our cabinets for us now? Josiah and Seth are the two oldest boys."

"Oh." Nicole nodded. She remembered her father saying something about a large homeschool family he had visited awhile back, but she hadn't made the connection. However, when her father had mentioned the family, somehow she had thought of the boys as teenagers. Nicole shifted awkwardly. "How long have you been in the cabinet business?" she asked, hoping to direct the attention to someone besides herself.

"Our dad started doing a bit of cabinetry about ten years ago, but it has only been the last four or five years that we've been working more steadily," Seth explained.

"All this talk of work is making me hungry." Jeremy walked over to the front window to peer out. "When is that pizza coming?"

"It should be here any minute," David commented.

The deliveryman arrived shortly, and the crew gathered on the living room floor to eat. Nicole was glad she had brought a pack of six drinks, because her father had obviously invited Josiah and Seth to join them for lunch. She glanced furtively toward the handsome men seated across from her. She noticed the gold band on Seth's finger as he reached for a piece of pizza, and her eyes unconsciously drifted toward Josiah's left hand. No ring. From her spot on the floor, Nicole casually studied the man's features. His closely trimmed beard and mustache neatly outlined the edge of his jaw and framed his mouth. She couldn't help but notice the striking contrast between his dark hair and deep blue eyes. When those eyes shifted to meet hers, Nicole self-consciously dropped her gaze.

"How was your morning, Nicole?" Her father leaned against the wall and stretched his legs out in front of him, lifting his pizza to take a bite.

"Pretty busy. I got another new client—a runaway. We were able to get her into a woman's shelter for now."

"Where do you work?" Josiah asked.

"I volunteer at Hope for Life, the Christian crisis pregnancy center. I'm a peer counselor, so I work mostly with the younger girls who come in." Nicole noticed Josiah's eyebrows rise as she spoke.

"Sounds interesting. How'd you get started in that?"

"My mom started volunteering there about seven years ago, and my sisters and I would go along to help out wherever we could. When I graduated, I wanted to continue to study at home and be involved at the center, so I applied for a peer counselor position. I really enjoy working with the girls; it's so rewarding."

"That's great. Do you get a chance to share the gospel with them at all?"

Nicole smiled as she looked at Josiah. She remembered now that her father had mentioned that the Thompsons were a Christian family. "I get a chance to share with some of them, if they're open to it. I've had a number of clients accept the Lord over the past few years."

"She's also been able to convince some of young girls not to get an abortion," Jeremy chimed in. "Nicole started a photo album of all the babies that have been born since she's been working there, and she prays for them and their mothers. It's pretty cool."

Nicole felt the intensity of Josiah's gaze upon her as Jeremy spoke. She avoided looking him in the eye.

Seth leaned forward to grasp another slice of pizza. "That's such a neat ministry. I wish more people understood the value God places on children. My parents have heard many negative comments over the years for having ten kids."

Nicole nodded as she looked at the older brother. "I know large families are often frowned upon in our society, but I admire them. It must have been challenging for your mom homeschooling all of you."

Seth paused before taking a bite of food and smiled. "It got a little crazy at times. My mom had her hands full, but the older kids often took turns watching the little ones or helping them with their schoolwork. My sister, Anna, helped a lot with the housework."

“And when any of the boys got too restless, she’d send us out to chop wood for an hour or have Dad put us to work until we were ready to sit again,” Josiah admitted.

“I’d have been chopping a lot of wood if my mom had done that,” Jeremy declared.

Nicole watched as a slow grin crept across Josiah’s face. Lifting her can of pop, she took a sip.

“We did chop a lot. In fact, we not only kept our woodstove going all winter, we also made a little money on the side selling extra wood to our neighbors,” Josiah told Jeremy.

“So I guess you’ve been working with wood for a long time, even before you started building cabinets,” David teased.

Josiah let out a low chuckle. “You could say that.”

Nicole enjoyed hearing more about the Thompson family while they ate. All too soon, it seemed, the pizza disappeared and the empty boxes and cans were stacked together. She rose to find a garbage bag among her supplies to put them in.

“We’d better get back to work.” Seth gave his brother’s shoulder a nudge with the back of his hand. He turned to David. “Can we pay you for half of the pizza?”

“Nope, my treat.”

“Thanks so much.”

“Yes, thank you,” Josiah echoed as he rose from his position on the floor.

After clarifying with her father what all she needed to do, Nicole headed to one of the bathrooms to scrub out the tub. She cringed at the grungy layer of mud and dust left over from the drywall finishers. Might as well get her least favorite job over with first. Tying her long hair back into a ponytail, she rolled up her sleeves and set to work.

When both tubs were sparkling clean, she gathered her broom and dustpan to sweep any debris from the floors in preparation for carpet installation. Her father generally tried to keep his job sites as tidy as possible, so his crew usually scraped and cleaned the floors once the drywall and painting were finished, making this task relatively easy.

She glanced occasionally toward the men working in the kitchen while she maneuvered her broom around the living room. Josiah knelt on the floor, his head and shoulders tucked inside the last cabinet unit as he screwed it to the wall. Seth had his attention focused on the hinge he was adjusting for one of the top cabinet doors. The two bantered back and forth, discussing who could take the other in a wrestling match. Nicole stifled a giggle, certain they had not heard her enter the room.

"C'mon, who are you trying to kid, Seth?" Josiah taunted from his position in the cabinet. "You know I whooped you the last time we wrestled. That's why you won't challenge me anymore."

Just then Seth turned and smiled when he saw her. "Maybe Nicole would like to be the judge."

"What?" Josiah jerked backward and cracked his head on the edge of the cupboard above him. "Ouch!" He eased out of the tight opening and turned around, one hand rubbing the back of his head.

Nicole brushed her hand across her face in an attempt to hide her smile. "Sorry, but I'm not much good at judging wrestling matches."

A sheepish grin crept across Josiah's flushed face. "Seth started it." He glared at his brother. "He always thinks that because he's three years older that he's tougher, but he's not. At least not anymore."

Seth laughed. "Fine, since you're so tough, I'll let you carry all the tools back out to the truck when we're through."

"I will, you wimp." Josiah socked his brother in the arm.

"I'm not a wimp; I'm just smarter than you." Seth drilled Josiah in the chest with his index finger.

"How's that?"

"I just got you to agree to carry everything out to the truck."

"That's not because you're smart, it's because you're *lazy*. That's why I'm stronger than you!" With a grin, Josiah jabbed his brother back and returned to his work.

Nicole smiled and shook her head. She couldn't imagine anyone calling either man a wimp. Both were tall with a solid build, obviously men used to heavy work. The men were quiet as she went back to her sweeping.

For the bulk of the afternoon, Nicole made her way from room to room, peeling the stickers off of windows. She washed each one as she went to remove any sticky residue. Her dad and Jeremy finished their work on the deck and came inside. The last half hour, Nicole helped screw cover plates onto the outlets and switches around the living room and kitchen, answering Josiah's occasional questions while she worked. The men soon finished off and started collecting their tools. She watched as Josiah effortlessly hoisted their toolbox in one hand and a large bin loaded with cordless screwdrivers, a level, and other paraphernalia in the other.

"Here, let me take that," Seth reached for the bin.

"Nope, it's too heavy for you," Josiah teased with a smile.

"You'd better be careful, or I'll let you carry it all the time."

"Good-bye, nice meeting you." Josiah nodded toward Nicole as he walked past.

"Bye," she waved and Seth waved back.

⌘⌘⌘

"How was your day?" Cassy asked Nicole when she got home.

"Good. I got another new client today from a rough background, but she was open to our help." Nicole washed her hands and joined her mother in dishing up supper.

"How was cleaning?" Cassy studied her daughter's face and thought she noticed a little color creep into her cheeks.

"It was fine. I got to meet a couple of the guys who are making cabinets for Dad. They seem pretty nice. Quite the characters. I smacked one of them with my broom when I came in." Nicole chuckled as she set a steaming bowl of scalloped potatoes on the table.

"Nicole! What did you do that for?" Cassy chided.

"It wasn't on purpose." Nicole explained what had happened.

"I missed that part. Great way to introduce yourself, Sis." Jeremy slid a piece of ham from the platter and popped it into his mouth. "Mmm, that's good."

"Well, supper is ready. Go call your sisters to the table."

Cassy heard a little more about Nicole's day over supper, and she noticed that Seth's and Josiah's name came up several times. It wasn't until later that evening, however, that she had a chance to get David's take on how the day had gone.

"They've just met, so it's hard to tell. They don't really know a lot about each other, but they seemed to get along well over lunch." David sat on the edge of the bed to remove his shoes. "Jeremy and I were working on the deck outside for a fair bit today, so I don't know what all happened while we were outside. I'm hoping I'll be able to get them together again down the road, but it will be two months before the next house is ready for cabinets."

"Won't they be back to finish off at this house tomorrow?"

"Yeah, but I don't really have anything more for Nicole to do there. It would look a little suspicious if I bring her along for no apparent reason."

Cassy ran her fingers through her hair and thought for a moment. "You could just happen to forget your lunch, and I could have her bring it to you."

David laughed. "And have her drive forty minutes round trip instead of me running out to pick something up? Now who's the schemer? That would be even more obvious."

"Two months just seems like a long time. If he's a good match for Nicole, I don't want him to forget about her."

"If he's at all interested, he won't forget, believe me. It might do him good to have some time to think about it. Besides, God's in control."

The next couple of months Cassy became preoccupied with Christmas preparations and holiday celebrations with family, but she often prayed for Nicole and the Thompson family. Though she had yet to meet them personally, she prayed that God would be directing in both Nicole's and Josiah's life, whether God chose to bring them together or not. When David finally lined up another day for Nicole to clean, she knew that Josiah would be there as well, and she began praying in earnest.

25

Getting Acquainted

Tuesday morning Nicole dragged herself from bed early and hopped in the shower, hoping it would help her to wake up. She hated the short January daylight hours, which meant getting up in the dark, and having the sun set before suppertime. Today she would see little of that sunshine, for she would be spending the full day helping her father. As she pulled a warm sweater over her head, she secretly wondered whether Josiah would be at the site. Probably not. He was not a regular member on her dad's crew, and her father hadn't mentioned him. She sighed. When would God bring the right man into her life? It seemed so hard to wait, and she longed to have a husband and family of her own. She twisted her hair up and fastened it with a clip before heading to the kitchen.

Nicole ate a quick breakfast and helped her mother pack their lunch. She still felt tired as she slipped on her coat, collected her cleaning supplies, and hurried to join her father, who was already loading some tools in the back of his truck. Jeremy opened the cab door and allowed her to hop in first before climbing onto the seat beside her. The temperature outside had been hovering around twenty below zero all week, and Nicole shivered as she snuggled down between her father and brother, hoping the heater would warm the vehicle quickly.

Twenty minutes later, they pulled up to the job site. Nicole hopped out of the truck, grabbed her things, and hurried into the house. She stamped the snow from her shoes on the mat by the door and made her way up a few stairs to the main floor.

"Hi Uncle Anthony, hi, Mack," she said, greeting the two men collecting some work lights from the corner of the living room.

"Hi, Nicole." Anthony turned to look at her. "We'll be out of your way in a minute. Sorry we're leaving a little more mess for you to deal with, but we're trying to get some heat hooked up in the other house today to make it bearable for the crew there. Your dad said he'd have you scrape the floors today."

"That's okay; you guys always do such a thorough job, there's never much left for me to clean. My bank account will appreciate the extra work."

"In other words, you like it when I'm messy." Anthony gave her a lopsided smile. "Unfortunately Sarah doesn't agree with you. Of course I don't pay her to pick up after me, so maybe that has something to do with it."

Nicole giggled. "The pay helps." She set down her things in a corner of the room and took off her coat, rubbing her hands together to warm them.

Anthony stopped to talk to David a moment before he and Mack carted the lights out to his waiting vehicle. Nicole couldn't imagine working on a construction site in this weather without any heat. Collecting her pail of rags and cleaning supplies, she headed down the hall in search of the nearest tub to scour.

"Actually Nicole, would you mind scraping the floors first, starting with the kitchen? The fellows should be here soon with the cabinets, and we need the floor clean for them."

Nicole stopped and worked to erase her tell-tale smile before turning to face her father. "Sure, where's the scraper?" She retraced her steps and set the pail back down with her other things.

"Right there." Her father pointed to a long-handled floor scraper propped against the far wall. "Jeremy and I will be in the basement staining trim, so you'll have to watch for Seth and Josiah and let them in."

"Okay." Nicole headed for the scraper and spotted her dad's radio on the floor. She stooped to turn on the Christian station, then set to work prying lumps of drywall mud off the subfloor in the kitchen. Quietly she sang along with the radio as she labored away, trying to get the floor clean before the cabinets arrived. Scanning the room, she spotted one last mound in the corner she'd missed. "Drywallers should be less messy," she mumbled to herself as she gave it a shove with the metal blade.

"Is your dad here?" a low voice rumbled just above her shoulder.

Nicole jumped and spun around, her hand flying to her chest. "Oh, I didn't hear you come in." Familiar blue eyes stared down at her. "My dad's downstairs; I was supposed to be watching for you."

Josiah fiddled with the gloves he was holding. "I didn't mean to startle you. I knocked, but—" he glanced toward the radio—"I guess you didn't hear me. I wanted to make sure it was okay to start unloading."

"Uh, sure. It'll only take me a second to sweep this up." She gestured toward the debris she'd scraped from the floor.

Josiah nodded. "I'll go help Seth then."

Nicole watched him leave, then quickly turned down the radio and grabbed the broom and dustpan. By the time the two men had carried the first batch of cabinets inside, she had started on the living room floor.

"Do you work for your father fairly often?" Josiah removed his coat and laid it on the floor against the wall.

"Not, really. I just do a little cleaning when they get to the finishing stage, or when they're extra busy. I'm not much good with a hammer," she added, a smirk tugging at the corner of her mouth.

"Well I…I didn't mean…" Josiah broke off with a low chuckle. "You don't look like the typical construction hand." His eyes locked onto hers for a moment, his smile slowly fading. He slid his hands into his pockets and dropped his gaze. "I'd better get to work." Josiah's voice was quiet. He threw her one more glance before turning toward the kitchen.

Nicole's eyes followed him a moment, her thoughts a jumble of confusion. What was it about this young man that seemed to grip her when he was around? Whatever it was, it was nonsense, she told herself. She hardly knew him. Chalking it up to infatuation over his good looks, Nicole gripped her scraper more tightly and tried to focus on her work. However, the intensity of those blue eyes haunted her.

As she rounded a corner of the room, she threw a sideways glance toward the men in the kitchen. They were already busy marking measurements on the wall for mounting the top cupboards. The rumble of their voices as they discussed their work easily carried across the open space and into the living room. Quietly Nicole finished off the floor and carried the scraper and broom down the hall.

When Nicole had completed all the floors, she once again collected her pail and headed for the bathrooms. She had just finished scrubbing the second tub and was collecting her dirty rags when she heard someone coming down the hall.

"You ready for lunch?" Jeremy popped his head around the doorway.

"Yes!" She threw the rags in her pail and washed her hands under the tub faucet, drying them on a paper towel. "Breakfast seems like a long time ago." She followed her brother out to the living room.

As Nicole collected their lunch from the corner of the room, she glanced toward the kitchen. Her father stood with Seth and Josiah, inspecting the progress of the cabinets. Taking a seat on the floor beside Jeremy, she watched the men as they talked. A moment later, her father directed them into the living room.

"Would one of you like to say grace for us?" David addressed the brothers.

"Sure," Josiah bowed his head and offered a blessing on the food.

Nicole appreciated the ease with which Josiah addressed his heavenly Father. Many young men she knew showed obvious discomfort when asked to pray in public. Josiah's prayer was neither mechanical nor lofty, as one conscious of impressing his listeners. Rather, it was a sincere offer of thanksgiving from one who clearly spent time in regular communion with God. She resisted the urge to peek at him while he prayed.

When he was finished, Nicole reached in their bag and handed her father and Jeremy each a sandwich before taking one for herself. She set it in her lap, opened her bottle of water, and took a long swig.

"So Nicole, what do you enjoy doing when you're not scraping floors or volunteering at Hope for Life?" Seth asked as he took a thick sandwich from his lunch bag and pulled it from the plastic wrap.

"Reading!" Jeremy cut in. "She always has her nose in a book."

Nicole smiled. "I do like to read, especially biographies or historical books, but I also teach piano, and like to sew and bake—though I don't bake as much as my sister, Anika."

"That's one thing that's nice about having sisters; there's always lots of baking around the house."

Nicole nudged her brother as he took a big bite of his sandwich. "You make it sound like that's the only thing we're good for."

"No, I said that's *one* thing you're good for," he said with his mouth full. "You're good at doing laundry too." Nicole raised her eyebrows at him. He swallowed and threw her a grin. "I'm kidding; I have great sisters. I could do without the times you guys stay up half the night giggling, though." Jeremy told Seth and Josiah about the night he shot bugs in their window to get his sisters back, and they cracked up laughing. "See, they thought it was funny." He looked at Nicole.

She shivered. "That was awful. I hate bugs!"

"I take it you're hoping God doesn't call you to be a missionary in some tropical place with lots of bugs." Josiah sat directly across from her, resting his elbows on his knees as he studied her face.

"The missionary and tropical part would be fine, the bugs—not so much. What about you? Any missionary adventures in your future plans?"

Josiah cocked his head and thought a moment before answering. "Not at this point. My brother, Benjamin, is planning to go to the mission field. I think it's great, but we have a lot of neighbors who need to hear the gospel and plenty of opportunities to minister right here. For now I plan to stay and continue to be involved in our house church and community outreach. I love living on the farm and working with the animals and hope to own a small farm of my own someday."

"What kinds of animals do you have?" Jeremy asked.

"Cattle, horses, a few sheep, and a couple dogs; we also have an assortment of chickens and barn cats, which the girls mostly look after."

"Sounds like a lot to keep up with. My dad and I used to help with some of the chores on my grandpa's farm when we'd go visit. I loved getting a chance to ride in the big combines when I was little, but he's retired now. He leases most of his land out to neighbors. I can't imagine doing all that and running a business on the side."

Seth nodded at Jeremy's assessment. "It can be challenging, but we have lots of help and we try not to book as many jobs during seeding and harvest."

"And since our shop is on the farm, that helps a lot," Josiah added. "We can still keep an eye on things during calving season, or take a break to do chores."

Nicole ate her lunch and listened quietly as the guys discussed work and farming. When there was a lull in the conversation, Josiah turned to her once again.

"So, I told you my plans, and I know Jeremy just finished his carpentry certification. What about you? What are your future goals?"

Nicole studied her half-eaten apple a moment before shrugging and looking Josiah in the eye. "I want to be a homemaker," she stated simply. "But until I get married, I plan to stay home and continue to study, teach piano, and be involved in ministry under the headship and protection of my father." She glanced over to her dad, who was sitting beside her, and he smiled at her. When she looked back, she found Josiah's gaze upon her, an expression on his face she found herself longing to decipher.

"No plans for college?"

Nicole shook her head and dropped her eyes to her apple once more. "I want a family, not a career or a college degree." Her voice was barely above a whisper.

"There aren't many girls nowadays who would share your opinion."

"I know, but I care more what God thinks." She glanced up at the man before her once more. He sat with a gleam in his eyes. "Did your sister go to college?"

A smile now tugged at the corner of his lips. "Anna? No, she took the same stand you're taking. I know it wasn't easy for her, and probably not for you either, but don't give up. You can be an encouragement for more young ladies to turn their hearts toward home."

Nicole flushed and looked away. It felt awkward discussing her desire for a husband and children with this single young man, but the admiration in his voice buoyed her spirits. To have a gentleman affirm her position meant a lot.

The conversation shifted to other topics, and Nicole thoroughly enjoyed interacting with these homeschooled fellows who seemed to share so many of her family's values. She felt reluctant to have the lunch break end. Before long, however, everyone headed back to work. Slowly Nicole rose from her spot on the floor, stretched, and began the tedious job of peeling stickers off the multitude of windows throughout the house, washing each pane as she went. It was dark once again when the workers slipped on their heavy coats, collected their things, and said good-bye to one another. Nicole hurried to her father's truck and climbed in.

"The Thompson boys sure do a nice job with the cabinets." David's words interrupted Nicole's thoughts and she glanced toward her father. He peered at her from the corner of his eyes for a moment before returning his gaze to the road. "They seem like neat fellows."

"Yeah, it's nice to meet another homeschool family with similar standards. It would be fun to get to know them better. I found it encouraging that Josiah supported my stance to stay at home and that his sister did the same thing. You don't find many Christians who think that way anymore."

"That's because too many Christians have compromised with the culture and no longer have a solid biblical worldview. But from what I've seen, Seth and Josiah seem to have a good foundation in Scripture."

"I wish there were more men like them," Nicole said quietly.

"Hey, what about me?" Jeremy asked indignantly.

"You're my brother; you don't count."

"Oh, thanks!"

David laughed. "No offense, Jeremy, you're just not a candidate for your sisters to marry." David gazed at his daughter a moment, and Nicole smiled at him. Her father understood.

26

Laying the Groundwork

The next morning Nicole slept longer than she had intended. She'd had a restless night. Every time she'd closed her eyes, thoughts of her conversation with Josiah the day before kept resurfacing, and her heart filled with longing. When would she meet that special someone who would love her and want to share her dreams of having a home and family? There seemed to be so few prospects of godly young men with a commitment to Scripture and vision to lead their family. Josiah was the first man she'd met for some time in whom she saw potential, but she had limited interaction with him. How could she get to know him or hope for a relationship when she had no idea when she'd see him again?

Crossing the room to her dresser, Nicole pulled a battered slip of paper from her top drawer. Her eyes scanned the list of qualities she hoped to find in a husband. "Please God, I know You're in control. Help me to be content where You lead me until the right man comes along," she prayed. With a sigh, she tucked the list back where she'd found it. "And help me to be content if no one comes along," she added, though her heart ached at the thought. Pushing her longings aside, she hurried to get dressed.

Nicole joined her mother and sisters for a quick breakfast before heading out for their morning at Hope for Life. Anika's and Kimberleigh's chatter filled the van as they drove. Content just to listen, she leaned her head back against her seat and closed her eyes.

"You feeling okay?"

Nicole tilted her head toward her mother, who eyed her with concern. "Yeah. Just tired I guess."

"Anything bothering you?" Cassy sounded unconvinced.

"You dated other guys before you met Dad, right?"

"Unfortunately, yes. It's something I regret, but everyone I knew was dating, and I never stopped to question it. Why?"

"Just wondering. How did you know Dad was the right one for you?"

Kimberleigh and Anika leaned forward from the backseat.

"Well, I knew your father loved God and that he was the kind of man I could respect and trust to lead our home. I knew he was a man of integrity, a hard worker, and that he would be a faithful husband. I also prayed a lot about our relationship."

"Did you have any doubts about your decision to marry him?" Nicole pressed.

Cassy smiled. "Doubts? I guess it's natural to feel a bit nervous about making such a big decision; it shouldn't be made lightly. If you believe that marriage is a lifetime commitment, you sure don't want to choose poorly. And once you're in a relationship, it can be difficult to be discerning. But to answer your question, I maybe felt uncertain at first, but by the time your dad proposed, I knew he was the right choice."

"But how did you know that what you were feeling was really love?"

"For starters, love is a choice, not a feeling. Girls who focus too much on romantic feelings instead of godliness and character often make poor decisions. Feelings fluctuate. Every couple has adjustments and struggles at times; if they are not committed to love one another and work through it, it will drive them apart. There have been moments over the years when I maybe didn't *feel* like loving your father, but I knew our relationship was built on something more solid than the current circumstances. You can always choose to love and show respect despite your feelings."

Kimberleigh gripped the back of her mother's seat and strained against her seatbelt, craning her neck to get a good look at her sister's face. "Okay, Nicole, what are you hiding? You obviously met someone and didn't tell me; I want to hear all the details."

"I'm not hiding anything...there's nothing to tell." She averted her glance out the window to hide the flush she felt creeping into her cheeks.

"You can't fool me." Kimberleigh poked her shoulder. "Wait a minute. Does this have anything to do with that nice homeschooled guy you mentioned awhile ago? You were working with Dad yesterday. Did you see him again?"

Nicole rolled her eyes. Kimberleigh knew her too well. Turning from the window, she gave her sister a rueful smile. "Yes, Josiah and Seth were there, but two days is hardly enough time to really get to know someone."

"But you like him, I can tell. I've got to meet him. There's no way you're going to start a courtship with someone I haven't given my approval of yet!" Kimberleigh slapped the back of the seat. "Why didn't you tell me?"

Nicole shrugged. "Because there's nothing to tell, and no one said anything about a courtship. We just met, for goodness' sake. Besides, it's Dad's job to give the approval."

"Of course he needs Dad's approval, but no guy is going to steal my sister and whisk her away to who knows where unless I think he's good enough for her."

"Kimberleigh, stop being overly dramatic, and stop yanking on my seat please," Cassy chided.

"Me? Overly dramatic?" Kimberleigh let go of her mother's seat and sat back with a "humph."

"Do you like him, Nicole?" Anika asked anxiously.

Nicole twisted around in her seat to peer at her younger sister. "I don't know, Anika. He seems like a very nice guy, but like I said, I don't know him that well." She gave her sister a tender smile. "But I was wondering how I *will* know when the right guy comes along someday."

Cassy pulled into the narrow drive of the pregnancy crisis center and drove around to the back of the building. She turned off the engine and reached to place a hand on Nicole's knee. "That's why your father and I want you to follow God's standards for your relationships and in choosing a husband. You can never eliminate all the emotional ups and downs, and seeking God's direction can be confusing at times, but with lots of prayer, you're less likely to make a decision you'll come to regret."

Nicole bit her lip. "I know," she murmured.

Cassy reached for her keys and opened her door. "For your information, your dad likes Josiah."

"I thought so." Nicole's face brightened as she climbed out of the van.

"I knew it!" Kimberleigh said triumphantly.

But Nicole ignored her. It was too early yet for her to admit that she felt attracted to him. Time would tell.

⌘⌘⌘

That evening Cassy told David about the discussion she'd had with Nicole. She felt sure their daughter was at least somewhat interested in Josiah, and David admitted he'd gotten the same impression. For now, all Cassy could do was to pray about the situation and wait.

A full week passed before the topic came up again. It had been a long day, and Cassy felt tired as she climbed into bed. She closed her eyes and heaved a sigh as David put his arm around her and pulled her against him.

"I got an interesting phone call today," David whispered against her hair.

"Uh huh," Cassy mumbled.

"It was from Josiah."

Cassy's eyes flew open and she spun to face her husband, all thoughts of sleep vanishing. "What did he say?"

David chuckled. "I thought you might be interested. He said he'd like a chance to get to know Nicole better, and he'd like to talk to me about it."

"And...what else did he say?"

"He said he doesn't know her well enough to make a decision about a possible courtship or anything, but he wondered whether I would be open to meeting with him over lunch sometime. He thought it would allow me to get acquainted with him, and he could find out more about Nicole and our family before he pursues anything further."

"Ooh, I can't wait to see what Nicole thinks of it." Cassy propped herself up on one elbow, hardly able to contain her excitement.

"Josiah doesn't want her to know," David cautioned.

"What? I can't tell her?" Cassy's face fell.

"Not yet. He wants to be sure of his intentions before we say anything to her, to avoid any awkwardness or hurt feelings in the process. I think he is being wise and very considerate of Nicole."

"That makes sense, I guess. I respect him for it, even though I'll find it hard not to say anything. So when do I get to meet him?"

David smiled. "Patience, my dear. Let's see how this progresses before you start making any wedding plans. He's just laying the groundwork for getting to know Nicole; he's not ready to commit to anything yet. He offered to take me for lunch tomorrow; we'll see where it goes from there."

⌘⌘⌘

For a month David met with Josiah twice a week for lunch, and Cassy received regular updates on the meetings. Their conversations covered a broad range of topics, from issues of theology and family values, to personal interests and goals, and Cassy coaxed as much information out of her husband as she could when he came home. David admitted that Josiah seemed a bit nervous at the start, but the young man soon began to relax and answer his questions with confidence, and Cassy could tell that the maturity of his responses pleased her husband. At the same time, she knew David had been sharing many things about their family with Josiah as well.

It wasn't hard to see that her husband looked forward to these informal lunches, and she found it more and more difficult to contain her desire to meet this prospective young suitor. Therefore, when David came home one evening with an invitation for the family to go to the Thompsons for supper the following Saturday, Cassy was ecstatic. Both Josiah and David were ready to pursue the possibility of a future courtship, but Josiah needed to spend more time with Nicole first and wanted their families to meet. Josiah still requested they not tell Nicole the reason for the invite until he was ready to ask her permission to court.

Though Cassy longed to give her daughter some assurance of Josiah's interest, she knew she must honor his request. It was for the better, she reasoned. For if Nicole knew and got her hopes up, only to have them dashed, it would be much harder on her. She had been waiting so long already, she could wait a little longer.

The next morning, Cassy entered the living room where Nicole sat at the piano playing a song from a new music book she had recently purchased. Kimberleigh lay on the floor writing in her notebook, and Anika sat on the couch reading. Cassy took a seat where she could see the profile of Nicole's face before telling them about the invitation to the Thompsons' farm. A faint flush came to her eldest daughter's cheeks as she stared down at the piano keys, her fingers paused in their playing.

"Ooo, we finally get to meet the elusive Josiah?" Kimberleigh looked up from her paper with a smile.

"We get to meet the whole family," Nicole stated simply without raising her eyes. "They do business with Dad, you know."

"Don't try to tell me you aren't interested in one particular member of the family," Kimberleigh teased. "I've seen it in your eyes when you've mentioned his name, which you've done a number of times lately."

Nicole glanced up for just a second. "It doesn't matter whether I'm interested or not unless he's interested in me," she said quietly, her fingers gently caressing the keys once more.

Cassy desperately wanted to tell her that he was, but she bit her tongue. "You'll find the right fellow in God's timing, sweetheart," she said instead.

Nicole threw her a tentative smile while she played. "I know, Mom."

"Dad said we could go early if anyone is interested in trying some horseback riding before supper, so you'll have to dress appropriately for the weather."

"They have horses?" Anika squealed. "I like the Thompsons already! I always thought Grandpa Knight should keep horses on his farm."

"Yeah, well once your father and uncles left the farm, Grandpa found it a lot to keep up with on his own. He didn't want to be tied down with animals," Cassy explained. "He got rid of the few animals he did own."

"He still has cats," Anika countered.

"Probably to keep down the mice." Nicole glanced over her shoulder. "Besides, cats eat considerably less and take less care than horses."

"But horses are so much more romantic," Kimberleigh said dreamily.

"I can't say I'm interested in a candlelight dinner with a horse." Nicole laughed at the thought.

Kimberleigh grabbed her eraser and whipped it at her sister, hitting Nicole on the shoulder. "I meant going horseback riding is romantic, you goof. Poor Josiah's going to have his work cut out for him in order to woo you."

Nicole picked up the eraser and flung it back. "Who said he's trying to woo anyone?"

Kimberleigh ducked and the eraser just missed her head. "We'll see. Maybe you'll fall off your horse, and Josiah will have to rescue you!"

"I'd rather not fall off my horse, thank you very much." Nicole rolled her eyes at her sister.

"Aw, you're no fun," Kimberleigh muttered.

Cassy chuckled. However, if she'd had any doubts about Nicole's interest in Josiah, they were quickly fading. Even though Nicole wouldn't come out and admit it, Cassy felt certain her daughter's interest had been piqued. She could only pray that it wouldn't lead to disappointment.

27

The Horseback Ride

For days Nicole's emotions were in a turmoil as she thought about the upcoming trip to the Thompsons' farm. She felt excited at the prospect of getting to interact with Josiah again and meeting the rest of his family. But what would the day hold? Could Josiah be the one she had been waiting for? Reason told her not to let her heart race ahead, but it was hard to hold her longings in check.

When Saturday finally arrived, Nicole pulled her favorite sweater from her closet and slipped it on. It was a cream-colored angora. She tucked her jeans into the tops of her brown suede boots and went to the mirror to arrange her hair. Then she reached for her Bible from the corner of her dresser. Settling herself on her bed, she opened it and began to read where she had left off. This morning she found it difficult to focus on the words before her, and after reading the same verses several times, she set it aside and closed her eyes in prayer. She poured out her struggles again to the Lord and asked for His direction in the day, praying that whatever the outcome, she'd be able to rest in God's peace.

Later that afternoon, the Knights piled into the van and headed to the farm located between Red Deer and Rocky Mountain House. They had been sure to collect gloves, hats, and scarves, for even though the sun looked warm and inviting, it was late February and the temperatures were still below freezing. Nicole sat quietly in the van, but Kimberleigh and Anika talked excitedly about getting to go horseback riding.

"Those poor guys don't know what they're getting in for, inviting a pack of giggling girls over." Jeremy shook his head.

"They have sisters, don't they?" Anika frowned at her brother.

"Three, but one is married and living further away, and the twins are younger. At least they have plenty of boys to balance things off."

"You get to work with a bunch of guys all week, so don't act so hard done by." Kimberleigh socked her brother in the arm.

When they pulled into the farmyard a little while later, a large dog came running to meet their van. "Here comes Chomper," David said as he turned off the ignition.

"Chomper?" Anika's voice sounded wary.

David laughed. "Don't worry, he's friendly."

At the door, they were greeted by two enthusiastic young girls, who looked amazingly identical. "Hi, you made it," said the one holding the door. "My name is Rachel."

"I'm Rebekah. Come on in," the other quickly added. "We've been waiting for you to get here all day."

"Waiting very impatiently, I might add," said the kind-faced woman who joined them by the door. "These two have been dashing to look out the window every time the dogs barked since first thing this morning. I couldn't convince them you wouldn't be here until afternoon. I'm Miriam, by the way."

"Hi, Miriam." Cassy reached to shake her hand before introducing each of her family in turn.

"Do you want to go horseback riding?" one of the twins asked as soon as the introductions had been made.

"Yeah, the boys are all out at the barn getting the horses ready," the other girl quipped, her blue eyes dancing with excitement.

Nicole had already lost track of which girl was Rebekah and which was Rachel. "Sure, we'd like that." She smiled at the girls.

The two were already grabbing their coats from the closet and hurrying to put on their boots. Miriam just shook her head.

"Let me take your coat," she offered Cassy. "Jacob is in the shop, if you want to join him, or you're welcome to come in and wait." She looked questioningly at David. "I don't imagine he'll be too long, but you can never tell once he gets his mind set on something that needs doin'."

"I'll go find him, thanks." David turned and waited for the young people to all clear the doorway before following them out.

Once outside, the twins took up their posts on either side of their company like matching bookends. "The barn's this way," they said in unison, causing their guests to laugh.

"We do that all the time." The girl on the right snickered. "We can't help it."

"So, which one are you—Rebekah or Rachel?" Nicole turned to the girl on her left.

"I'm Rebekah, but don't worry. People get us mixed up all the time. We answer to either name. The only difference is that I'm a half inch taller than Rachel, but it's hard to tell."

"Especially if we aren't standing next to each other," Rachel added.

"How old are you guys?" Anika questioned.

"Thirteen," they answered together again.

"It must be so cool being twins." Kimberleigh looked from one to the other as they walked.

"It's a lot of fun," Rachel admitted. "Especially when we can trick people."

"I imagine that's not too hard to do." Jeremy was a few paces ahead of the girls, but he turned to eye them with a smile.

"When we get done riding, we'll have to show you our new baby lambs," Rebekah offered. "We have one we have to feed with a bottle..."

"She's named Snowflake because she was born in a snowstorm," Rachel interrupted.

"Her mother had twins and won't nurse the smaller one," Rebekah finished.

Nicole felt like she was watching a tennis match as she tried to keep up with the two girls on opposite sides of her. "I'd like to see her."

They had reached the large barn and as her eyes adjusted from the bright sunlight, Nicole was immediately struck by the number of horses and boys that seemed to fill every corner.

"They're here," announced a young boy just inside the door.

"That's Jesse; he's ten," Rachel explained.

"C'mon." Rebekah tugged on Nicole's arm. "I'll introduce you to all of them." She led the girls down the aisle between the stalls where her brothers were finishing saddling the horses. "This is Caleb; he's twenty-one. Benjamin is nineteen, Micah is eighteen, and Nathan is fifteen." She pointed each brother out in turn, and they nodded toward the girls. "Of course, you've met Josiah." The twins looked at each other and giggled, causing Josiah to raise his brows at them.

"I haven't met all of them yet," he told his sisters.

"Oh yeah." Rebekah smirked. She turned to Kimberleigh and Anika.

"That's Josiah, and he's twenty-three."

"Seth's at home with Vanessa and our little niece, Bethany, but they'll be over later for supper," Rachel added.

Rebekah looked around the room at her brothers. "This is Kimberleigh and Anika," she indicated the girls beside her, "and this is Nicole and Jeremy," she introduced for her brothers who hadn't met them yet. She shrugged. "I don't know how old they all are."

"That's okay, Rebekah." Josiah gave his horse's nose a pat as he stepped out of its stall to join them. "So, you all ready for a ride?"

"I think so," Kimberleigh piped up. "None of us have ever ridden before, but we'd like to give it a try. How bad does it hurt if you fall off?" Nicole subtly reached to pinch her sister's leg, and Kimberleigh jerked in surprise. "Ouch, I'm just asking." She glared at Nicole.

Josiah smirked. "Why, do one of you plan on falling off?"

"No!" Nicole answered with a glance to silence her sister. "I don't think that sounds like much fun."

Josiah chuckled, and some of his brothers laughed outright. "Good. I wouldn't recommend it."

"There's just eight horses; should we take turns?" Jeremy asked.

"That's okay." Josiah motioned toward his younger siblings. "Jesse and the twins are going to double up with some of us. We'll lead the horses out to the corral fence so we can mount."

Rachel and Rebekah directed them back outside to wait while the boys led each of the horses out and looped their reins over the top rail of the fence.

"We'll give you guys the four gentlest horses. Just be careful not to walk right behind them; if you take them by surprise, they may kick," Caleb instructed. "Jeremy, if you want to come over here, we'll give you Bandit." Jeremy made his way over to the black horse beside Caleb.

"This is the smallest one, Anika," Benjamin offered. "She's easy to handle and pretty much follows the horse in front of her. Her name is Hop Scotch."

Anika giggled as she walked carefully over to the multi-colored pony and allowed Benjamin to help her mount. "That's a cute name."

"We named her," one of the twins said proudly.

"You can ride Starlight," Micah offered to Kimberleigh.

"Ooo, he's pretty." Kimberleigh patted the flank of the dark Appaloosa as she walked past.

"He's a she." Micah smiled as he offered her a hand up.

"Oh." Kimberleigh smiled back. "No wonder she's so pretty."

Nicole watched as each of her siblings mounted their horse. She turned to see Josiah standing waiting for her.

"Would you like to ride Velvet?"

"Sure." She followed him to a sleek black horse further down the rail.

Josiah stopped beside the horse and waited for her to grab the saddle horn and place her foot in the stirrup. He grasped her elbow and gave her a gentle boost as she pulled herself into the saddle.

"That's a long way up." She shifted nervously in her seat, her toes barely touching the stirrups.

"I'll adjust these for you so your footing is more secure." Josiah cranked the stirrup up a notch or two before crossing in front of the horse to adjust the other side. Then he came back to check that the cinch was tight. "How does that feel now?"

Nicole wiggled her feet in the stirrups as she gripped the saddle horn. "Better."

"Don't put your feet too far forward; you don't want to get the stirrup caught around your ankle," he cautioned. Lifting the reins from the rail, he handed them to her. "If you want to back up, pull gently against the reins and give her a little kick. To turn, lay the reins against her neck on the opposite side you want to go, like this…." He demonstrated to make sure she understood.

Nicole nodded uncertainly. "Will they go very fast?"

"We'll take it slow and make sure you're feeling comfortable. I'll stay beside you in case you need help." Josiah grabbed the reins of the massive buckskin horse beside hers and swung easily up into the saddle.

"He's a big horse; what's his name?"

"Samson."

She eyed the horse with wide eyes. "Good name."

By then everyone was mounted and ready to go, so Nicole cautiously followed Josiah's lead as he backed his horse from the fence and turned it toward the gate leading across the field. She held the reins with one hand and gripped the saddle lightly with the other as her horse fell in beside Samson. Each of the brothers paired off to ride side-by-side with their visitors in order to guide them.

At the gate, Josiah halted and slid from the back of his horse. Unhooking the wire closure, he swung the gate wide to allow the riders to pass. Nicole prompted her horse through the gate but, unsure where to go, she reined Velvet to the side and stopped. Once all the horses were clear, Josiah led Samson through the opening and fastened the gate. The others had continued their brisk walk across the frozen field.

Nicole hesitated, unsure whether to follow behind them or wait for Josiah to join her. As soon as he had remounted, she gave Velvet a sharp nudge with her heels, and the horse bounded forward in a fast trot to catch up to the others. Nicole's fingers tightened around the saddle horn at the sudden movement and she dug her feet into the stirrups to keep from losing her footing as she bounced in the saddle. Velvet tugged at the reins, straining to gain her head. Immediately Josiah was at her side and reached over to slow her horse to a walk, guiding the frisky mare to fall into step behind Hop Scotch.

"In this brisk weather, they're looking for a chance to run. You just need to show her who's boss with a firm hand on the reins. She needs a little slack, but don't give her too much freedom."

Nicole nodded shakily. What would she do if her horse decided to run? Maybe Kimberleigh would get her wish after all.

"You okay?" Josiah eyed her face.

"I think so. I just wasn't expecting that." Feeling silly, Nicole glanced sideways with a smile to reassure him that she was fine.

One of the twins rode behind Benjamin. She glanced back and waved to Nicole. "Don't worry. Velvet's a good horse, but likes to be at the head of the line. Josiah will make her behave." She grinned at her brother.

As they made their way across the field and along the tree line, Nicole began to relax and feel more comfortable in the saddle. She felt a little self-conscious with Josiah riding by her side, asking her questions about her childhood and homeschooling, and she hoped he would credit the cool air for the flush in her cheeks. At breaks in their dialog, he would pause to point out certain aspects of their farm. She could tell he was proud of their herd of cattle and expansive fields, lying dormant now under a dusting of snow. Even though her fingers and toes had started to tingle, she wasn't ready to head back.

"That's Seth's house you can see behind those trees." Josiah pointed to the row of poplar just ahead. "My house is just beyond his. It's not finished yet, but do you want to see it?"

"You're building a house?" Nicole asked in amazement.

"I'm working on it." Josiah nodded. "Four years ago Dad subdivided off a few parcels of his land for some of the older boys. Seth built his home on one before he married Vanessa, and I've been working away at mine when I have the time and money. I hope to have it done before I get married."

Nicole felt her heart sink at the words. So, Josiah was getting married. She should have known he'd be engaged. All the good men were always spoken for. Nicole chided herself for allowing her own desire and imagination to trick her into thinking he might be interested in her. Josiah was only being friendly. She stifled a sigh before turning to answer.

"I'd love to see your house," she said as enthusiastically as possible. Nicole thought she detected a trace of disappointment on Josiah's face. He probably expected her to ask about his wedding, but she couldn't bring herself to do it.

"Are you guys ready to pick up the pace for a bit to that stand of trees over there?" Josiah called to the others. "I thought I'd show you the house I'm building."

Everyone seemed anxious to try, so Josiah directed Nicole to follow him as he maneuvered Samson around to the lead. "If you find a trot too rough, nudge your horse into a canter, it's smoother." He turned to Nicole. "Ready?"

She looked at him with wide eyes and nodded. This time she prepared herself for the jolt as she gave her horse a kick. Tightening her knees, she tried to grip Velvet's sides to keep from jostling in the saddle so much.

"You want to try a canter?" Josiah asked as he rode smoothly along beside her.

Nicole wondered how he kept himself from bouncing with each stroke of the horse's hooves. Swallowing the apprehension she felt, Nicole gripped her reins tighter, clung to the saddle horn until her fingers ached and nodded once again.

Josiah smiled. "You don't have to if you're afraid."

"No, I want to try it," she answered with steely resolve. Before she could change her mind, she gave Velvet another nudge with her heels.

Velvet needed no further coaxing to quicken her pace. Nicole felt like she was flying as the wind whipped her face, but Josiah had been right. It was easier to hold herself in the saddle with the smoother stride of the horse. She felt Josiah watching her as Samson kept pace beside Velvet. Realizing she'd been holding her breath, Nicole tried to relax her taut muscles and breathe normally. However, not until they reached the trees and reined in their horses could she release her vise-like grip on the saddle. Her cold, cramped fingers seemed reluctant to unbend.

"Whew, that was fun—I think." Nicole brushed her hair from her face.

Josiah let out a deep, rumbling laugh. "You think?"

"Well, it takes some getting used to, clinging to the saddle of a horse going that fast." Nicole slowly flexed her fingers to revive the circulation.

"You're not supposed to *cling* to the saddle."

"That's better than falling off. I heard it's not recommended." She smiled at the man beside her. He seemed even taller now, seated on Samson. Looking into those blue eyes, Nicole's pulse quickened, and she turned away in confusion. She had no business feeling such things for an engaged man.

The others had gathered behind them and she twisted in her saddle to see how her siblings had enjoyed the experience. They all sat securely in their saddles, talking excitedly.

"My house is just through these trees a little ways," Josiah explained once the commotion had settled.

He led them single file through the brush, ducking a few branches as he went. Nicole kept her eyes on the ground, watching where her horse stepped as Velvet plodded behind Samson. When they had reached the clearing on the other side, she looked up to see a charming, beige-colored house with rustic rockwork along the front and a covered veranda. She stared at the pleasant scene before her, nestled in the small clearing. She could see another farmhouse in the distance, on the far side of the gravel road, and Seth's home lay a few hundred yards to the right.

Suddenly realizing that Josiah was waiting for her, she turned to him. "Sorry, I guess I stopped to enjoy the view. It's beautiful. I'm sure when you get married, your wife will love it."

"I hope so." Josiah's eyes were shining.

She's one lucky girl, whoever she is, Nicole thought ruefully to herself. When they reached the house, everyone dismounted and looped their reins around the railing of the veranda. Josiah led them inside and took them through the as yet empty rooms. The walls had been drywalled but remained unpainted, and the floors were bare.

At one point, Kimberleigh sidled up to Nicole and whispered, "You didn't tell me that Josiah was so handsome!"

"It doesn't matter," Nicole hissed back.

"No, but he is just the same."

Nicole rolled her eyes. Now was not the time to explain to Kimberleigh that he was engaged. Someone might hear her. Besides, she didn't want to talk about it.

On the ride back to the barn, Nicole was lost in thought. The horses strode in more of a cluster, and Nicole was content to let the others talk around her. Though Josiah stayed close to her side, she felt certain he did so only to make sure she arrived safely back at the house. When they came in sight of the barn, the horses started to prance in anticipation, and Jeremy suggested one more canter back to the gate. Nicole was thankful for the chance to let the wind rush against her face as her horse's hooves ate up the distance across the field. Maybe it would help to clear her mind from the distracting thoughts caused by the presence of the blue-eyed rider at her side.

28

Family Dinner

When they reached the barn, they all dismounted, and each of the Knights enthusiastically thanked their hosts for the ride. Nicole felt stiff as she led Velvet back to her stall to have her saddle removed and receive a good brushing.

"Can we take the girls to see Snowflake?" One of the twins questioned.

"Yeah, it's time to feed her a bottle," the other chimed in.

"Sure, we'll take care of the horses." Josiah nodded at his sisters.

The twins grabbed the arms of their guests and pulled them to a small pen at the back of the barn where a tiny lamb bounded to the rail and started bleating. The girls climbed between the slats of the pen to snuggle their little friend.

"C'mon." One of the girls motioned for their guests to join them.

"Awe, it's so cute!" Anika exclaimed.

Nicole pulled off her gloves and reached to pet the lamb. "And warm," she added, sinking her cold fingers into the lamb's wool.

"Jesse," the twin closest to Nicole called, "go get Snowflake's bottle for us please, so we can feed her."

"What's wrong with your legs?" Jesse mumbled as he headed for the barn door.

"Are you Rachel?" Nicole asked the girl beside her.

"Nope, Rebekah."

"I can't figure out how to tell you two apart." She looked from one to the other.

The twins grinned.

The lamb squirmed and nuzzled each of the girls in turn, causing them to giggle. "She's looking for her supper," Rachel informed them. "If you hold out your finger, she'll suck on it."

Each of the girls let the lamb suck one of their fingers while they waited for Jesse to return. Nicole was surprised at the amount of suction the little thing had. Finally Jesse appeared, and Snowflake started bleating with a frenzy when she saw the bottle.

Rebekah took the bottle from her brother and handed it to Nicole. "Here, you want to try first?"

Nicole sat down in the straw and stroked the lamb's head as she held the bottle for the hungry creature. The bottle bobbed in her hand as the lamb sucked greedily at its contents.

"Oh, you're so adorable," she cooed as she nuzzled her face against the furry ear of the animal. Glancing up, she noticed Josiah watching them over the side of the stall.

"Looks like you made a friend."

"I could take this little one home." Nicole buried her face in Snowflake's woolly neck to hide her confusion. After a moment, she saw Josiah reach for a brush hanging on a nail in the wall and turn back to the horse he was tending.

Kimberleigh and Anika both took turns holding the bottle until it was empty, but the lamb still tugged at the nipple, hoping to gain a little more. The girls giggled again.

"That's all until later, you greedy little thing," Rachel chided as she took the bottle away. "We should go get cleaned up for supper."

They stood and brushed the straw from their jeans. Nicole would be glad to get inside and warm up. Her toes were beginning to feel numb. After removing their coats and washing up, they joined the ladies in the kitchen. Miriam seemed to have everything under control but told the girls they could set the table.

Nicole was shocked at the size of the long, custom-made table that seemed to fill the dining room. The twins brought the stacks of plates and cutlery to one end, while Nicole and her sisters managed to squeeze nineteen place settings around the perimeter. It was a tight fit, but not many people she knew had a table large enough to accommodate that many people.

Just as they were finishing their task, the guys came stomping noisily into the house. They all crowded around the sink in the back entrance, taking turns to wash up before coming into the kitchen. When Seth and his family arrived, they were ready to eat. Miriam gave quick introductions, then directed everyone to their place. Her parents were seated at one end of the table with Mr. and Mrs. Thompson, Seth and Vanessa, and everyone else circled the rest of the table. The twins requested to sit between Nicole and her sisters, so the boys were seated across from them.

Nicole took her seat and looked up to find Josiah seated directly across from her. *Oh God,* she prayed silently, *how am I going to avoid looking into his eyes all through supper?* Jacob Thompson led the family in grace, which erupted into boisterous conversation the moment he said amen. Heaping bowls of mashed potatoes and large platters of roast beef were passed around the table, and Nicole tried not to stare at the amount of food loaded onto the plates across from her. It must cost a fortune to feed this family of farm boys.

Thankfully, Rebekah seemed so overjoyed to have some more girls sitting beside her that she monopolized much of Nicole's attention during the meal. She found the twins enchanting as they excitedly told the girls of all their projects on the farm and tried to outdo one another with stories of their brothers' many antics. Nicole couldn't help but laugh at all their tales.

"You should have seen the time Josiah decided to try riding Brutus," Rebekah snickered as she leaned to whisper to Nicole.

"Who's Brutus?" Nicole bent toward the girl.

"Rebekah, I think you've told quite enough stories already." Nicole glanced up to see Josiah giving his sister a warning look.

Rebekah ignored her brother. "Brutus is our bull."

Nicole smiled at the man across from her. "I take it that it didn't go so well."

Josiah's mouth cocked in a crooked grin, but he didn't say anything.

"He got Caleb and Benjamin to help him pin Brutus in the corner of the corral, and they managed to get a rope around him. Then Josiah climbed over the rail onto his back and they let him go. Josiah lasted about five seconds before Brutus managed to throw him over his head into the mud. He barely missed Brutus' horns on his way over. Jesse thought he was going to get trampled so he ran to call Dad, but Josiah jumped up and ran with Brutus hot on his tail. You should have seen him fly over the corral fence! He got away from Brutus, but I thought Mom was going to kill him when she found out."

"That sounds pretty dangerous." Nicole eyed Josiah. "How old were you?"

"It was a long time ago," he assured her.

"He was twenty-one," Rachel cut in.

"Wow, I never considered trying to ride a bull before." Jeremy regarded the fellow beside him in awe.

"And *your* mother *would* kill you if you tried it!" Kimberleigh said sternly.

Josiah grinned. "It was quite a bit tougher than breaking a horse. I don't think I'll try it again."

When everyone had their fill, Miriam got up to serve the pie Vanessa had brought. Following dessert, the parents stayed at the table to visit over coffee, while the others retired to the living room. Nicole took a seat on the floor to play with two-year-old Bethany, coaxing the shy little girl onto her lap. Vanessa was obviously expecting their second child, and she seemed tired. She and Seth didn't stay long, as they wanted to get their daughter home to bed.

After they left, Rebekah and Rachel went to fix another bottle for Snowflake. They brought it to the living room and stopped beside the couch where the girls sat.

"Do you want to come out and help us?" one of them asked.

"Yeah, please come," the other pleaded.

Nicole smiled up at the two girls. "That would be fun," she told them as she rose from her seat.

"Me too," Anika jumped up, and Kimberleigh followed.

"We should go check a few of the cows that are ready to calve." Micah looked at Jeremy. "You can join us if you'd like."

"Sure. I don't know what I'm checking, but I'll come."

The gang headed to get on their coats and boots, and the boys grabbed several flashlights. They escorted the girls to the barn, then meandered to a nearby corral holding a couple dozen head of cattle.

Inside the barn, the girls flipped on a light and made their way to the back pen. The stalls were now empty, the horses having been released into the pasture. Snowflake greeted them eagerly, her ears twitching. The girls once again took turns feeding the lamb until the bottle was empty.

"You want to see if we can find the kittens?" Rachel asked.

Kimberleigh and Anika squeezed through the slots of the pen to follow Rachel, while Nicole opted to stay and help Rebekah give the lamb some fresh straw for its bed.

"So, when is Josiah going to get married?" she asked casually when her sisters were out of earshot.

Rebekah stopped and stared at Nicole with surprise. "Josiah?"

Nicole nodded.

The younger girl screwed up her face and fiddled with the straw in her hands. "Um, I'm not sure exactly; he's kinda figuring that out yet," she said evasively. "I think he's hoping it will be soon." Rebekah turned away and Nicole thought she saw the girl struggling to stifle a giggle. "I'll be glad when he does, 'cause it will be nice to have another girl around the farm." Rebekah glanced back and grinned.

Nicole sighed. So it was true. He hadn't picked a date yet, but it would be in the near future.

"Josiah's never kissed a girl before," Rebekah whispered. "Just thought you might like to know."

Nicole stared at her, not sure how to respond to that bit of information. "That's a good standard to have. I haven't kissed a boy either," she said quietly as she helped Rebekah with the straw.

When the two were finished, they went in search of the others. She could still see the guys out in the corral, but when Rachel and her sisters turned up empty handed, they headed back to the house.

⌘⌘⌘

Meanwhile, Jeremy accompanied Josiah to the far end of the corral to check the cows furthest from the barn. "How often do you have to check the cows?"

"During calving season, several times a day to make sure none of the cows are having complications in birthing. We take turns getting up during the night to check them."

"Whew, I didn't realize how much work it is to look after a farm. My grandpa mainly farmed grain. He didn't have to get up during the night to do that."

Josiah gave Jeremy a sideways glance. "Do you think Nicole would like farm life?"

Jeremy shrugged. "She likes animals, especially baby ones, but I never really thought about it." He walked a few more paces, then stopped. Why would Josiah be asking such a question unless.... Josiah had stopped as well, and Jeremy studied his face in the dim light of the flashlight. He thought he read the answer in the young man's expression. "You're seriously interested in my sister?"

Josiah didn't flinch beneath his gaze. "I am."

"Good." Jeremy slapped his shoulder and grinned. "I think you'd suit Nicole. Just don't mess with her heart, or I may have to hurt you."

Josiah chuckled.

"I mean it, man. I like you and all, but you break her heart, and I'll hurt you." Jeremy started to walk again.

"I don't doubt it." When they reached one of the cows, Josiah stopped again. "I've already been talking to your father, but I haven't said anything to Nicole yet. How do you think she'll respond if I approach her about spending a little more time together to see if she would be interested in a courtship?"

Jeremy thought for a moment. "It's fairly sudden, but Nicole is pretty discerning. She knows what she's looking for in a husband, and I think she'd be able to give you an answer."

"But do you think she'd say yes?"

"Can't say for sure, but I think she'd be thrilled."

Josiah let out his breath in a rush. "Good. At times today I thought I saw a spark of interest in her eyes, but at other times I wasn't so sure."

"That's just women's emotions. Who can keep up to them? I've been living with three sisters all my life, and I still can't figure them out." Jeremy shook his head. "Good luck!"

29

The Misunderstanding

Late that night, Nicole's head had barely hit her pillow when Kimberleigh sneaked into her room. Plopping down on the end of her bed, Kimberleigh breathed a dreamy sigh.

"That was sure a fun day."

"Uh-huh, and I'm tired, Kimberleigh." Nicole pulled the covers around her shoulders and flipped onto her side.

"How can you be tired at a time like this?" Kimberleigh asked incredulously. "I'd say Josiah's a Sir Faithful if ever I saw one. He's a regular prince, horse and all."

"Yeah, well, he's someone else's prince." Nicole swiped at the tears that threatened to spill over.

"What? No way! Who told you that?" Kimberleigh grabbed her sister's leg.

"He did, and Rebekah verified it; now let me go to sleep." She couldn't keep her voice from shaking.

"I don't believe it, Nicole. I saw the way he looked at you. The way he stayed by your side the whole time we were out riding."

"He was just being nice; that's all."

"What did he say?"

"He said he was hoping to get his house finished before his wedding, and Rebekah said they hadn't set a date yet, but she hoped the wedding would be soon."

"What's her name? I'll buy her a one-way ticket to Timbuktu!"

Nicole threw her sister a disgruntled look. "I don't know her name, and it doesn't matter. Good night, Kimberleigh."

"I don't get it; he seemed so perfect for you."

"Good night, Kimberleigh!"

"I'm sorry, Nicole." She leaned to give her sister a hug. "I guess he wasn't Sir Faithful after all. Don't worry; he'll come." Kimberleigh flipped off the light as she made her way quietly from the room and shut the door.

Nicole's tears hit her pillow before she heard her sisters' bedroom door shut a moment later. "Why God?" she asked softly. "Why couldn't this one have been for me?"

⌘⌘⌘

Over the next few days, Cassy noticed that Nicole was more quiet than usual. She had asked her daughter earlier that morning if she was feeling okay, and Nicole had assured her she was fine. Now, as she watched Nicole staring aimlessly out the window, her book lying idle in her lap, Cassy felt certain something was indeed bothering her daughter. Cassy pushed aside her unopened mail and went to join her daughter on the couch.

"What is it, honey?" She placed a hand on Nicole's knee.

Slowly Nicole turned to face her with a sweet smile that didn't quite reach her eyes. "What do you mean?"

"Something seems to be bothering you. What is it?"

"Oh, Mom." Nicole stared down at the pages of her book. "I'm trying so hard to be patient and see what God has for me; truly I am. It is just so hard waiting sometimes. I long for a family of my own."

Cassy frowned. Hadn't she noticed Josiah's attention the other night? Cassy wished more than ever that she could talk to her daughter about Josiah's meetings with David, but she had promised. Besides, David was still waiting to hear from him since their visit to know how he wanted to proceed. "You are still quite young, Nicole. God knows what He's doing; you'll see."

"I know, and I know many girls have been waiting much longer than I have. You and Dad have been so great to support and encourage me. I just wish I knew how to plan. What if I'm still here when I'm thirty?"

"Like I've told you before, then we'll still support and encourage you, but I don't think that's going to happen."

"But what would people say? What would they think of me? Some girls never get married. What if..."

Cassy held up her hand to stop her daughter. She could see the raging battle in her eyes—the battle between her longing and her desire to trust God with her future. "There will always be 'what ifs,' Nicole. We can't rest in God's hands if we are always worried about the 'what ifs' in life—I know. I've struggled with worry all my life. God knows your heart."

Nicole blinked back her tears and gave a tremulous smile. "I know, Mom." She reached to give her mother a quick hug. "I'm trying to be content where God has me right now, and most days I am."

"In the meantime, you have lots of worthwhile things to fill your time." Cassy shifted to a more comfortable position. She desperately wanted to know how things had gone with Josiah without giving away her secret. "How'd you enjoy our visit at the Thompsons the other day?" she asked, trying to sound casual.

Nicole's face brightened. "They seem like a really neat family. I got such a kick out of Rebekah and Rachel, but they're impossible to tell apart. I imagine the Thompson house is a lively one."

"I'm sure it is with that many boys in one household." Cassy watched her daughter's face for any tell-tale signs.

Nicole smiled. "Yeah, but I think it's cool having such a big family. I really enjoyed Saturday and hope we can see them again sometime."

"I'm sure we will," Cassy offered, feeling more assured. "Your dad and I enjoyed visiting with Jacob and Miriam too. They think a lot the way we do."

"I know. It would be interesting to talk to Vanessa or Anna sometime, just to see how they handled the whole courtship thing. I don't actually know anyone else who has been through it before; I think it would help to hear some of their experience."

"I did talk to Miriam about that," Cassy admitted.

"Really." Nicole perked up. "What did she say?"

"Well, it worked a little different for Anna than it did for Seth, since Anna's husband lived further away at the time. Vanessa's family goes to the same house church as the Thompsons, so they had been friends for a long time. Seth had a more natural setting to interact with her on a regular basis. But Anna met her husband at a Bible Prophesy Camp their families both attended. Tyler talked to Jacob at length during the week, and with Jacob's permission, he pursued getting to know Anna further through emails. Jacob kept in contact with Tyler by phone as well. After a few months, they felt ready to start a courtship, so Tyler came to stay with one of their church families for a month. He worked alongside the Thompsons on the farm, and they all got to know him really well. From there the courtship progressed quite quickly."

Nicole asked a number of questions, and Cassy did her best to answer them. By the end of their talk, Cassy felt Nicole's hesitation to express interest in Josiah was due to her uncertainty about his feelings. She didn't want to come right out and ask her daughter about him, for fear she would be pressed to reveal more than she should. Cassy would just have to wait and pray.

Two days later, David received some news. He phoned Cassy at noon to let her know that Josiah had called him at work to ask permission to come and talk to Nicole that evening.

"Finally! What took him so long?" Cassy carried the phone into her bedroom to avoid being overheard.

"He said he needed a few days to pray about how to approach Nicole regarding a possible courtship, but he is certain he wants to move in that direction if she is interested."

"I'm sure she will be. Can I let her know?" Cassy asked hopefully.

"Josiah wants to present the idea to her, but I'll tell her he's coming when I get home."

Cassy's shoulders slumped. She'd have a few more hours to wait. She busied herself for the rest of the afternoon cleaning house, but she could hardly keep herself from smiling. She worried the girls would guess something was up as she seldom cleaned with such enthusiasm. Thankfully, they were busy with their own tasks and didn't seem to notice.

All through supper, Cassy fidgeted and waited for David to speak, but he merely smiled at her and calmly ate his dinner. Cassy felt like kicking him under the table.

Finally, he pushed back his chair and cleared his throat. "Josiah Thompson called me today, and he wants to stop by this evening," he said to Nicole. "He has something he wants to ask you about; is that okay with you?"

Nicole gave her father a perplexed look. "He wants to talk to me?" she asked hesitantly, as she fiddled with the fork beside her plate.

"Yes, he'll explain more when he gets here. I've talked with him and given my approval, but I wanted to make sure you're okay with him coming."

Nicole stared at her mother with wide eyes, and Cassy smiled reassuringly. Her reaction wasn't quite what Cassy had been expecting; David's announcement seemed to have flustered her. But then again, Nicole had never been through this before, and they hadn't given her much notice. Cassy nodded toward her daughter, and she seemed to recover her composure somewhat.

"Sure it's okay." Nicole directed her response to her father, though she still looked a little uncertain. "When is he coming?"

David glanced at his watch. "He should be here in about an hour. But if you don't feel comfortable talking to him, I'll give him a quick call and let him know."

"No, that's fine." Nicole shrugged. "Why wouldn't I want to talk to Josiah? I like the Thompsons," she assured her father.

Jeremy sat at the end of the table grinning from ear to ear, and for once, Kimberleigh sat speechless—looking from her father to Nicole with her mouth hanging open. Cassy didn't know what to think; she had seen the initial confusion in her daughter's eyes. Had Josiah's interest really taken her completely off guard? When Nicole got up from the table to go to her room, Cassy followed.

"Are you sure you're okay, Nicole?" she asked from the bedroom doorway.

"Yeah, I'm surprised, that's all. I just need a moment."

Cassy felt reassured. "Okay, if you're sure." Maybe she was merely nervous now that a man was finally coming to call. She closed the door to give Nicole a little time to herself.

⌘⌘⌘

The minute the door shut, Nicole started pacing. Of all the unexpected things! She was at a loss. What in the world could Josiah be coming to talk to her about, and why had her parents made such a big deal of him stopping by? All their attention made her feel more self-conscious. If it hadn't been for the knowledge of his upcoming wedding, she would be ecstatic. But now she didn't know what to think. She hadn't wanted to admit to her mother how quickly she had let her heart get ensnared by a man she had only interacted with a few times. An engaged man no less.

Nicole plopped down on her bed. "Oh God," she moaned, "I know it's wrong to have feelings for a man who's promised to another, and I've been trying not to think of him all week. Why do you have to bring him here? Please, God, help me not to feel anything more than friendship for him."

Nicole rose to check her reflection in the mirror and brush her hair. Feeling foolish, she tossed her brush onto the dresser and began puttering around the room, trying to get her thoughts under control. All too soon a knock came at her door, and Kimberleigh poked her head into the room. "He's here. What do you think he wants?" she whispered.

"I have no idea." Nicole headed slowly for the door.

"Whatever it is, Dad said to give you some privacy, and we'll find out later." Kimberleigh studied her sister's face. "It doesn't make sense."

"I know." Nicole watched her sister disappear down the hall before making her way to the kitchen. Josiah stood by the table talking to her father. He looked a lot different out of his work clothes she thought, eying his crisply ironed Western shirt and stiff new jeans. When she entered the room, he turned to smile, his hands shifting from his side to slide into his back pockets. Everyone else seemed to have mysteriously disappeared to another part of the house.

"Hi, Josiah," Nicole said as she walked slowly into the room. "My dad said you had something you wanted to talk to me about?"

David cleared his throat and gave Josiah a pat on the back. "I'll be in my office." He pointed to the door off the living room and smiled at Nicole as he walked past.

Nicole watched him leave. "You can have a seat if you like." She offered her guest a chair at the table.

"Thanks." Josiah removed his hands from his pockets and pulled out a chair.

"Can I get you a drink or anything?"

He shifted. "Uh, a glass of water would be fine."

Nicole went to the cupboard and retrieved two glasses, glad for something to do in the awkward silence. She set one glass before Josiah and took a seat across the table from him. "How's Rebekah and Rachel?"

Josiah let out a nervous laugh. "They're fine. They said to tell you hi."

"Oh, tell them hi for me; I enjoyed getting to meet them."

"They really liked you too. Actually, all my family liked you."

Nicole looked startled. "You took a vote?"

"Not exactly, but it means a lot to me that they like you," Josiah said with a penetrating look.

She looked away. "Why?"

"Well, because I really like you, and I was hoping we could spend some more time together." Josiah quickly picked up his glass of water to take a drink.

She looked at him in shock. "What about your fiancé?" she faltered.

Josiah's eyes nearly popped as he choked on his mouthful of water. "My what?" he sputtered.

"Your fiancé. The one you're building the house for." Nicole stared at Josiah in confusion. "You said…you said…" What exactly did he say? Her thoughts were swirling now.

Josiah gave her a dumbfounded look. "I didn't say anything about a fiancé. I've been working on my house for over three years. I-I don't have a fiancé. I'm sorry you thought…whew." He rubbed his face with his hand. "Why did you think I came to see you?"

"I…I didn't know. But Rebekah said she thought you were hoping to get married soon." Nicole's voice was shaky; she couldn't look Josiah in the eyes.

"Rebekah? My family knew I was interested in you, but they weren't supposed to say anything!"

"It's not her fault," Nicole mumbled. "I asked her when you were getting married. She probably didn't know what to say." Oh, how had things gotten so mixed up? She peeked up and saw Josiah grinning. "It's not funny. Why are you smiling?" Nicole didn't know whether to laugh or cry.

"Why did you ask my sister when I was getting married?" Josiah was gazing at her so intently, she couldn't bring herself to look away.

"Because you said that you hoped to have your house finished before you got married. I thought you must be engaged, so I asked her when you were going to get married."

"Did that bother you that you thought I was engaged?" he pressed.

Nicole shifted uneasily. "Maybe…sort of…" She let out a long breath. "Yes."

Now Josiah's face lit up. "I am hoping to get engaged someday, Nicole, but I'm hoping to marry you. I've been talking to your father for some time now, and he's given his blessing for me to pursue a courtship with you."

Nicole could hardly believe what she was hearing. "Really? You've been talking to my dad and he didn't tell me?"

Josiah shrugged. "I asked him not to until I could pray about it and be sure and until he could give his approval. I didn't want to hurt your feelings if it didn't work out. I guess it would have saved some confusion if you had known, but I never dreamed you'd think I was engaged."

Nicole was remorseful. "That was my fault. I jumped to conclusions and I should have clarified things. It was kind of you to want to protect my feelings."

"Nicole, I know you haven't known me long, but I know that you're the type of girl I would like to marry. I wouldn't ask to pursue a courtship unless I was serious about marriage. I don't want to ask you to make a decision about anything yet, but would you be interested in spending some time together, either here or with my family? I want to give you some time before I ask you to commit to anything more formal."

Nicole was so happy she thought she would burst. "I'd really like that, Josiah. I think you're a great guy, and you seem to have a heart for God—that's important." Nicole looked at him mischievously. "Oh yeah, and you have another thing going for ya."

Josiah cocked his eyebrow. "What's that?"

"You've never kissed a girl." She smirked.

Josiah's eyes widened in surprise. "Let me guess, Rebekah?"

Nicole nodded. "She thought I might like to know, although I wasn't sure at the time why she would think that."

"Sisters." Josiah laughed. "They're so helpful."

⌘⌘⌘

When the family joined them in the kitchen later for some brownies and ice cream, Nicole could hardly keep from beaming. Her father explained to the others why Josiah had come over.

"I knew it!" Kimberleigh declared with a pointed look at Nicole.

Josiah appeared taken aback. "Really? Well, it took Nicole by surprise."

"I know. She wouldn't believe me that you weren't engaged." The minute the words were out, Kimberleigh covered her mouth in horror.

"Engaged!" David and Cassy exclaimed in unison as they looked at their daughter.

Nicole propped her elbows on the table and covered her face with her hands. "I'll explain later," she mumbled through her fingers.

"I guess my coming was a bit of a surprise." Josiah smiled at Nicole. "But once the misunderstanding was cleared up, it went better."

"I guess so." David shook his head. "Sorry for the confusion."

"That's okay." Josiah shifted in his chair. "I thought you might all like to visit our house church on Sunday," he said, changing the subject. "It's our turn to host the service, and Mom said to make sure and invite you to stay for dinner and the afternoon."

"We'd love to come," David responded.

"It really should be our turn to have your family here for dinner." Cassy looked from her husband to Josiah.

"My mom is used to cooking for a crowd, and she volunteered. Besides, I know you've been interested in our house church, and I thought it would give you a chance to see how we operate."

"That's fine. I'll call your mom later to see what I can bring."

When everything was settled, Josiah politely excused himself and wished the family good night, heading to the entrance way to find his coat. "See you on Sunday at ten," he added with a nod toward Nicole before slipping out into the cold.

Once Josiah had departed, Nicole gave her father a hug. "Thanks, Dad, for looking out for me. I had no idea you were meeting with Josiah in order to protect me. It means a lot that he has your approval."

"Josiah has a good head on his shoulders, and I think he suits you, but ultimately you'll have to decide." David gave her shoulders a squeeze. "I'm just sorry you got the idea he was engaged. Both your mother and I thought you would welcome a chance to get to know him better, and I thought you understood his intentions for wanting to meet with you. I certainly would have cleared up the misunderstanding, had I known."

"How did you get the idea he was engaged?" Cassy wanted to know.

Sheepishly Nicole explained how she'd come to that conclusion. Jeremy shook his head and laughed.

"That explains your mood earlier this week," Cassy said. "I couldn't understand how you could be so unaware of his interest. He seemed so attentive to you on Saturday, I thought it would be obvious. I'll have you know that I found it very difficult not to tell you what was going on, but Josiah had requested we not say anything until he was sure."

It was late by the time everyone finally headed to bed, but Kimberleigh and Anika still managed to convince Nicole to sleep with them so they could hear the details of Josiah's visit. They giggled as she told them of her embarrassing blunder.

"I knew Josiah looked like a Sir Faithful." Kimberleigh nudged her with an elbow.

"And now it's only a matter of time until you get married and leave us," Anika said with a mixture of excitement and sorrow.

"I'm not going anywhere yet," Nicole said tenderly.

"I know, but you will. Then I'll be stuck with just Kimberleigh."

Kimberleigh grabbed her pillow and reached across Nicole to wallop her sister. "You make that sound awful!" she accused.

Anika giggled and took her pillow to strike back. In the midst of the ensuing pillow fight, someone pounded on their bedroom door, and they grew quiet a moment.

"Can't a guy get any sleep in this house?" Jeremy's voice demanded from the hall.

The girls covered their mouths to stifle their giggles.

"It's just Jeremy," Kimberleigh whispered as she whacked Anika with her pillow once more.

30

Moving Forward

That Sunday Nicole helped her mother gather the bags of homemade buns and salad they'd promised to bring to the Thompsons. Now that a prospect of courtship had presented itself, she felt a bundle of nerves. It had been easier when she hadn't known that Josiah's whole family would be evaluating her. Now she was going to feel like an ant under a microscope. However, the thought that Josiah actually liked her and had been meeting with her father on her behalf buoyed her spirits. She'd been praying for the last two days that God would give her wisdom to know how to proceed, and that He would guard her heart, should the relationship not work out.

By the time they reached the Thompsons, another family had already arrived. Josiah greeted them at the door, and the twins raced to collect their coats. They were grinning ear to ear.

"I'm glad you could come today and that I don't have to keep a secret anymore," Rebekah whispered into Nicole's ear.

"I'm glad I could come too," Nicole answered with a smile. She wondered if Josiah had told her how her words had been misinterpreted.

When the girls disappeared with their armloads down the hall, Nicole picked up the large bowl of salad she'd set on the wash stand in the entry. Josiah led them toward the kitchen to deposit their food, pausing to introduce the Knights to the other family.

"This is Carolyn and Samuel Hawkins." He indicated the couple visiting with his parents. Mr. Hawkins immediately reached to shake David's hand. "And this is Kent, Terry, and Jenny." Josiah pointed out each of the others in turn.

"Hi, Jenny." Nicole greeted the blond-haired girl who appeared to be about her age.

"Hi," Jenny answered. Nicole couldn't help but notice the way the girl studied her, before turning her attention to Josiah. "Hey, you guys want to go skating at the pond later this afternoon?"

"Sorry, not today; we have company." He looked down at Nicole standing at his side. "Here, let me take that to the fridge for you." Josiah reached for the bowl in her hands. "I'll be right back."

As Jenny watched him go, the smile on her face vanished. The twins returned and started chatting with her sisters, and Jeremy was already preoccupied with the guys.

Nicole shifted uncomfortably. "So, do you live on a farm near here?" she asked in an attempt to befriend the girl.

Jenny hugged her arms across her chest and pursed her lips before glancing at Nicole once again. "No, we live in Rocky Mountain House."

"Have you been attending this house church for long?"

Jenny cocked her head as she studied Nicole once again. "Our family helped start it. We've been good friends with the Thompsons for years. How long have you known them?" There was an edge to her voice.

"The Thompsons started making cabinets for my dad's business a few months ago. We're just getting to know the family."

"I see," Jenny stated flatly as Josiah approached them again.

"Sorry. The kitchen fridge was full; I had to run your salad down to the extra fridge in the basement," he explained to Nicole with a smile.

"Excuse me. I think I'll go find a seat in the living room." Jenny turned and brushed past Nicole, lightly clipping her shoulder as she passed.

Nicole sighed. "I don't think she likes me," she whispered.

He frowned and bent toward her. "I'll explain later."

By now more families were coming in the door, and Jacob made sure to introduce them to everyone. Slowly the group crowded into the living room. Younger children found places on the floor or on parents' laps, while the rest filled every available seat. A number of adults spilled over onto the kitchen chairs, which had been lined up in a couple of rows along the edge of the room. The house seemed to be bursting at the seams.

Once everyone was settled, Jacob opened in prayer. Then Josiah rose from his place beside Nicole and made his way toward his guitar propped against the piano. Miriam had already taken her place on the bench. Nicole noticed everyone leafing through the songbooks, which had been distributed on the chairs before people arrived.

"You can make a request for a song if you want," Rebekah whispered over her shoulder from her place at Nicole's and Kimberleigh's feet. Anika had joined the twins on the floor.

Family members from around the room called out page numbers at random, and the house reverberated with music. Nicole found it difficult to avoid watching Josiah as he strummed away on his guitar in the corner. Once she caught Jenny eying her from across the room, causing her to focus on the book she shared with Kimberleigh.

Following the singing, Josiah came back to join her, and an extended time of prayer and sharing ensued. Being a visitor, Nicole sat back and quietly took it all in. The camaraderie of the tightly knit group revealed many insights into each family as they prayed for one another. One of the men requested prayer for another family in the area. Though they appeared to be a non-Christian family, many in the room seemed to know them. Apparently the mother had been admitted to the hospital with pneumonia, leaving the father at home with four young children. Several of the women quickly organized a schedule to take meals to the family over the following week.

Next Caleb read a short Bible story from an illustrated book for the children on the floor. They all shifted to get a good view of the pictures. It was obvious that Caleb felt quite comfortable ministering to the younger members of the group. When the story ended, Jacob led the time of study from the book of Philippians. Everyone took part in reading the Scripture and discussing the insights Jacob presented. And though some of the toddlers grew restless on occasion, the rustle of children didn't seem to bother anyone. One mother took her fussy baby to the edge of the kitchen, where she could continue to listen while she settled him down.

Mr. Hawkins ended the morning with prayer and reminded everyone that the service would be at his home the following week. He made sure to invite the Knights to join them, and informed David that he could get directions from Jacob if he wished. Nicole glanced in Jenny's direction. She stared at the floor, her lips clenched in a firm line.

Soon the room was abuzz, a number of the ladies dispersing to the kitchen to have more space to visit. Youngsters grabbed their coats and bounded outside to race around until it was time to leave. Rebekah and Rachel did their best to make sure their visitors met the majority of young people in the room, before the families gradually began to leave. When the last of the people had departed, Jeremy headed to the basement with some of the boys, and Nicole headed to the kitchen with the girls. Josiah lingered by the table.

"Is there anything I can do to help?" Nicole asked Mrs. Thompson.

Turning from the stove, Miriam smiled. "I think we have lots of helpers for now; dinner won't be ready for half an hour. The younger girls can set the table; why don't you relax for a bit, and I'll call if I need you."

Kimberleigh brushed past Nicole and gave her a subtle nudge. "Go talk to him," she said under her breath. Her sister's face remained masked behind a smile, her lips barely moving.

"How'd you enjoy the service?" Josiah asked when Nicole turned toward him.

"It was great, and I enjoyed the music," she said shyly. "Everyone was so friendly." *Well, almost everyone*, Nicole thought as she remembered the blond-haired girl who had watched her furtively from a distance.

"Let's go to the living room." Josiah indicated for Nicole to have a seat on the couch, and he pulled a kitchen chair over and placed it before her. Straddling the chair, he draped his arms across the back. "I'm sorry about Jenny's reaction to you," he said, as though reading her previous thought. "The Hawkins are good friends of our family, and we've done a lot together. Anna and Jenny were best buddies growing up. I think a few people in the church assumed she and I would someday get together. In fact, her father questioned me about a year ago to see if I'd be interested in a courtship with Jenny, and I spent a lot of time praying about it. In the end, I told him no, and I think Jenny felt hurt. When I introduced you to her today, I think she put the pieces together. She may have been hoping I'd eventually change my mind."

"I wondered if there had been something between you."

"Not really. At least not on my part." Josiah paused. "Your dad said you haven't had any relationships with a guy before either."

Nicole glanced at her father, who sat across the room visiting with Jacob. "Nope. There were a couple of guys who wanted to date me years ago, but my dad and Jeremy took care of them. I was too young and not interested in dating."

"I heard about that." Josiah smiled. "I feel like I've had a chance to learn a lot more about you and your family through talking with your father. If you have any questions about my family, don't be afraid to ask."

Nicole couldn't help but wonder what all he'd heard. Her mind raced, trying to replay what she knew of this man. "You mentioned before that you'd like to have your own farm. I don't know much about farming. I grew up on an acreage, and I know a little bit about my grandpa's farm—my dad used to help him with harvest when I was little. But I don't know the first thing about cattle or taking care of horses and sheep."

"I could show you around and teach you about the animals." Josiah looked like the prospect pleased him.

"I'd like that. I think I'd also like to talk to your mother about her role as a farmer's wife, so I have a better picture of what's involved. Like does she help butcher and pluck chickens and all that?" Josiah burst out laughing at her words. "What? What's so funny?"

Nicole thought her question had been legitimate.

"I'm sorry." Josiah tried to wipe the smile from his lips. "It's just that by the grimace on your face when you said that, I take it that the idea of butchering chickens doesn't appeal to you."

"I've never done it before, but I can't say it's been my dream to pull feathers from a dead chicken." Nicole involuntarily shivered. "I don't mind cooking them once they're dead, but they're not looking at you when you put them into the pan."

"They're not looking at you once you chop their heads off either." Josiah smirked, and Nicole crinkled her nose at him. "It would be a good idea to talk to my mom. She didn't grow up on a farm either, but I don't think she'd trade it. Of course she doesn't do as much of the work now as when we were all little, so I'm sure she found it much tougher at first. Farm life isn't without its challenges; she could tell you about all that."

"How hard is it to get started in farming these days, with the cost of land and equipment and all?"

"It's not easy," Josiah admitted, "so for now I will continue on with Dad. He gave each of us kids a heifer when we graduated. We could either sell her calf each year to help with school expenses, or use the calves to start our own cow and calf operation. I kept mine and have been able to start building a bit of my own herd. Eventually I may have the opportunity to buy some of my dad's land and equipment, but it would be a big investment." Josiah went on to explain some of his dreams and how he hoped to accomplish them, until the call to dinner halted their discussion.

Nicole enjoyed the interaction with the others around the table. The two families got along so well, it seemed hard to believe they'd known each other such a short time. No one seemed too anxious to clear the table, as they shared family stories with one another and relaxed over coffee and dessert. Nicole got the impression that the Thompson family were highly regarded within their community. It seemed they had countless tales of neighbors they had banded together to help through difficult times, harvesting fields or offering services to those in need.

Finally Miriam rose to put away the food, and the girls all helped load the dishwasher. Jeremy joined Josiah and his brothers as they headed out to do a few chores, and the twins prepared a bottle for Snowflake.

"You want to come to the barn with us?" Rachel asked her visitors.

Kimberleigh and Anika quickly agreed, but Nicole decided to stay and help wash the dishes, since she hadn't helped with dinner. Besides, it would give her a chance to visit with Mrs. Thompson. The four girls scurried outside. Cassy offered to wash and have Nicole dry, so that Miriam could put things away, and the dishes were finished in no time as Nicole questioned Josiah's mother about farm life.

The minute the girls came back inside, Rebekah and Rachel disappeared, returning a moment later with a stack of games. The men weren't far behind, and they spent the afternoon around the table, playing an assortment of board and card games. As the day wore on, Nicole found it easier to relax and be herself. She had expected to feel like she was on trial, under pressure to prove herself before a jury, but that wasn't the case. Miriam had been warm and inviting, gladly answering her questions, and the atmosphere for getting to know one another seemed natural. There remained much to learn, however, and the process would take time.

As the Knights prepared to leave that evening, plans were made for the Thompsons to come for dinner the following Saturday. Josiah said he'd like to join them for church on Sunday, so he would have a chance to see where they attended and meet some of Nicole's friends. Nicole felt both elated and nervous as they drove home. She hoped things weren't moving too fast. The last thing she wanted to do was rush into a relationship and hurt Josiah. She also wanted to protect her own heart from getting emotionally involved before a definite commitment had been made. But at the moment, conquering her emotions seemed about as difficult as telling the earth to stand still.

31

Courtship

Clad in her pajamas, Nicole tiptoed down the hallway to her parents' room. She couldn't settle down to sleep without talking to her father. A sliver of light escaped from under the door; they were still awake. Hesitating, she tapped gently.

"Come in," David's voice invited.

Nicole turned the knob and peeked inside. Her father sat in a chair by the bed, Bible in hand, and she could hear her mother brushing her teeth in the en-suite bathroom. "May I talk to you?"

David nodded toward the bed. "Have a seat."

Slipping into the room, Nicole shut the door behind her and climbed onto the bed facing her father. "You've talked a lot more with Josiah than I have. Am I doing the right thing?"

David studied her. "Is there something in particular bothering you?"

Nicole stared at her hands in her lap. "I don't know. Not really, I guess. It's just that I haven't ever done this before, and I don't know if I'm merely excited about a possible courtship, or if Josiah's the right one for me. I don't want to get too involved and then change my mind."

"Before I say anything, what do you think of Josiah?"

"From what I know of him, he's a great guy and a solid Christian. We share a lot of the same values, and I think I could come to love and respect him. But I don't know him well enough to see how our personalities fit together, or what conflicts we might have." Nicole glanced over to her mother, who had just entered and joined her on the bed. "I wish I knew for sure I'm doing the right thing." She turned back to her father.

"That's why we haven't established an actual courtship yet, to give you a chance to get to know Josiah better. However, no matter how much you have in common, there will always be some areas of conflict. Don't let that scare you away. The bigger thing is knowing you're able to work through them, and making sure the conflicts aren't because of major differences in belief and vision. From my time with Josiah, I don't see that as being an issue. If I did, I'd never have given him my permission to talk to you."

"But what about the fact that I have no experience living on a farm? Managing a farm takes a huge amount of investment and can be very stressful with all the ups and downs due to weather and changing markets. Farm girls have to be pretty tough to help with all the work involved. Playing the piano and pulling a calf are two very different things."

David laughed. "You're right, and that's something you do have to consider, but it's possible to learn. If you are dedicated to helping your husband, and you apply yourself, there's no reason you can't learn some of those things. The question is, do you think you would enjoy that type of life?"

"I think I would," Nicole said slowly. "I like the country and animals, but I think I'd get really stressed if we have a tough year and can't pay our bills."

"There's no guarantee you won't have that problem even if you aren't on a farm." David looked at his daughter sympathetically. "Life is like that. At least you would always have food on your table."

Nicole smiled and nodded. "I do like Josiah," she admitted. "So you think I'm doing the right thing?"

"If I didn't, I wouldn't have gone out of my way to arrange a chance for the two of you meet," David said with a smirk.

Nicole gasped. "Are you serious?"

"Totally serious!" Cassy laughed and patted her daughter's shoulder. "You should have seen your father scheming."

"I just arranged the meeting, Josiah took it from there," he clarified.

Nicole hopped from the bed and bent to give her father a hug. "I love you, Daddy."

"I love you too, sweetheart. You're doing fine. Just take it slow till you sort out your feelings."

⌘⌘⌘

Nicole did take it slow over the next couple of months, spending time with Josiah in group and family settings. She spent much time on the farm, getting used to the routine and particulars of farm life. She witnessed the birth of a calf, and grew more confident around the horses through her numerous rides. Rebekah and Rachel were great little teachers, including Nicole in the care of their new chicks and all their farm tasks. Josiah had also become a regular visitor at the Knights, and had even stopped in at Hope for Life to see where Nicole worked and hear more about the ministry.

"So, what do you think of my relationship with Josiah?" Nicole asked her sisters one night as they got ready for bed.

"I think you'd be crazy to pass him up," Kimberleigh said, her mouth full of toothpaste. "If you do, then you'll have to go to the back of the line and wait your turn, because the next Prince Charming to come our way is mine!"

"You two suit each other," Anika assured her.

"I think so too." Nicole beamed. "And what's more, I think I will truly enjoy living on a farm."

"You'd have horses for us to ride; that's definitely a bonus." Anika added.

"Josiah asked me this afternoon if I am ready to commit to a courtship. I've prayed about it a lot, and Mom and Dad have given their approval. I told him yes."

Kimberleigh squealed and reached to hug her sister, dripping toothpaste on her sleeve. "Oops, sorry." She swiped at it with her hand. "You should have waited until my mouth was empty to tell me that."

"So you're sure you want to marry him?" Anika asked.

"Yes, I am. I really struggled at first to separate my emotions from the whole process so I could be discerning, but the fact that we haven't had any physical involvement helps, I think."

Kimberleigh spit the remainder of her toothpaste in the sink and rinsed her mouth. "When do you think you'll get married?"

"I'm not sure. Josiah wants me to help pick out colors for the house so that he can get it finished. I plan to help him with the painting. I don't think he wants to wait real long, but I don't know just what he's thinking."

"You have to sleep with us tonight so we can start planning," Anika insisted. "Besides, we don't know how many more chances we'll have."

Just then Jeremy peeked around the corner of the bathroom. "You girls plan to camp out in there all night, or can I have a turn?"

"Nicole is planning to get married, and all you can think about is getting into the bathroom!" Kimberleigh brushed past her brother with a humph.

Jeremy's eyes flew to his sister. "Really?"

"Well, he hasn't formally asked me to marry him yet, but I've agreed to a courtship. That's the plan." Nicole grinned at her brother.

"It's about time." Jeremy socked his sister in the arm. "I could have told you to go for it a month ago. Congratulations!"

"Hurry and get your pillow and come to our room," Anika called back to Nicole as she headed for her room.

"Oh great. First a guy can't get into the bathroom; now I won't be able to get any sleep."

"You'll miss me when I'm gone," Nicole teased.

It surprised her to see Jeremy's eyes suddenly fill with tears. "Yes, I will," he stated huskily.

Nicole stretched to give her brother a kiss on the cheek. "I'll miss you too."

32

The Wedding

One warm June evening, Josiah asked if Nicole would like to join him for a horseback ride. Following Josiah out to the barn, Nicole noticed he had already rounded up Samson and Velvet and had them waiting in their stalls. Josiah and his brothers had always saddled the horses whenever they'd gone riding before, but Nicole had watched on occasion and thought she could figure it out.

"I'll saddle Velvet," she offered.

Josiah gave her a questioning look. "You sure? I can saddle them both; it won't take me long."

"No, I think I can do it. I'd like to give it a shot."

"Okay, you know where her tack is."

Nicole nodded and went to select a bridle from the dozen or so hanging on the barn wall. Carrying it to Velvet's stall, she entered and talked soothingly to the mare. She fiddled with the straps until she had them figured out, then slipped the bit into the horse's mouth as she reached to situate the straps around Velvet's ears and brow. She leaned back to see if everything looked like it was in the right place. "So far so good," she whispered. She noticed Josiah peeking at her every so often to see how she was getting along.

Next she grabbed the striped blanket, which was draped over the side of the stall, and flung it across Velvet's back. Now for the saddle. Nicole headed to the thick wooden beam lined with saddles at the end of the aisle. Selecting the big Western saddle she usually used, she gripped the back and the saddle horn and pulled it off the beam. The saddle thumped against her legs and she nearly dropped it on her toes. "That's heavier than I thought," she mumbled to herself as she glanced back to see if Josiah had been watching. Though he was busy adjusting Samson's bridle, his smirk told her he'd seen her reaction.

Gritting her teeth, she heaved the saddle as high as she could to keep the stirrups from dragging and carted it back toward the stall. Josiah had already managed to get Samson saddled and ready to go, so he met her halfway down the aisle.

"Need some help?"

"I think I can get it," Nicole insisted, hoping her voice didn't sound strained.

She squeezed past him into the stall, but Velvet's back suddenly looked a lot higher now as she realized she was holding the heavy saddle well below where she needed to lift it. How would she keep the stirrups out of the way and lift this thing over her head? She wasn't used to lifting something so heavy and awkward that high.

With a smile, Josiah reached for the saddle and easily lifted it from her hands and onto the horse. "Heavier than you thought?"

"Just a bit," Nicole admitted. "Besides, you're about a foot taller than I am."

Josiah chuckled as he pulled the cinch tight and adjusted the stirrups into place. He handed her the reins and went to lead Samson from his stall.

As Nicole rode alongside Josiah, she inhaled the welcome aroma of the lush green landscape, still fresh from the recent rain. The crop was off to a good start, and Josiah seemed pleased as he scanned the fields around them. Now more comfortable on the back of a horse, she was able to relax and enjoy the ride. When they reached the familiar strand of trees, they wove their way through to the clearing on the other side. Josiah dismounted by the front veranda of his house and reached to help her from the saddle. Once her feet were on the ground, Josiah did not release her hand. Nicole looked at him in surprise. For the past months, he had kept their physical contact to a minimum.

"The house is finished," Josiah stated simply as his eyes penetrated hers.

She smiled. She knew the house was complete except for the basement, which would be finished at a later time. Josiah's dad had offered him a loan so he could continue, and the whole family had chipped in to get the work done.

"I want to share my home with you, Nicole. I want to spend our future together and to grow old with you."

Nicole's eyes glistened with tears as she gazed into the eyes of the man she had grown to love. She waited quietly for him to finish.

"You know it has been my intent all along to make you my wife. I love you with my whole heart and will remain faithful to you alone," he said huskily. "Nicole, will you marry me?" Josiah reached into his shirt pocket and pulled out a small velvet case. He flipped open the lid with his thumb and held the case for Nicole to view the tiny gold ring. Delicate strands of gold intertwined around a shimmering diamond, set off on either side by two smaller diamonds.

Nicole gasped when she saw the ring, and tears of joy spilled over as she reached to accept it. "Nothing could make me happier than to be your wife, Josiah."

With a warm smile, Josiah lifted the ring from its satin confines and gently slid it onto her finger. He drew her close for just a moment, then released her. Nicole had felt his arms tremble against her, and she knew in that instant the vulnerable position many couples placed themselves in when they pursued physical intimacy before marriage.

"We'll wait until I can call you Mrs. Thompson to seal it with a kiss." Josiah looked into her eyes a moment longer and then cleared his throat. "We should head back." He reached to help her onto Velvet's saddle.

"I like having your ring on my finger," Nicole murmured, admiring the glistening diamonds while she waited for Josiah to mount his horse.

"I hope to add another one to it very soon." He turned Samson's head in the direction of home.

⌘⌘⌘

It was a bright September afternoon, not long after Nicole's twenty-third birthday. Cassy reflected on Nicole's courtship as she sat in the front-row seat reserved for the mother of the bride. The prelude music drifted in the background, mingling with her memories. The integrity and purity of her daughter's relationship with Josiah had been a testimony that brought glory to God. It had been a much better path to marriage than the one she herself had taken. No compromises. No regrets of stolen intimacies shared with another.

A moment later the music changed, and Cassy watched as Josiah stepped onto the platform, along with three of his brothers and the little ring bearer. The anticipation on his face spoke volumes. Slowly Kimberleigh, Anika and Melissa made their way down the aisle, followed by a very hesitant Bethany carrying a basket of flowers.

Cassy stood when Nicole appeared in the doorway. Even beneath the veil, Nicole's face glowed as she clung to her father's elbow. When they reached the front of the church, David placed his daughter's arm in Josiah's, a symbol of the transference of headship and the covering of protection from one to the other. With one last hug for his daughter, David joined Cassy in the front row, his eyes suspiciously ready to overflow.

More than once, Cassy had to dab her own eyes during the ceremony as her daughter pledged vows before God to love and honor her husband. Before they exchanged rings, Jeremy played a song on his guitar while Kimberleigh and Anika sang.

Finally, with the golden bands sealing their covenant to one another firmly on their hands, Pastor Nelson pronounced them husband and wife. Then, with a smile, he uttered the famous words, "You may now kiss the bride."

Josiah lovingly lifted the veil from his wife's face. Tenderly gripping Nicole's shoulders, and with his heart in his eyes, he bent for the first time and their lips met.

Author's Note

As Christian homeschooling parents, we are each on a journey—seeking the best for our respective families. What I hope to have challenged you with through this story is to keep your eyes on the goal of raising godly offspring. We are but stewards of the children God has entrusted to us. We need to nurture in them a strong faith, founded solidly on God's Word, so that we may present those children back to Him.

At the time of this writing, we have not completed the full cycle of this story. We are on the brink, searching for godly husbands for some of our daughters. As readers, your children may be at varying stages along this road. However, if you are dedicated to a path of purity and godly femininity for your daughters, you will most certainly meet opposition along the way. You can't help but clash with our strongly feministic culture. Though your daughters may at times feel lonely in their pursuits, may you encourage them to press on. There are more and more young women choosing this path.

For those of you raising sons, may you be challenged to mentor them into godly young men—mature and ready to be the spiritual leaders in their homes. In our materialistic, entertainment-driven society, where men's and women's roles have been turned upside-down, our young women are not the only ones floundering. We desperately need more serious-minded men who are willing to confront their culture and take a stand for the truth.

For me, as a mother, this path has been a new one, but the journey has been very rewarding. I was not homeschooled. I went to college—though not to pursue a career. And I did not follow the path of courtship. I had never heard of courtship, other than to read about it in novels from bygone centuries. However, I feel extremely blessed that God saw fit to provide me with a godly and faithful husband, and that He has given me the grace to lead my daughters down a path I had not traveled.

God bless each one of you as you strive to do the same.

About the Author

Elizabeth Wiens and her husband, Gary, have four daughters and live in Alberta, Canada. Their family has enjoyed working together in children's ministry for almost sixteen years while serving full-time with Child Evangelism Fellowship. They are now ministering with GoodSeed Canada.

Elizabeth feels passionate about God's call for parents to purposefully mentor their children for Him. She and Gary have been home educating their family for fifteen years, and Elizabeth is involved in homeschool leadership in her community. In her spare time, she enjoys writing and doing research—seeking biblical answers to life's issues. *As for Me and My House* is her second book, and a sequel to *Bringing Them Home.*

You may reach Elizabeth via email at: gbwiens@shaw.ca

www.elizabethwiens.com
www.oaktara.com